The Case of the
Man Who Died Twice
A Sherlock Holmes Adventure

by Ken Courtenay

(Based on characters created by Sir Arthur Conan Doyle)

Hardcover ISBN 978-1-80424-675-7
Paperback ISBN 978-1-80424-676-4
ePub ISBN 978-1-80424-677-1
PDF ISBN 978-1-80424-678-8

Published by MX Publishing
335 Princess Park Manor, Royal Drive,
London, N11 3GX
www.mxpublishing.com

Cover design by Awan

Dedication

This novel is dedicated to my family: my wife for her unending support; our sons and daughter-in-law for keeping me grounded; and our grandchildren who continue to help me see the world through wonderous eyes. Their love, support and encouragement have been critical during the writing of this novel.

Table of Contents

Roll Call of Major Characters

(in order of appearance)

Dr. John H. Watson	Physician and colleague of Sherlock Holmes
Sherlock Holmes	Consulting detective
Simon Rhoads	Convicted of the murder of Paul Watts
Mycroft Holmes	Sherlock Holmes' older brother
Inspector Tobias Gregson	Scotland Yard inspector
Det. Sergeant Jeffery Cummings	Scotland Yard detective sergeant
Asst. Comm. Charles Sanders	Scotland Yard assistant commissioner
Comm. Sir Richard Haliford	Scotland Yard commissioner
Chris Ross	American business partner of Paul Watts
Inspector Jack Hall	Retired Scotland Yard inspector
Asa Bloom	Identified Watts' body

Basil Hart	Former business partner of Rhoads
Inspector G. Lestrade	Scotland Yard inspector
Colin Dunn	Watts' part-time employer
Mrs. Frances Dunn (née Hillsdale)	Formerly Mrs. Simon Rhoads
Clint Hatch	Publican at the Fox and Goose
Harvey Wise	Day labourer
Kelwin Hooper	Itinerant seaman

Part I:
Wednesday - October 31, 1894

Chapter I: Dr. Watson Is Summoned

Of the many adventures I shared with my good friend Sherlock Holmes, none has made as significant an impression on my consciousness or psyche as this case. As one ages, one develops the sense that one can distinguish right from wrong, just from unjust. It can be a shattering and humbling experience to suddenly find that you may have been too cavalier in your beliefs and perhaps too trusting in how the law is applied.

My involvement in this extraordinary case (a case which, unbeknownst to us, would span more than eighteen months) began late Wednesday afternoon, the 31st of October, 1894. It was the day prior to All Saint's Day and Holmes and I were in our rooms at 221B Baker Street. The day had been brisk and the small fire crackling in the fireplace kept the cool afternoon temperatures at bay.

Holmes was playing his violin, whilst I was seated in my chair, an open newspaper on my lap, staring out the window deep in my own thoughts. When Holmes ceased his playing, I hadn't noticed, so distant were my ruminations.

"My dear Watson," Holmes began, "why do you volunteer for such duties if it makes you so melancholy?"

I hadn't mentioned anything to Holmes concerning my troubles, and I wasn't in the mood to enter into a discussion about his powers of observation. Yet he had pinpointed my mood exactly.

"How do you know what has set me in this 'melancholy' mood?" I sighed.

"When I see an opened telegram from Newgate Prison on the table, my usually energetic friend sitting quietly staring out the window, and today's newspaper on his lap open to an article concerning an execution that is scheduled to take place tonight, it is the height of simplicity to conclude that he has been requested to serve as the attending physician at a hanging."

"Your powers of observation never cease to amaze me, Holmes," I sarcastically replied.

"Oh, it is simple deduction," Holmes continued, missing my petulant tone. "Although why you volunteer for such duty escapes me."

"Some time ago I was asked if I would be willing to serve as an alternate attending physician for the prison if the need ever arose. I felt it was my civic duty and would help serve the cause of justice. In the event that Dr. Raff, the prison physician, could not be in attendance, either myself or Dr. Taylor in Walworth would serve as his alternate. As it happens, this morning Dr. Raff was called away for a family emergency."

Lifting the telegram, I concluded. "Hence, I have been summoned."

"Well," Holmes said as he sat across the table, "you have never been one to shirk your responsibilities. At least they have ceased with public executions and have brought the gallows inside the prison walls. Make sure you are thorough in your duties. You don't want another incident like that William Duell hanging."

After pausing for a moment, Holmes said, "Pray, tell me about the case."

Referring to the newspaper, I briefly recounted the affair.

"It seems that Mr. Simon Rhoads was convicted of the murder of Mr. Paul Watts. The trial took place late last month. You and I were in France attending to that business for Colonel Charles Maret and his wife."

"Yes. A simple enough case and not very challenging."

"Well," I continued, "it says here that Mr. Rhoads was tried and convicted for the murder. He had been seen quarrelling with Mr. Watts in a pub the evening before the murder. Witnesses said they saw the two men leave together. Both men were found the next morning lying in Battersea Park, across from the pub. Mr. Rhoads was asleep from a night of drinking; Mr Watts was dead from a severe stab wound. The newspaper says the weapon was a letter opener that Rhoads' wife had given him. Both the letter opener and Rhoads' clothes were covered in blood, as of course, was Mr. Watts. Even though Rhoads protested his innocence loudly throughout the trial, he was convicted of the crime and sentenced to hang."

"And the requisite three Sundays have passed, so the execution is tonight?" Holmes enquired.

"Yes, Sunday last was the third. And I'm afraid that since it is the eve of All Saint's Day there will be an even larger and more unruly crowd outside the prison than usual."

"Yes, they'll make quite a festival of it."

We were silent for a few moments until my eyes fell upon another story in the newspaper.

"And here is an article relating that several members of Parliament have asked the Home Secretary to commute Rhoads' sentence. They have even considered petitioning the Queen. But there are other members of Parliament, led by this Lord Oliver, demanding that the sentence be carried out. They've made statements like 'brutal criminals should be treated brutally' and 'blood will have blood.' It appears they will win the day."

Holmes considered this for a moment. "Well, putting brutality and *MacBeth* aside for the moment, Lord Oliver would seem to have a point. The man received a fair trial by the finest justice system in the land. A life was taken, brutally it seems, so a debt is owed to society. A society can only survive if it has laws that are fair and enforced. You are simply serving as confirmation that the final step in the enforcement of the law has been carried out." He paused another moment, then asked, "Tell me, why does this distress you so? I recall the other times you served in this capacity you have also been in an agitated state."

I shook my head.

"It is my own wrangling with my conscience. As a physician I am duty bound to ease suffering. However, as you say, justice must be carried out. A wrong must be punished. I have sat here turning this over and over in my mind. I can find no other solution, yet I feel an uneasiness that neither justice nor society is being well served."

We were each silent for several moments, considering the arguments for and against the issue that was laid before us.

Then Holmes sighed. "Well, we shan't resolve the matter tonight and I can see that you are out of sorts. It was inconsiderate of me to draw you into such a discussion. Please forgive me."

We left the issue there and one hour later I was on my way to Newgate Prison.

# # #

During my journey to the prison, I was thankful for the shelter of a cab as the weather had turned foul. Unfortunately, I was forced to abandon the carriage some two blocks from the prison as the streets were choked with all manner of activity.

Upon exiting the cab, I encountered a mass of people cavorting in the streets and outside the prison walls. Hangings still attracted a large number of people and one could describe the overall mood as festive. Even the heavy mist couldn't dampen the celebratory atmosphere. Men, women and even children were laughing and playing games in the streets outside the prison. Some were dining on sandwiches. Many more were wearing costumes or masks and guzzling beer in celebration of All Saint's Day. This was particularly ghoulish given the event about to take place. Boisterous laughter accompanied by drunken singing added to the cacophony of sounds. As I picked my way through the madness, I observed the very worst of human nature on display.

Street vendors and all manner of folk had set up small stands or tables to sell baubles, trinkets, or anything else that could be peddled wherever there was a crowd of people. One vendor sold masks with the image of a skull painted upon it. Another sold a three-foot length of rope with a hangman's noose on the end. I witnessed several children running through the streets waving the ghastly symbol over their heads.

With a glance down one of the alleys, I paused to watch two gaudily dressed women sitting on the back rails of a buckboard wagon. The male driver, dressed in an overcoat and shoddy hat, sat on the front seat holding the reins of the two horses. All three were gazing at the back of the wagon where I saw the upstretched legs of a third woman, her block-toed shoes in the air. A group of four men stood behind the wagon, quietly watching, waiting, and apparently unconcerned that their activities showed them to be little more than animals. A fifth man came up and spoke to the driver. After money was exchanged, he went and joined the others.

Then one of the seated women rose, apparently in preparation for taking the place of the one lying in the back of the wagon. The third woman, upon seeing me observe them, winked, blew me a kiss, and lifted her skirt slightly. I hastily averted my gaze and moved on.

As I continued making my way through the clamouring mayhem, the stench of burnt sausage and the odour of horse manure from the alley penetrated the damp air. Passing between groups of people, jostled by the rowdy crowd, the strong smell of body odour assailed my senses. From across the street, I could hear discordant singing accompanied by a small accordion. Elsewhere, a fife played as a woman sang an old Scottish dirge. The constant gaiety and laughter were occasionally punctuated with the sound of loud belching, angry cursing, or a random scream.

Pressing on to the prison, I had to step over a man sitting against a lamppost, his hat in his lap, swilling beer purchased from a street vendor. Under a canvas tarpaulin, a busy cadre of *tricoteuses* sat laughing in anticipation of the main event. Then several children with painted faces suddenly surrounded me, and holding hands, danced around me in a circle of gleeful laughter, before running down the pavement.

Finally, I made my way through the melee to the main gate of the prison. The guard was none too happy to see me request entry, believing that I was part of the general rabble celebrating outside.

"We don't let spectators inside! Now be off with ye'," he stated gruffly.

"Sir! I am Dr. John Watson. I have been requested to attend the execution this evening," I declared as I showed him the telegram.

"Oh, aye!" said he. "I didn't recognise ye'. Let me get this here gate open." He fumbled with a heavy set of keys until he found the correct one that unlocked the gate. As I passed through, several people behind me attempted to push forward and enter, but they were harshly forced back by the guard.

With the gate closed, the guard said, "Follow me, Doctor," and led the way across the prison compound towards one of the large wooden prison doors some thirty yards from the gate. As we walked through the prison yard, I saw the execution shed through the mist.

The shed itself had been constructed some years ago when hangings were moved inside the walls of the prison. It was a massive stone structure that stood about fifteen feet tall and some ten feet wide at the top. It protruded away from the prison's west wall by some thirty feet. A large passage connected the condemned cells up on the first floor of the prison with the gallows platform standing at the top of the structure. The upper half of the gallows could be seen from where I was in the prison yard, perhaps to serve as a constant reminder of what awaited those convicted of a capital crime. I have to say that just gazing at the apparatus unnerved me greatly.

"This ought to be a good one tonight, Doctor," the guard said over his shoulder. "He's been telling anyone who'll listen that 'e's innocent."

With a knowing chuckle he continued, "Of course, they're all innocent in 'ere." As the guard spoke, it was evident that he was anticipating the hanging with much enthusiasm.

Once we were inside the prison, we walked up a set of spiralled stone steps to the condemned cells on the first floor. Our footfalls echoed off the stone stairs and condensation could be seen on the walls.

"We 'ave quite a crowd outside tonight," said the guard, the echo of his voice carrying down the steps. "I 'aven't seen a crowd this size in years. What with it comin' up on All Saint's Day and all, this'll be quite a celebration."

"I'm sure that there is a great deal to celebrate, sir," said I grimly.

The guard turned to give me a look of disdain, but I was unconcerned with his opinion. I had found that it was one thing to hold a belief in how justice should be carried out, but it was quite another to actually be a part of the process. I do not mind saying that I was not looking forward to any part of the affair that I was about to witness.

Without any further discussion, the guard took me to an upstairs hallway. As we walked, I saw massive wooden doors at the far end of the corridor. I knew that through those doors, the gallows awaited.

Finally, I was shown to a room where I was told to sit and wait until I was sent for. As I stood at the entryway, I observed that the room had been a cell at one time, with crude messages scratched onto the stone walls and barred windows that looked out onto the back of the prison yard. A small table, upon which I set my medical case, stood against one wall. I sat on the only wooden chair, alone with my thoughts, and waited to be summoned.

As I waited, the sounds around me began to make their way into my consciousness. I could hear the muted rumble of merriment and carrying on of the crowd outside the prison walls. I could also hear an occasional whoop or scream from somewhere deep within the prison as well as the echo of insane laughter. The air in the cell remained chilled and the odour of damp rock was prevalent throughout. The stone floor and walls were cool and damp to the touch due to the inclement weather. Yet I noticed that my mouth was parched from nervous anticipation of the events that were about to take place.

I had seen death many times before. In the war I saw comrades killed by the enemy and in the many cases I shared with Holmes I had viewed dead bodies as the result of all manner of murder. But tonight, this was going to be a death that was to be orchestrated by order of a court. This was a planned, anticipated, and scripted killing that I was going to witness as it took place.

Chapter II: A Morbid Celebration

Some minutes later, as I sat in the empty cell with my thoughts, I heard another group of footsteps approaching. Two gentlemen paused to place something outside the cell, and then were shown in by the guard. I stood, but no introductions were made. The two gentlemen were left standing as the guard simply walked away. They both then silently turned to me. We remained that way, the three of us standing quietly for several seconds.

As we stood, I looked over my new companions to try to determine why they had been brought here. Both were dressed in dark suits, white shirts, and black boots covered in mud. It was apparent that they had walked over dirt roads or pastures prior to arriving.

One was slender and quite tall, possibly six feet four. He had piercing blue eyes and slick dark hair. Long sideburns framed a gaunt face and long arms extended out of too-short coat sleeves. The other man was smaller, perhaps five feet six, and appeared somewhat thick as his clothes seemed to strain against his broad chest and shoulders. He possessed a bushy head of hair, long side whiskers, and discoloured teeth. His smaller stature was due in no small part to his bowed legs, which to my mind appeared to be painful to walk upon. He kept looking from me to the taller man and then back to me as if waiting to see if we were going to come to blows.

Finally, since no introduction seemed to be forthcoming, I said, "I am Dr. John Watson," and extended my hand.

"My name is Robert St. John," the tall man said, "and this is my associate, Harley Yates." There were handshakes all around.

As there were no other chairs, we all remained standing.

"Doctor," Mr. St. John asked after a few additional moments, "do you serve as part of the prison staff?"

"Oh, no," I replied. "I have been asked to substitute for Dr. Raff this evening. He had a family emergency."

"Ah," Mr. St John said nodding. "I was fairly sure I had not seen you at the prison before."

"What are you gentlemen here for?"

"We are here to collect the body for burial after the...sentence has been carried out."

"I thought after an execution the body was placed in a pauper's field," said I.

"Aye, usually that is the case, but his wife has paid for us to collect the body and take it for burial in a private cemetery in Essex."

"Oh, I see," was my reply, and we said nothing more.

Finally, I heard the distant creak of grinding metal hinges followed by a great commotion far down the hall. A man began yelling and screaming. Several other voices could be heard loudly shouting instructions.

"All right! Time to go!"

"Get your hands off me!"

"Behave yourself!"

"You can't do this!"

"Act like a man!"

"You've known this day was coming!"

And loudest of all was the structured cadence of what sounded like prayer or gospel verses being recited over the din. The turmoil made its way up the hall as I and my two companions watched through the open doorway of our room.

When the entourage finally passed by, I could see one man, Simon Rhoads I presumed, struggling as he was physically carried down the hall by four guards. A robed priest followed closely behind with an open Bible reciting the Lord's Prayer.

All the commotion caused other distant voices throughout the prison to begin to scream and shout in a loud cacophony of sounds. Some were laughing, some were shouting encouragement to Rhoads, and some were simply making noise to add to the tumult. At this point the prison had become little more than a madhouse.

The guard who had let me through the prison gate finally came up and said, "This way, gentlemen," and motioned us up the hallway behind the noisy procession. Grasping my medical bag, I stepped into the corridor, my two companions following, with the gate guard bringing up the rear. I noticed that the large wooden doors I had seen at the end of the hallway were now open, the grey sky visible behind the distant guard towers. A rush of cool, damp air had filled the corridor. Beyond the open doors and out in the weather stood the gallows, a solitary rope hanging over the third drop. All appeared to be ready atop the execution shed.

Our progress was slow as the guards were having difficulty keeping hold of Rhoads. As I followed, I tried to imagine what the condemned man must be experiencing, knowing that these were his very last steps. Knowing that these were his very last moments of life. Knowing that he was about to leave this world. If his faith was strong, he possibly took some comfort in what might come next. If not, he was going into the terrifying unknown.

"Murder! You're all committing murder!" Rhoads yelled. "Each of you guards! You're all murderers! I've never killed anyone! I'm innocent, I tell you!"

He violently turned his head to try to look at the priest behind him. "You're participating in a murder! How about that! A murdering priest!" The priest, undeterred, continued his recitations.

As we went out to the gallows, the heavy mist had turned to a light rain. Indeed, the inclement weather had not dampened the raucous crowd outside the prison walls. Laughter, singing, and music could be heard clearly from the street. But for those of us standing on the platform, the solemn sense of approaching death stood in stark contrast with the joyous noise of the crowd outside.

Rhoads was placed on the drop underneath the noose. When the signal was given, the executioner would pull a lever and the floor would fall open.

As his hands and legs were being tied together, Rhoads wildly looked around. Seeing my medical bag, he brought his focus upon me.

"You! Doctor! You're participating in a murder and you're supposed to be a healer! Physician! Heal thyself!" He followed this outburst with a maniacal laugh, spittle ejecting from his mouth. It was at that moment that I could discern the true level of fright and panic in the man's eyes.

I looked behind me and saw that in addition to the two gentlemen who had joined me in the cell and the gate guard, there were four other individuals standing nearby to observe the execution. I recognised Warden Harrison, whom I had interacted with several times over the years. I also saw Inspector Jack Hall of Scotland Yard. Even with his hat and damp mackintosh I recognised his compact figure. From the newspaper reports I knew that he had led the investigation that had resulted in Rhoads being found guilty. There was another, younger man standing beside Inspector Hall, whom I did not recognise but assumed was a member of the police. The last fellow, an older gentleman, was standing back and to the left of everyone else, quietly taking notes. I assumed that he was the lone newspaper reporter who had been allowed to witness the proceedings. There were no witnesses from the victim's family, as Mr. Watts had no family. Rhoads' wife was not in attendance for obvious reasons.

Once Rhoads' hands and legs had been bound, the executioner prepared to place a black hood over his head. Rhoads violently moved to avoid the cover.

"No!" he roared. Then looking over at Warden Harrison he demanded, "As my last request, I demand that no hood be placed over my head! I want everyone here to see what a murder really looks like!"

Warden Harrison seemed unsure for a few moments, then nodded in the affirmative. The executioner tossed the hood to the side and then placed the noose over Rhoads' head and around his neck.

The warden solemnly retrieved a paper from his coat pocket and began to read:

"Simon Rhoads. You have been convicted of the wilful murder of Paul Watts, contrary to common law. The courts have heard the evidence; a jury of your peers has found you guilty; your sentence has been pronounced. Today that sentence will be carried out. Do you have any last words?"

Rhoads, his damp hair plastered upon his forehead, made an effort to calm his heavy breathing. After a few moments he spoke, and as he did so, he looked at each and every person who was in attendance.

"I am an innocent man. I never killed anyone. Tell my wife that I love her. And may God have mercy on all of *your* souls!"

This last caused Harley Yates to cross himself and begin to mutter his own prayer.

"Very well," the warden said as the priest again began his murmurings. The warden briefly turned towards the priest, paused a moment, then turned back to the executioner and promptly gave a nod. The executioner pulled the lever and with a loud, sharp groan of metal grinding against metal, the floor opened up and Rhoads fell through.

The rope snapped taut and for just a few moments Rhoads' arms and legs convulsed, restricted by their bindings. His face, however, was in full view just above the floor. His features were twisted in agony, eyes bulging and neck turning from white to bright red as the rope tightened itself.

Soon the body ceased its movements and began to slowly rotate. The rain fell a little harder, splashing on the gallows and the wooden walkway. We were all silent except for the priest, who quietly continued his readings. The commotion and uproar that had seemed so prevalent outside the prison walls just moments ago now seemed to have disappeared as we watched the lifeless body hang.

At this point we were required to wait at least fifteen minutes to ensure that the prisoner had expired. Our entourage retreated to the shelter of the prison corridor from which we had emerged in order to get out of the inclement weather.

As we stood silently, the festive sounds from the streets outside the prison were further muted by the clamour from within the prison. Somehow the prisoners seemed to know that the execution had taken place, and they were banging on their metal cell bars with whatever came to hand. And while each of us would have much preferred to be anywhere else, we were duty-bound to stand by, watching the body slowly twist as the rain softly fell and time crawled forward.

After fifteen interminable minutes, the warden mercifully said, "All right, let's get him up."

We all moved back out into the rain and onto the scaffold. Two guards grasped the rope and quietly hauled the body up to the platform before laying it out on the damp wood.

Turning to me the warden said, "Doctor, if you please."

I came forward and with my stethoscope checked for any signs of life: heartbeat, pulse, respiration. After a few moments, I pronounced Simon Rhoads deceased.

"Thank you, Doctor," the warden said as he handed me an official looking piece of paper. "If you'll sign this death certificate, we'll not detain you any further."

I read the certificate, signed it, and handed it back to the warden. He took it from me, folded it into his coat pocket and turned to Messrs. St. John and Yates.

"All right, gentlemen, he's all yours."

As I turned to leave, I saw the two men reach for a stretcher they had brought. They unfolded the stretcher and proceeded to place the body of Simon Rhoads upon it. A thick, oil-skinned sheet was placed over the corpse, like a shroud, to shield it from the worsening weather. I imagined they would take the body to a wagon at the back of the prison and quietly transport it to which-ever cemetery Rhoads' wife had selected.

With the guard following close behind, I made my way quickly back down the corridor, past the small cell where I and my companions had waited, and down the stone steps. Once I was out of the building, I strode across the prison yard towards the gate through which I had entered. I was anxious to return home and to be done with the place. Shortly, I arrived at the prison gate where I was let out. The rain continued to fall and the clamour of the crowd that had seemed to diminish only a few moments ago had become more pronounced as they continued their festivities in the streets outside the prison.

As I walked through the throng, a sudden roar of applause and cheering erupted. Looking back, I saw that the black flag had been raised over the prison. The crowd now knew that the execution had carried out. The celebration and singing continued, and I imagined it would be maintained well into the night.

As for me, I had to make my way back through the crowd for two blocks before I could finally hail a cab back to Baker Street. When I arrived Holmes could see that I was in no mood to discuss the events of the evening, so he simply continued playing his violin. I was so much out of sorts that I felt it best that I go to bed, but not until I had drunk two large shots of whisky to settle my nerves.

That experience, and those that followed in this case, have haunted me ever since. While I served as the prison's attending physician on only a few occasions, this was the last and most troubling.

Now, in writing about this case some twenty-odd years later, I am further reminded of the impact this experience had on my overall view of the world and the era in which it took place. On that day, the Victorian veneer had somehow lost its sheen, and seemed to have never really been as elegant as it had at first appeared. Like a velvet cloak that when seen from a distance appears to be stylish and fashionable, but upon closer examination is found to be tattered and moth-eaten. Perhaps it simply was the first time I had finally recognised the dark underbelly of the world we lived in.

Part II:
Day 1 – Monday

Chapter III: Mr. Holmes Gets a Case

It was on Monday, the 6th of April, 1896, that the events previously mentioned returned to occupy both our lives in a most extraordinary way. I recall the day exactly because it was the first day of the Modern Olympic Games that were taking place in Athens, Greece.

Holmes and I were in our rooms at Baker Street just finishing an early afternoon meal. We were discussing the resumption of the games after a fifteen-hundred-year absence.

"Well, I for one am very excited to see that the Olympic Games are being restarted in the modern era," I enthused. "And just imagine, we will be able to get eyewitness accounts of the events the very day they occur. Reporters will transmit their stories to the newspapers and we will read about the games that very evening. What a modern marvel! It is certainly a good time to be alive."

"Yes," Holmes calmly agreed as he stood gazing out the window. I could see that his enthusiasm was not as great as my own, but he had been out of sorts lately. There had not been very much for him to do after that affair with the submarine plans late the previous year. More than once, he would scour the newspaper for any hint of a potential case.

Holmes simply could not be idle. My concerns for the well-being of my friend had continued as the weeks passed. Would my friend seek the solace of the needle to alleviate the inactivity of his brain? I had recently made it a habit to keep him engaged in conversation and companionship, hoping that my efforts would keep his mind occupied. I also took the opportunity to surreptitiously look for any signs of abuse he might inflict upon himself.

Before anything further could be said, a soft knock came to our door.

"Ah," Holmes sighed heavily as he walked to the door. "This is probably someone who has lost their pet dog and wants my assistance in locating it."

Holmes opened the door and a messenger handed him a note. Holmes took the note and read it...twice. The expression on his face was at first puzzlement, followed by intrigue.

He turned to the messenger and handed him a coin.

"Thank you. There is no reply," and he closed the door.

"This does indeed seem to be the beginnings of a case," he said as he handed the message to me. It read thus:

S.

Most urgent I speak with you and Dr. Watson.

D.C. 3 PM. Please come.

M.

The note was from Mycroft, Sherlock's older brother. Holmes and I gazed at each other a moment, intrigued as much by its contents as by its brevity. As I put the note down, I could see that Holmes was anxious to be on our way.

"Get your hat and coat, Watson. The matter must be most urgent to cause Mycroft to be at the Diogenes Club prior to his customary quarter to five. If we leave now, we can have a pleasant walk to the club and be there at the appointed hour."

After gathering our hats, coats, and walking sticks, we made our way down to the street. It was a blustery day as London had been slow to come out of a long winter. I for one was thankful that at least it wasn't snowing.

We walked towards Oxford Street in silence as the frantic pace of the London environs engulfed us. Carriages and pedestrians dodged one another as the ever-present stream of commerce ebbed and flowed. Knowing Holmes would never hypothesize on any matter without data, it was useless to try to induce him to speculate on what the urgent matter might be. So, I endeavoured to enjoy the short walk, the sunshine, and the brisk, fresh air.

In just a few minutes we turned onto Pall Mall and shortly thereafter came to the nondescript door that gave way to the Diogenes Club. Passing through the entrance, we came to a wall of glass panelling through which one could see a large room where several men sat reading silently. And that was the point of the club: to provide a place where gentlemen could go and read the day's news without the need or obligation to socialise with one another. It was a most unique organisation.

Once inside we were shown to the Stranger's Room, the only room in the club where visitors *and* talking were allowed. The room was small and contained several oversized chairs scattered along two walls; a large bookcase covered a third wall, and along the fourth wall a bow window looked out upon Pall Mall. In the middle of the room were several chairs and a long table.

Upon entering, we encountered two other men who were standing by the large window, looking out. They turned at our arrival and we recognised one of them.

"Why if it isn't Inspector Tobias Gregson of Scotland Yard," Holmes said as he shook the man's hand. I also shook his hand and as I did, I couldn't help but notice the almost sick expression on the inspector's face, as if he had eaten something that greatly disagreed with him. He was a tall man with square hands and flaxen hair. His normally bright eyes appeared dull from lack of sleep and his beard was in need of a trim.

"Hello Mr. Holmes, Dr. Watson," the inspector sighed. "I don't mind telling you you're a sight for sore eyes."

Then turning to the other man standing next to him he said, "Let me introduce Detective Sergeant Jeffery Cummings of Scotland Yard. Sergeant, this is Mr. Sherlock Holmes and Dr. Watson."

"A pleasure to meet you both, I'm sure," the sergeant said as he shook our hands. The young man looked familiar to me, but I could not place where I had seen him before. He stood about five feet ten inches tall and seemed unusually thin. I would have placed his age at no more than thirty-two years. Bushy, brown hair reached to his collar and his hazel eyes appeared to continually move about his surroundings.

His clothes were of moderate quality and he wore sensible shoes that were well-polished.

"Well, Inspector, do you know what this is all about?" enquired Sherlock.

"Aye, I do, Mr. Holmes. But I've been instructed not to say anything until everyone is here."

"Who else is coming, besides Mycroft?"

At that moment the door opened and Mycroft Holmes' rotund figure came into the room. While he was still a large man, he appeared to have lost some weight since I had seen him last, as evidenced by the loose fit of his shirt collar and jacket. When he entered, he didn't present his customary confident manner, and I could see he wore a troubled expression.

So rarely did Sherlock speak of his own family, it was quite some time after my initial acquaintance with him that I discovered he even had an older brother. Mycroft held some nebulous government position that brought him, and occasionally Holmes, in contact with problems of a critical nature that could be of drastic import to the government.

Mycroft was followed by two other men, dressed in formal police uniforms. Both Inspector Gregson and Sergeant Cummings quickly came to attention as they entered. Once everyone was in the room, Mycroft closed the door.

"Sherlock, Dr. Watson, I'd like to thank you for coming so promptly," Mycroft said as we shook hands, his large hand engulfing my own in greeting. Then turning to the two men who entered with him he said, "Let me introduce Assistant Commissioner Charles Sanders and Sir Richard Haliford, Commissioner of Scotland Yard."

Both men were dressed smartly in their freshly pressed uniforms. Assistant Commissioner Sanders was a gentleman of about fifty-five years of age and stood about six feet tall. The hair on his head, moustache, and beard had gone to grey, and his sharp eyes peered out from underneath unruly grey eyebrows. While I had never met the man, I knew of him from his dealings with the Fenians prior to joining Scotland Yard. He had also had some involvement with the Ripper murder investigations.

Commissioner Haliford stood about five feet eleven inches tall and appeared to be approximately sixty-five years of age. He too possessed grey hair and a grey moustache, yet I noted he had piercing blue eyes that quickly surveyed the room and seemed to miss nothing. He had lost the lower part of his left arm years ago while in service during the Indian Uprising; the partially-empty sleeve of his dress jacket was pinned neatly under his upper arm. It was evident that he had not let the amputation interfere with his life's pursuits.

After the introductions, there were handshakes all around. The assistant commissioner waved the inspector and sergeant to stand at ease and then Mycroft motioned towards the large table and asked everyone to sit.

I do not mind saying that my mind was reeling from what had just transpired. This must indeed be an important case to get both the assistant commissioner and the commissioner of Scotland Yard to take a personal interest. I took out my notebook and prepared to take notes.

"Ah, sorry, but we can't have any notes taken at this meeting," Commissioner Haliford said looking sternly at me.

Before I could react, Sherlock stood.

"Then we shall take our leave," he said matter-of-factly and began to make his way to the door.

"Sherlock, this is a most distressing business and your participation is critical," Mycroft stated as he turned towards his brother.

"That may be, but I will not be dictated to regarding how I work and whether we take notes or not. It is a simple decision but we need to get this settled before we go any further."

I felt extraordinarily conspicuous since I had inadvertently started this stand-off, but all eyes in the room were on the commissioner. After a few moments, he acquiesced.

"Very well," he sighed. "I apologize, Dr. Watson."

Mollified, Holmes resumed his seat and we again settled down to get to the reason we had all been summoned.

"Gentlemen," Mycroft began, "for over eight hundred years, English Common Law has been faithfully applied and carried out in this country. It has inspired the legal foundations of foreign governments and is the standard by which other countries measure their own judicial systems. Every Englishman in the realm is not only proud of, but has the utmost faith and confidence in, the sanctity of British law."

Mycroft paused a moment, then continued.

"You have been asked here today because it may be that a mortal stain has been placed upon our judicial system. That a miscarriage of justice has taken place so egregious that if it were to become known, not only would confidence in the justice system be shaken to the core, but it would not be an exaggeration to say that confidence in the current government could be in peril."

Finally, Holmes could take no more.

"Mycroft, what has happened?"

Mycroft focused his gaze first at me, then he turned to his brother.

"It seems that Great Britain executed a man for the murder of someone who wasn't dead."

Chapter IV: An Injustice Uncovered

The room was silent. Even as I wrote the words, I could hardly believe I had heard them. The worst fear of any true justice system is the miscarriage of justice, but an execution would be a miscarriage of the greatest kind, one that could not be rectified. The worst fears of those opposed to capital punishment would be realized, and the common citizenry would begin to question the entire judicial institution.

Holmes was the first to recover.

"Mycroft, why do you, and I assume these other gentlemen, believe that this has happened? What is the specific case that is of concern here?"

"The specific case," Mycroft replied, "involved the murder of Paul Watts and the execution of Simon Rhoads for that murder."

I felt my heart almost stop. The images and sounds from that execution suddenly came roaring back to my mind. The damp smells of the prison, the priest's mutterings, and Rhoads' frantic accusations that we were all participating in murder came flooding back to my senses. I also realized that it was at the execution where I had seen the young sergeant. He had been standing on the platform next to Inspector Hall.

I must have made some sort of unconscious sound or movement, for when I looked up everyone had fixed their gaze upon me.

"Are you not well, Doctor?" Mycroft asked.

I gathered myself and responded. "It was Simon Rhoads' execution in which I served as the attending physician. The entire affair was most distressing."

"How extraordinary," Mycroft said to himself after a moment.

Sherlock turned to me. "Do you wish to continue?"

"Oh, yes, yes," said I. If such a miscarriage of justice had occurred, then indeed I wanted to get to the bottom of it, no matter how stressful the situation became.

"Well," Mycroft continued, "at the time the case seemed straightforward. I will not get into the details of the case at this meeting. That will be for another time. But there was not much doubt as to Simon Rhoads' guilt in causing the death of Paul Watts during the trial and leading up to the execution.

"However, in the early hours of this morning, the body of Paul Watts was found down by the London docks. Detective Sergeant Cummings was the first investigator on the scene."

Mycroft turned to Sergeant Cummings and said, "Why don't you tell us what you found."

Sergeant Cummings had been quietly listening. When his name was called, he sat up straighter to provide his information. It was apparent that he was ill at ease speaking to so many high-ranking members of Scotland Yard. After clearing his throat, he began.

"Well, I arrived to the docks in the early morning hours. I'd say about five-thirty. The body was on the pavement, and a constable was standing with another man. I learned that the other man was Mr. Chris Ross from

America. He said that he and the victim, whom he referred to as Paul Watts, had disembarked from a ship from America a few hours previously. They had come to London because they were considering expanding their export business. After checking into their hotel, Ross said Watts wanted to walk a bit before going to bed."

He stopped and took a breath, his nervousness still evident.

"When he told me the victim's name I was surprised, but initially not too concerned. The Watts murder was the first case I worked after I achieved the rank of detective sergeant. I worked the case with Inspector Jack Hall, a good investigator. So, I asked the constable to accompany Mr. Ross back to his hotel room and to remain there with him until he heard from me. Once I saw them off, I began to search the body.

"I found the man's cruise line ticket in the name of 'Paul Watts' and it showed that he had arrived several hours before. I also found a British passport for 'Paul Watts' in his coat pocket. I quickly looked through the passport and found that it had been stamped with today's date when he arrived from America with his business partner. I looked back through the passport for any previous stamps and found that the passport showed he had departed from England on the 13th of September, 1894, and had arrived to America on the 20th of September, 1894. The 13th of September, 1894, was the morning we found Simon Rhoads and a body purported to be that of Paul Watts in Battersea Park."

Sergeant Cummings paused again clearly unnerved. He was not unaware of the part he may have played in both an incorrect conviction and the discovery of the body of a man thought dead several months previous.

"Now gentlemen," Sergeant Cummings continued, "I'm aware that there could be several men by the name of Paul Watts in the London area, so I wanted to be sure of my facts. When Inspector Gregson here arrived on the scene, I told him what had transpired and my fears that this could be the Paul Watts from another case. I requested that he allow me to search the cruise line's passenger logs to see if a 'Paul Watts' had travelled on their ship during the fall of 1894 to America. He agreed to continue working with the body but to use the name 'John Doe' for the victim until he heard from me.

"By this time the cruise line offices had opened for the morning, so I went to look through their archived passenger logs. It was short work to find that Paul Watts had indeed departed from London harbour on the morning of Friday, the 13th of September, 1894."

The two high-ranking police officials had remained silent so far during this oration. But a brief glance at the commissioner showed the man had a stoic expression and clear eyes that were focused on Sergeant Cummings as he gave his account. The assistant commissioner, however, had one hand on his forehead, shielding his eyes, while his other hand made markings on the paper in front of him. Both men listened intently since they would ultimately be responsible for the outcome of this case.

After a moment's pause, Sergeant Cummings continued.

"After checking the passenger logs, I went to the tax office and found that there are two other men by the name of 'Paul Watts' living in London, and both are still alive and paid their taxes this past year. The tax records also showed that a third Paul Watts paid his outstanding taxes in full on the 10th of September, 1894, with a note on the account stating that he was 'emigrating to America.' This led me to conclude that the real Paul Watts was found murdered this morning near the London docks and that Simon Rhoads did not murder Paul Watts on the 13th of September, 1894, as he was convicted of doing."

The room was silent as we all digested the implications of this discovery.

"Once I verified the records at the tax office," Sergeant Cummings concluded with a sigh, "I reported my findings to Inspector Gregson. I also sent another constable to relieve the constable I had assigned to stay with Mr. Ross. They are still at Ross' hotel room as we speak."

Inspector Gregson, who had been silent throughout this narration, now spoke up.

"When Sergeant Cummings reported back that the body was indeed that of the once-thought-deceased Paul Watts, I felt that unusual measures were called for. I had kept the victim's name as 'John Doe' in all reports up to this point, and I believed that now this issue had to be escalated quickly. I contacted Assistant Commissioner Sanders and apprised him of the situation."

"You leapt over several lines of command in doing so," Holmes pointed out.

"You're correct Mr. Holmes," the assistant commissioner interjected, "he did. But the inspector and I have a personal relationship as well as a professional one. My wife is a cousin of Inspector Gregson's, so we see each other at family gatherings. It is not unusual for us to be seen speaking together while at the Met."

31

It seemed fortunate indeed that a personal relationship existed, or this issue might already be spreading throughout the entire police force.

"To get back to the matter at hand," Assistant Commissioner Sanders resumed, "I contacted Commissioner Haliford here and brought him up to date with where matters stood and what had been found."

"And I," Commissioner Haliford added, "promptly, and quietly, spoke to Sir Harold Bixby, the Home Secretary, and provided all the information that we had for his consideration."

"That, Sherlock," Mycroft said, "was how I became involved. The Home Secretary asked me to deal with this case. So, I sent for you and Dr. Watson."

Now that we were current on the happenings that had taken place since the early hours of this morning, it seemed that a great deal had transpired prior to our meeting. High-level discussions at Scotland Yard leading to the involvement of the Home Secretary all pointed to an incident of the utmost importance and concern.

But that wasn't the end of it.

"I should also tell you," Commissioner Haliford added, "both I and the assistant commissioner submitted our resignations to the Home Secretary this afternoon. He has not accepted them, but is holding them until this case is brought to a close."

"There is another matter pertaining to this case that you should be aware of," Mycroft interjected. "Lord Oliver was quite vocal at the time of Rhoads' execution that it should take place, even while others were asking for the sentence to be commuted. Now that he is the Prime Minister, if it comes out that the executed man was innocent, those who oppose Lord Oliver in Parliament and in the press will waste no time sowing discontent. The moderates in Parliament, not wanting to be seen as supporting the execution of an innocent man, will also throw their support to the Prime Minister's opponents and he will no doubt have to call for new elections." Mycroft sighed and concluded. "We thought it best not to inform the Prime Minister of the situation until we have all of the facts."

After considering what he had heard, Holmes said, "So if I have this correct, the only person outside of this room who knows that this morning's dead man is a man who was supposed to have been killed eighteen months ago is the Home Secretary?"

"Yes, that's correct," Mycroft agreed. "No one has informed the former Home Secretary and there are no plans at this time to do so unless it becomes necessary."

"Such as the need to deflect blame away from the current Home Secretary for something that happened during the former Home Secretary's tenure?" Sherlock chided.

"Perhaps," Mycroft responded matter-of-factly. "Watts' business partner, Chris Ross, who travelled with Watts, obviously knows he is dead now, but is completely unaware that it was thought Watts had been murdered eighteen months previously here in London." After a moment's thought he added, "I think we had better keep it that way."

"I agree," Holmes said, but I could tell his mind was working on something else.

At that moment, Commissioner Haliford cleared his throat as he prepared to speak.

"Gentlemen," he began, "the assistant commissioner and I discussed on our way over here how devastating this case could be if it became known that a man was executed for the murder of someone who wasn't dead. Devastating to the police force, devastating to the judicial system, and most likely devastating to the Prime Minister. Absolute secrecy must be maintained, at least until we know what happened and we can decide how best to address the situation." As his eyes scanned the group in the room, they came to rest upon me.

Sergeant Cummings, having lost his reticence to speak, said, "Well, Simon Rhoads may have killed the man found in the park with him. We just don't know."

Mycroft took that as his opportunity to give us our task.

"That is essentially what the four of you – Sherlock, Dr. Watson, Inspector Gregson and Sergeant Cummings – are to find out. We are asking that you get to the root of the matter. Investigate and find the answers to several questions. For example, who was the body that was identified as Paul Watts in September, 1894? Who killed him? Why did the investigation find Rhoads guilty of the murder of Watts when it seems that Watts was on a transatlantic voyage to America at the time? Was the police investigation mishandled? Was any evidence overlooked? Was any evidence manufactured?"

Mycroft paused, then concluded, "Sherlock, find out everything you can about that case and the murder this morning."

The assistant commissioner said, "Inspector Gregson, Sergeant Cummings, you both are on official leave, with pay, while you work on this case. You may have access to anything you need at Scotland Yard, just be discreet. If you encounter any obstacles, come directly to me."

"Sir!" both men responded smartly.

"Assistant Commissioner?" my friend interjected. "I believe we will need as much information regarding the Rhoads case as we can gather. I'd like to suggest that you request the initial autopsy report and the transcribed trial notes, as well as the Prosecution's files for this case, so that we may have them by this evening. The request may not seem so unusual coming from you. Perhaps you could say that you are considering using that case as an example for your inspectors."

The assistant commissioner considered my friend's request for a moment before replying.

"Very well, Mr. Holmes. I'll collect the files as soon as I depart from here." Then turning to Inspector Gregson, he said, "I'll place all of the files in a box that will be behind my desk. I'll write your name on it. When you are ready to collect the box, you'll find it there."

"Thank you, sir!"

Turning to Mycroft, the commissioner said, "We would like to receive updates on the investigation's progress, perhaps here at six o'clock on Wednesday evening."

"Yes," Mycroft added, "I've been requested to update the Home Secretary as well."

"Just one more thing, gentlemen," Sherlock interjected. addressing the two senior Scotland Yard officials. "I want to be clear that I understand the precarious position the two of you, as well as the Prime Minister, are in due to this situation. But I need your complete assurances that regardless of where the evidence leads us, there will be no effort to stifle or curtail the investigation. Now, I don't for a moment believe that either of you or the Prime Minister had a direct hand in this affair, but regardless of whether the evidence paints Scotland Yard or the Prime Minister in a favourable or unfavourable light, I intend to follow the investigation to the very end and see that justice is done."

Both senior Scotland Yard officials exchanged glances, then Commissioner Haliford said, "We would expect nothing less, sir."

"Thank you, gentlemen," Holmes said with a nod of his head.

After another moment, both the assistant commissioner and commissioner rose to leave. Inspector Gregson and Sergeant Cummings stood smartly.

"Gentlemen," the commissioner said as they walked to the door, "we are relying on your utmost discretion. I don't want to consider the ramifications if this information were to become public. The citizens would demand answers. I doubt if the Prime Minister would survive the scandal. Well, we'll leave it with you. Good day."

After the assistant commissioner and commissioner had left, Inspector Gregson and Sergeant Cummings resumed their seats. We were all quiet for a moment, each contemplating the issues and questions that had been discussed.

Finally, Holmes said, "I usually work with only Dr. Watson by my side, but in this case, I believe the aid of the inspector and Sergeant Cummings will be most welcomed. I'm sure there will come a time when we will need additional files and information held only at Scotland Yard."

Then turning to the two policemen, he said, "I suggest that we utilize Baker Street as our primary base of operation. I do not believe it would be prudent to be seen investigating a closed case at police headquarters."

"Aye, that's a good point," Gregson agreed.

"Has the medical examiner completed the autopsy of Mr. Watts yet?"

"Most likely, he's doing it now," Gregson replied. "He was told to push everything else aside to do the autopsy. He was a bit angry and confused about the urgency of an autopsy for a John Doe. But he should be finished shortly. He's been instructed not to leave until he speaks with me on the matter."

"Good," Holmes said. "Then I suggest that we interview Chris Ross, Watts' business partner, at his hotel. Let's see what he knows, or if Watts said anything to him about any danger he might face once he arrived in London. I think the sooner we can send Mr. Ross on his way back to America the better. For all we know, he may be in danger as well."

"Aye," the inspector agreed. "And by the time we finish with Mr. Ross, the medical examiner should have completed the autopsy of Watts and we can collect the autopsy report."

"Very well," Holmes said as we all rose from our seats.

"Good luck, gentlemen," Mycroft said, "I have every confidence you'll get to the bottom of this affair."

As we all made our way to the street, I must admit I did not share Mycroft's confidence. It seemed a whirlwind of dangerous events had been unleashed eighteen months ago, festered for a year and a half, and were only now coming to a head. And I felt that we were, all four, in the centre of it.

Chapter V: The Investigation Begins

It was late afternoon when we left the Diogenes Club. I, as well as my companions, were still in shock, and that shock was in evidence as the cab took us to the London docks. We rode in silence, each man holding his own counsel.

"Sergeant Cummings?" Holmes asked finally breaking the silence. "Forgive me, but I must ask what your feelings and intentions are since we will be investigating a case that you played a major part in. I, in fact we all here, must have confidence that you will provide complete and unbiased information regardless of whether it reflects well upon you or any of the other officers involved in this case. I know this cannot be easy for you."

Sergeant Cummings was silent for several moments as he gave consideration to what Holmes had asked.

"You are right, Mr. Holmes," said he. "This is not easy for me. Prior to this morning, I maintained a fairly confident view of not only my abilities but those of Scotland Yard. This entire incident has come as a great shock to me. When I learned the name of this morning's victim, I suppose I could have just said nothing and let the murder investigation move along as normal. I'm pretty sure that no one else would have made the connection of the victim's name with a case eighteen months previously."

Sergeant Cummings turned to look earnestly at Holmes. "But I *did* make the connection, and it would have haunted me for the rest of my life not knowing for sure whether our initial investigation had resulted in a terrible mistake. I wanted to know what had happened. How had that man come to be on the London docks this morning when we had convicted and executed someone for his murder several months before? No, Mr. Holmes, I'll investigate this case with the appropriate commitment and thoroughness it deserves."

"It does speak well of you, Sergeant, that you did take the extra steps to verify your suspicions. And I believe that you will give a good account of yourself and Scotland Yard on this case. Very well. I think we can also benefit from your first-hand knowledge of the first crime and the investigation."

We rode the rest of the way in silence.

The pace of commerce seemed to quicken as our carriage neared the London docks. Ships unloaded their cargo at the end of the piers. Large boxes of goods bundled in netting were hauled through the air by cranes and pulleys, then set down on the dockside. Fully laden lorries drawn by two-horse teams moved up and down the roadway. Dock workers focused on their tasks with very little patience for anyone who might impede their efforts. An inescapable wind ladened with the odour of fish engulfed us as we approached the piers.

We arrived in front of the Seaway Hotel where Mr. Ross' room was located and exited our cab. The foundation of the hotel consisted of stonework, which covered the exterior of the ground floor; brick covered the exterior of the two upper floors. A set of double doors at the centre of the building provided entry into the establishment. A long hallway leading to a registration desk could be seen through the windows of the doors. Two large bow windows were located on either side of the building entrance. A dining room could be seen through the left window with candles, plates, and chairs set up along a handsome table. Through the right window, a large library or sitting room was occupied by three or four guests.

Before entering the hotel, Holmes turned to Inspector Gregson.

"Inspector, before we speak to Mr. Ross, I wonder if I might have a look at the scene where the body was found this morning."

Inspector Gregson and Sergeant Cummings looked at each other.

"We can certainly take you there, Mr. Holmes," the inspector said, pointing, "it's just down the way there. But the body has been removed, and I'm sure all manner of foot traffic and lorries have trampled over the place."

"That may be, but nevertheless I'd like to see it, if you please."

"By all means," and Inspector Gregson led the way down the pavement towards the docks.

In a very short time, we approached a place on the pavement where it was obvious that something of significance had taken place. A darkened oblong stain, about four feet by three feet in size, was evident on the pavement. Even though the matters of commerce had not been stopped by the terrible event that had occurred here, evidence of the tragedy remained.

Holmes took out his lens and spent several minutes studying the stain and looking around the general area. I also took time to gaze at the surroundings. Alongside of the pavement there were coils of large rope and stacks of wooden boxes awaiting further shipment. Wastepaper and detritus were blown about on random gusts of wind.

After a few minutes, Holmes said, "There appear to be a number of places where one or more assailants could lay in wait for a victim to come along. Those stacked boxes would provide ample shadowing for someone to remain unseen even in moonlight."

He then turned to Sergeant Cummings and asked, "Exactly how was the body positioned when you came upon the scene?"

"Well," Sergeant Cummings began, "the victim was lying flat on his back with his feet together and his arms down by his sides. I could see the blood pooling out from beneath him. There was more blood on the victim's back left side, so I believe that is where the stab wound will be, but we'll need to wait for the autopsy to be sure."

"I see," Holmes said after a moment. "So, if someone came up and stabbed you in the back, how do you suppose you would naturally fall?"

He had posed the question to no one in particular, but it was Sergeant Cummings who responded.

"I should think that I would fall in a heap; body crumpled, possibly forward a bit. Not laid out as if I were in bed asleep."

"Right you are, Sergeant Cummings. So, what does that tell us?"

"That the murderer took time to lay the victim out?" asked Inspector Gregson.

"Perhaps," responded Holmes. "But why? Why take the time to lay out the body? For what purpose? For now, we don't know, but we should keep this piece of information in our minds as it may provide some insights later. I also draw your attention to the fact that there are no other bloodstains in evidence anywhere else on the pavement. Only where the victim lay. That may also prove to be important."

Holmes spent another few moments looking at the scene, then after returning his lens to his pocket said, "All right. I think we've learned all we can here. Let's go speak with Mr. Ross."

Chapter VI: What Mr. Ross Had to Say

The four of us began to retrace our steps back to the Seaway Hotel. It was approaching twilight now and the seedier side of the London docks were beginning to emerge. I could not help but notice the suspicious glares that were focused in our direction. Women dressed flamboyantly had begun to present themselves along certain doorways. This was certainly no place for gentlemen, and I was hopeful that we would get what information we could and leave this area straightaway.

As we entered the hotel, Sergeant Cummings guided us through the lobby and up the stairs to the first floor. Mr. Ross' room was on the left at the top of the stairs. A constable answered our knock and we entered a small room with a bed, dresser, chifforobe and washing bowl. A lone window looked out on an alley located at the backside of the hotel.

"Gentlemen, this is Mr. Chris Ross," Sergeant Cummings said, and he made the introductions. Chris Ross looked to be about thirty years of age with a lanky figure, dark hair and narrow eyes that looked around a hooked nose. His face was clean shaven and his hands, while thin and bony, possessed hidden strength. It was evident from his grimace that he was in quite a state of agitation.

"Sergeant Cummings!" Ross exclaimed after shaking our hands, "I must protest being kept locked away in this hotel room. It is bad enough that my friend has been murdered only hours after our arrival, but now I am being held captive and watched over by Scotland Yard. I must ask to what purpose? We only came to this wretched place to consider opening a new office!"

"I can answer that," Inspector Gregson said. "We were concerned, and in fact are still concerned, that perhaps the murder of Mr. Watts was a targeted attack and that you may very well be at risk. Since this incident occurred so soon after you both disembarked from your ship, we felt that extreme precautions should be taken."

This seemed to mollify Ross somewhat, but I could see that he still harboured some ill feelings about the situation, which I have to say I found understandable.

"May I ask, Mr. Ross," Holmes interjected to move the interview along, "What did you and Mr. Watts do after your ship arrived?"

"We departed the ship," Ross began, turning to Holmes, "and we came to this hotel to check into our rooms. I was exhausted so I remained in my room, but Paul left for a brief walk. The next thing I knew, the police were knocking on my hotel room door telling me Paul was dead."

After a moment, Holmes asked, "How did you come to know Mr. Watts?"

"Well, I met Paul almost two years ago here in London; in late May, 1894, I believe it was. I had travelled to England on holiday to meet some friends in the Alpine Club. We were then to travel to Spain for some mountain climbing in the Pyrenees. It was they who introduced me to Paul, who was also an Alpine Club member. Paul worked as an accountant, or rather a part-time accountant. He would work just long enough to fund his mountaineering travels, then take off for an adventure, only to return to work and start saving for the next trip."

Ross paused a few moments, as if trying to decide how to relate the next part. Then he plunged ahead.

"After a few days, he confided in me that he had become disillusioned with his job. He had mentioned to his employer that he would like to take on some additional duties or perhaps clients of his own. But his employer was not very keen on the idea and discouraged him. He told me that after he had expressed his dissatisfaction, the atmosphere at work had worsened to the point that it was almost intolerable.

"Anyway, on that trip, I also met Paul's good friend Jeremy Bales. He had joined us, and we spent several days climbing along various routes in the Pyrenees.

"Tragically, on the first of June, Jeremy died in a climbing accident. He had gone out alone to climb a popular route and didn't return. After a search, his body was found in a valley. It seemed one of his ropes had frayed to the point of breaking and it had cost him his life.

"Paul was devastated by his friend's death, and we cut our excursion short. When he returned to London after the trip, he became more disenchanted with his own life. After several weeks, he wired me to say he was ready to make some drastic changes. I believe the death of his friend was the trigger that made Paul decide to alter his life.

"While we had been mountaineering, Paul had mentioned to me that he'd like to start an export business. At the time I had told him that I was interested, so after I received his wire, I wired back that he should migrate to America and we would become business partners. Over the next several weeks we made our preparations.

"Paul came over to America eighteen months ago, September of 1894, never intending to return to England. He gave away most of his possessions before he left. We called the new company *Cross Seas Export* and set up our headquarters in New York City. In short order the business began to do so well that we set up offices in several nearby cities. Finally, after a year or so, we decided to expand to London. On this trip we intended to find suitable office space."

"I see," Holmes said as he considered what he had heard. Then he asked, "Did Mr. Watts have any family in America?"

"No, he did not."

"Who knew of your journey to London?"

Ross paused a moment, thinking about the question, then responded. "No one, other than my secretary who made our reservations with the cruise line. We were keeping our journey quiet so as not to alert our competitors to our plans. In fact..."

Ross paused as if he had just recalled something. We waited while he considered it.

"Well, I don't know if this is important," he finally said, seemingly unsure.

"Please, Mr. Ross," Holmes implored, "a seemingly insignificant detail could become a vital key to our investigation."

"Well, there was one odd thing that Paul spoke about during our journey. Several months prior to our travels, Paul said he'd written to some friends in London that he was planning to be back and wanted to see them. He also told me he had received a return letter some weeks later from his friends encouraging him *not* to return. He was quite put out by the thing. Why would friends not want to meet with an old acquaintance?"

We were all as perplexed by the situation as Ross seemed to be. Then he continued.

"He told me he wrote back saying when he would be arriving and that he hoped they would be able to at least join him for dinner one night. Then just before our departure he received another letter telling him that his friends were looking forward to seeing him again. He was quite pleased at the apparent change in their attitude and was looking forward to the reunion."

Holmes seemed to consider this for a few moments, then asked, "I don't suppose he mentioned any of their names?"

"No, I'm afraid not."

"How about an envelope? Did he show you either of the envelopes of his correspondences, or perhaps did he bring any of the letters with him on this trip?"

"I never saw the letters or the envelopes. He never showed them to me. And whether he brought any of the letters with him, I just don't know. I'm sorry."

He seemed genuinely regretful that he was unable to shed any additional light on this awful affair. It was evident that he had just lost not only a business partner, but a good friend.

"What are your plans now, Mr. Ross? Will you be returning to America soon?" Holmes asked after a moment.

"Yes, I have passage booked on the next ship back, but it does not depart until Wednesday night. There are a number of things I need to do now that Paul is no longer part of the business."

"I think that's wise," Holmes said. Then turning to Inspector Gregson, he said, "I suggest that a constable accompany Mr. Ross on any excursion he may wish to make up until he is safely back upon the ship."

"Very well, Mr. Holmes," the inspector responded. "We'll see to it."

"Mr. Ross," said Holmes, "May we have your address in America? In the event any additional questions arise, we may be in contact."

"Certainly, and I hope that you will keep me informed as your investigation progresses. Paul was such a good man, I can't understand why anyone would want to hurt him, or as you seem to suspect, target him."

"Very well," Holmes said as he turned to Inspector Gregson. "I'd like to see Mr. Watts' room and his belongings, if you please."

After collecting Ross' information, we made our way down the hall to Paul Watts' room and entered. His room was very similar to Ross' room with much the same furniture and layout, except the window looked out towards the London docks. A small valise had been placed on the bed and a heavily scarred trunk sat on the floor. Both were unopened. No clothes hung in the chifforobe, leading us to think that Watts had not yet unpacked.

Holmes carefully opened the valise and looked through its contents. He found file folders and receipts for the ship voyage and hotel room, along with a set of keys and twenty pounds.

"There are no letters in here," Holmes said almost to himself. Then he began a search of the trunk. Clothes, coats, razor, and an additional pair of shoes were neatly packed in the trunk along with notebooks and a ledger. There was also a folded map of London with several markings indicating street intersections.

"Well," Holmes said after looking closely at the map, "it would seem that Mr. Watts planned to travel throughout London to look at several potential sites for their new office. Looking at the map, he seems to have made notations on streets that bear a close proximity to banks with an American affiliation."

Holmes continued through the trunk until finally he said, "But I have not found any letters or envelopes."

We looked throughout the room for some other place where a letter might be placed or hidden, including under the bed and inside the drawers of the dresser.

Finally, Holmes said, "Well, there doesn't seem to be anything else to be gained from here. I suggest we make our way to the medical examiner's office so we can get apprised of the autopsy results."

We agreed and left Watts' room, going down to the street. The four of us stood on the pavement outside the hotel as Holmes summoned a cab. In short order a growler approached drawn by two horses.

Just as the cab pulled up to our position, the loud report of a shot pierced the air. The bullet must have struck the stone wall of the Seaway Hotel behind us, for the sound of a ricochet could be heard and bits of stone exploded from the building's side. The loud noise startled the horses, causing the beasts to rear back upon their hind legs, ready to bolt.

Thinking quickly, Holmes took hold of the bridle of the nearest horse as the cabman jumped down and ran to the other horse in an effort to calm the creatures. In a few moments the horses were settled.

"Is everyone all right?" I shouted.

"I believe that shot may have been meant for one of us," Holmes exclaimed as he pointed. "It came from across the street."

We all stated we were uninjured as we looked across the street for anyone suspicious. Drunks sat in doorways and women slowly walked along the pavement and down alleyways. But no one seemed to have taken any notice at the sound of a gunshot, most likely because it was a common occurrence in this area of London and it was better to mind one's own business.

"Why would anyone take a shot at us?" Inspector Gregson asked as he continued looking across the street.

"'cause this is as dangerous a place as I'd ever want to be," the cabman said, after tightening the harnesses on his horses. "I don't usually bring my cab down this way 'cause there are guns firin', stabbin's, thievin', an' all sorts of mischief goin' on 'round 'ere."

Holmes went over and took a closer look at the damage the bullet had caused to the hotel's stone façade. Using his walking stick, he tried to judge the path the bullet had taken in an attempt to pinpoint its origin. But there were several places from which the shot could have been fired. As Holmes tried to trace the path of the bullet, the rest of us looked around in search of our assailant. We saw no one.

Finally, the cabman was anxious to get moving.

"Either you gentlemen get in the cab, or you can find another," he stated as he climbed back upon his cab. "I'm leavin'."

"Very well, cabman," Holmes said and gave the cabman our destination as we all climbed in. I don't mind saying I was glad to be leaving that troubled place. This was one area of London to which I had no desire to ever return.

On our ride to the medical examiner's office, we were quiet as we considered the narrow escape we had just experienced. Had that shot actually been intended for one of us? Or was it just a random act of violence that had transpired in a violent part of London, and we just happened to be close to the event? I know none of us could be sure.

And had the unfortunate Paul Watts actually been the target of some nefarious scoundrel, or was his death just the result of some random act committed upon him because he happened to be in that particular place? Again, none of us could know.

I also began to consider the progress, or rather the lack of progress, we had made so far. For all of Mr. Chris Ross' desire to assist us, we had received precious little useful information from him. The only new information, to my mind, that we had gathered was how Watts and Ross met and why they were in London. I suppose we also received confirmation that Paul Watts had spent the last eighteen months in America, but Sergeant Cummings had arrived at that conclusion this morning.

I must say that as we travelled through the London streets, I kept turning this whole affair over in my mind, trying to assemble the pieces we had so far into a coherent picture. Looking over at Holmes, I could see the eagerness my friend usually possessed during the early stages of a case.

I knew he would not cease his efforts until a satisfactory resolution was found.

Chapter VII: The Medical Examiner's Findings

We finally arrived to the medical examiner's office, and Inspector Gregson ushered us through the complex to the primary examining room. As we approached, our footsteps echoed off the stone walls as our senses were assailed by the odours of antiseptic, formaldehyde, human waste, and other chemicals. Once we were through the door and inside the examining rooms, these became even stronger.

In the main examining room, scales, hoses, and various medical implements hung along the walls and from tables. To the untrained eye the place might appear to be a chamber of horrors, but I recognised each tool used in the practices of healing and dissection.

There were three exam tables in the main examining room, each occupied by a body covered with a sheet. A man in a white coat stood at the back counter making some notes as we entered. He did not look up as we approached but continued his notations. We quietly waited for him to finish before we spoke.

I recognised Dr. Jackson, the medical examiner, from my previous visits. He was a rotund man who stood approximately five feet eight inches tall. A close-cropped beard covered most of his face, and his brown eyes looked out from under heavy eyebrows. A man known for his meticulous manner and adherence to procedure, he viewed the examination room strictly as his domain and would not suffer any fool who believed they could dictate the activities within his realm. I knew him to be a skilled medical doctor who was very thorough in his examinations and rarely missed anything of importance.

When he turned to face us, I could tell that his temper had been riled and he was none too pleased with having been instructed to complete the post-mortem on "John Doe" when there were other more pressing corpses awaiting his attention.

"Inspector," he intoned as he removed the covering sheet from the middle examination table, "perhaps you can enlighten me as to why Mr. John Doe here is of such importance that I was required to forego all manner of protocol and perform this autopsy forthwith? It is all highly unusual." He waved to one of the other examination tables. "I have the body of the son of a council member who is demanding that we determine the cause of his son's death. They wish to proceed with making their arrangements. I have been dealing with almost hourly enquiries."

"We believe," Inspector Gregson replied in a conciliatory manner, "that John Doe is tied to another case. And, Dr. Jackson, we very much appreciate your understanding and assistance in this matter." I was unaware that Inspector Gregson had a flair for diplomacy, but he seemed to be soothing the doctor's irritations.

Dr. Jackson looked doubtfully at all of us, then said, "Well, I recognise Mr. Holmes and Dr. Watson, so if this case has their attention, it must indeed be a critical issue for Scotland Yard."

"Thank you, Dr. Jackson," Holmes interjected in an attempt to move things along. "Have you been able to complete the autopsy on John Doe?"

"Aye, I have. And I've just finished my notes as well. I have been instructed to hand my notes and the victim's clothes to Inspector Gregson here when we're finished. The clothes are in that box over there." Dr. Jackson pointed to a box sitting on the back counter. Sergeant Cummings went and collected the box to take with us.

"Would you mind summarising your findings please, Dr. Jackson?" Holmes asked as he removed his lens and began to inspect the body.

"Very well," Dr. Jackson sighed and looked down at his report. "The deceased was a normal, well-nourished Caucasian male approximately thirty-to-thirty-five years of age. He measured five feet ten inches long and weighed twelve-and-a-half stone. No marks or scars were found on the body. He appeared to be a fit man but not someone who earned his living out of doors or with his hands. However, his hands showed light calluses. I will also say that his upper arm muscles were well developed as if he exercised them regularly.

"All internal organs, as well as the brain, appeared to be normal, and no disease was present. An external examination showed that he suffered one fatal stab wound from behind. The entry wound was located on the left side between the fourth and fifth rib. The knife penetrated the left lung and then into the heart, tearing the left ventricle. The knife blade was approximately eight inches long. The only other injuries that I could find were bruising on both upper arms between the elbows and shoulders."

"As if he were being held while being stabbed?" Holmes enquired, looking up from his examination.

"That would be my conclusion. Even with his well-developed upper arm muscles, if he were taken unawares or there were two assailants, he would have succumbed to an attack. There also appeared to be some slight skin irritations across the man's throat, but the cause of death was the stab wound."

After a few moments, Holmes said, "Yes. Look here, Watson. You can just see the bruising on both arms."

I moved to get a closer look, and it was as Dr. Jackson had said. Black and blue marks could clearly be seen on both upper arms near the elbows. It appeared there had been a significant amount of force used to hold Mr. Watts while he was being attacked.

Holmes stood and returned his lens to his pocket. Then he looked at Dr. Jackson.

"Is there anything else you can tell us, Doctor?"

Dr. Jackson thought for a moment, then said, "It appears to me that this young man never had a chance. I found no defensive wounds, no bruising on the knuckles, or anything else that would indicate that he tried to defend himself. I think he was taken completely by surprise, and it cost him his life."

"Very well, Dr. Jackson," Inspector Gregson said after a moment's contemplation. "Thank you again for your help in this matter."

"Now Inspector, I'll get this autopsy report back?" Dr. Jackson asked as he handed the folder over to the inspector. "This is very unusual. Of course, this whole case is unusual."

"Yes, Dr. Jackson," Inspector Gregson assured him, "I'll personally make sure the autopsy report is returned."

With Dr. Jackson satisfied, we made our way out of the main examining room to a nearby hallway. The stale air of the closed building was a welcome relief to the odours of the examining room.

Holmes turned to Inspector Gregson and Sergeant Cummings.

"Gentlemen," Holmes began, "are there any notes from the initial investigation of the Rhoads case?"

"Aye, there are," Sergeant Cummings said proudly. "That was a habit that Inspector Hall possessed, and I picked it up as well. We made notes in our notebooks of questions, ideas, thoughts, even hunches, as well as facts. Once the case was closed, we put all of our notes in the evidence box along with the murder weapon, the bloody clothes, and anything else we had as evidence. It is all stored down in the basement and should be there now."

"Very well," Holmes said. "Sergeant Cummings, if you would, go collect the evidence box for the Rhoads case and anything else you think might be helpful. Bring whatever you can to Baker Street tonight."

"I know right where the evidence box is," the Sergeant said.

"Good man. I can take that box to Baker Street." Holmes took the box from this morning's murder from the sergeant.

Turning to Gregson, Holmes said, "I believe by now Assistant Commissioner Sanders has most likely gathered everything we requested this afternoon. Perhaps, Inspector, you can collect the box from his office at Scotland Yard and bring it to Baker Street."

"All right," the inspector said.

After a moment's thought, Holmes said, "One other thing, Inspector."

"Yes?"

"Would you send word to Inspector Hall that you intend to travel to see him tomorrow afternoon? Tell him that you very much need his recollections regarding one of his former cases that may have a bearing on a current case. But do not tell him to which case you are referring. Tell him you are sorry to impose, but it is most urgent that you speak with him."

Holmes paused, then continued. "I would like to accompany you; however, I believe he will be more willing to meet with an inspector than with someone not affiliated with Scotland Yard."

"Do you feel it is absolutely necessary to speak with Inspector Hall regarding this case? He may not take too kindly to having one of his cases reopened. He also will have to be told the true reason we are carrying out our investigation."

"Yes, I understand the risks we are taking by involving Inspector Hall in our enquiries. But I believe he may provide some additional insights into the investigation and all of the previous lines of enquiry. Perhaps he will possess some additional information that is not contained in his notebooks that might assist us."

"Very well, Mr. Holmes," Inspector Gregson agreed.

Holmes continued, "Dr. Watson and I will return to Baker Street and prepare a work area for us to use." Then checking his pocket watch he concluded, "Shall we meet back at Baker Street at, let's say, seven o'clock?"

"We'll see you at seven," the inspector said as he and Sergeant Cummings left to execute their tasks.

Once outside, Holmes and I hailed a cab back to Baker Street. It being just the two of us, Holmes began to share something that had been on his mind for some time. I must say I was shocked by his next statement.

"Watson, I hope you realize there is likely a criminal enterprise behind this murder. And, I fear, possibly behind the execution of Simon Rhoads."

"How have you arrived at that conclusion?" enquired I.

"Because of the letters Mr. Ross referred to. Whoever corresponded with Paul Watts concerning his intention to return to England had to be in possession of several critical facts.

"First, they knew that Paul Watts was alive and living in America. Yet no one came forward when Simon Rhoads was tried and executed for Watts' murder. Why did they not come forward? Why not provide the information they had as to the fact that Paul Watts was in America? Instead, they remained silent, and allowed an innocent man to be executed.

"Second, even if they actually thought that Paul Watts had been murdered by Simon Rhoads eighteen months ago, when they received the first letter from Paul Watts announcing his intention to return to London, I would have thought they would have brought it to the attention of the authorities that Paul Watts was still alive. Instead, they attempted to dissuade Mr. Watts from returning to London, I suspect in an effort to keep his existence a secret. For what purpose?

"Third, Watts was killed just hours after departing the ship. I suspect that he was followed from the ship to the hotel where he obtained his room. When he came back out of the hotel, whoever followed him saw their opportunity.

"Combined with the shot fired at us outside the Seaway Hotel earlier, I'd say there is very little doubt that there are sinister forces at work here."

Holmes paused a few moments, his eyes searching the dark confines of the cab. Then he concluded his thought.

"Watson, I suggest that you keep your service revolver close at hand. We may have need of it."

I was silent, wrestling with the points Holmes had just made. As the horse hooves echoed off the passing buildings and darkness began to fall over the city, I had to admit that I could not find an error in his thinking. This entire affair was becoming more sinister by the moment.

Chapter VIII: A Review of Rhoads' Arrest

Just before seven o'clock that evening, Inspector Gregson and Sergeant Cummings arrived at Baker Street with the items they had been charged with retrieving. We had been quite busy all afternoon with no time for refreshment, so in anticipation, Holmes had requested that Mrs. Hudson make sandwiches and tea, which were very much appreciated by our two Scotland Yard companions.

While we ate, Holmes informed Inspector Gregson and Sergeant Cummings of the theory he had shared with me regarding the likelihood that there was a criminal element at work. Both men agreed that there seemed to be a strong possibility, as unsettling as that might sound. Once the meals were finished, we cleared the table and turned our attention to the three boxes.

We first began to carefully unpack the contents of the Rhoads evidence box Sergeant Cummings had retrieved. The box contained a bag in which the ripped, bloodstained clothes and shoes of the Battersea Park victim had been stored, as well as a second bag with the bloody clothes and shoes of Simon Rhoads. The murder weapon that had been found at the scene was in a third bag. It was a letter opener, a gift from Simon Rhoads' wife, with the initials 'S. R.' inscribed on the pearl handle. Caked blood was still in evidence upon the handle, causing the initials to be barely legible.

Lastly, the box contained three well-worn pocket-sized notebooks which had been used by Inspector Hall and Sergeant Cummings during their investigation. Inspector Hall's notes had filled two of the small notebooks, while Sergeant Cummings had used his notebook to write down his tasks and the results of any assignments he completed.

The second box that Inspector Gregson had obtained from Assistant Commissioner Sanders' office held several large notebooks containing the transcribed trial notes, as well as the notes and various memoranda from the prosecutor's office. The original autopsy report for the Battersea Park victim was the last item the inspector removed from the box and placed on the table for us all to see.

We gazed in silence at the items that had effectively caused the judicial system to execute an innocent man. On the face of it, there did not seem to be very much. That fact gave me pause as I considered that it seemed to take so little to condemn a man.

We then unpacked the box we had taken from the medical examiner's office. It contained Paul Watts' bloody clothes: a pair of neatly tailored trousers, a coat, a silk shirt monogrammed with 'PW' on the cuffs, and a pair of shoes.

Holmes was anxious to begin. It had been a long day and we were only now really getting started on this case.

"Gentlemen," Holmes began, "I propose that we divide these documents amongst ourselves and become familiar with their contents. Watson, perhaps you can read and compare the two autopsy reports. Look for anything similar or unusual between them. I will start reading the trial transcript. Inspector Gregson, perhaps you could review Inspector Hall's and Sergeant Cummings' case notes. Sergeant Cummings can read the prosecution's notes. Then

I suggest that we all exchange with one another until everyone has read all of the material we have gathered."

We all agreed that this seemed to be the best approach to get each of us familiar with the original case. But there was yet one more step we needed to take in preparation for our review of the case.

"But before we began," Holmes said, "I would like to ask Sergeant Cummings to give us a summary of what you remember when you first approached the murder scene in the Simon Rhoads case. I know we'll see your case notes, but perhaps you can provide a summary of what you recall?"

"Aye, Mr. Holmes," Sergeant Cummings said. "I have been reliving that day over and over in my head all day as we have been going through our investigation. There are some striking similarities that are beginning to concern me."

"Then pray, let us hear your thoughts."

For the second time that day Sergeant Cummings found himself the centre of focus. With a nervous clearing of his throat, he began to recount his recollections of that day in September, 1894.

# # #

"We were notified," Sergeant Cummings began, "that two bodies had been found in Battersea Park early on the morning of the 13th of September, 1894. It must have been an hour or so after dawn. Two patrolling constables found the bodies, at first thinking they were roustabouts sleeping rough. But when they saw both were covered in blood, they checked and found one man dead, his clothes ripped and torn all over. The other body was that of a man in a heavy sleep. The senior constable remained at the scene and kept the growing crowd away from the bodies. The other constable notified Scotland Yard.

"As I said, I remember the day clearly because it was my first case after being promoted to detective sergeant. I arrived to Battersea Park just as Inspector Hall arrived, and we met in front of the Fox and Goose pub. As we approached the scene, we could see the constables standing near a large oak tree behind a hedgerow, perhaps fifty feet from the roadway. To get to the site, we had to walk around a small memorial area in the park, and then down beside a long hedgerow that was about five feet in height. The hedgerow continued for about forty feet into the park. Then we turned to the right, and still following the back of the hedgerow, made our way over to the oak tree. The bodies were lying on either side of the oak tree. I remember the leaves had already started to fall, and blood was staining the brightly coloured leaves underneath both the dead man and the sleeping one.

"The blood on both men made it difficult at first to determine which one was the victim. But one of the men, who we later learned to be Simon Rhoads, snored from a deep sleep. He did not awaken, even when we had him moved and taken to a cell at Scotland Yard. I don't believe he woke up for several hours.

"Once Rhoads was gone, we focused our attentions on the dead man. His clothes were ripped terribly; apparently during the stabbing attack as he had attempted to fight off his attacker. Both of his coat sleeves had been ripped away and his shirt had large tears in the chest and arms. It was apparent he had suffered an extremely violent attack. We searched his torn trousers and found a membership card for 'Paul Watts' from the Alpine Club, along with a few coins and five pounds."

Holmes interrupted, "As you observed the body, Sergeant Cummings, did you notice anything peculiar? For example, was the body dressed in the clothes of a man of means?"

"Aye, Mr. Holmes. He was dressed in tailored trousers and a dress coat; a tailor's mark inside both. The man's shirt was of good quality and monogramed with 'PW' on both shirt cuffs. Even though all of the clothes were terribly ripped and torn, you could tell the fabric was of superior quality. The shoes were also of high quality. The right shoe was on the ground near his right foot. The left shoe was about three feet away from the body."

Sergeant Cummings paused a moment, as if trying to collect his thoughts of that fateful day. Then he continued.

"As we were going through the man's pockets, a man from the crowd called out, 'Hey, that's Paul Watts!' Both Inspector Hall and I were keen to confirm the identity of the victim, so we called the man forward."

"How was this man dressed?" Holmes asked.

"He was dressed as a gentleman. He said he was on his way to work when he saw the commotion in the park. You will find his name and address in my case notes. I recall that he stood about six feet tall and wore a long, heavy beard. I seem to remember that his eyebrows were also heavy. But the one peculiar thing about him: the skin on top of his right hand and his upper neck was significantly lighter in colour then the skin on his left hand or his face. I assumed that he wore his beard long in an effort to conceal the discolouration on his neck.

"He said he recognised the dead man as Paul Watts. He could tell by the face, and he also recognised the heart tattoo present on the victim's left arm. We turned to look and the heart tattoo was there. You could see it through one of the rips in the shirt.

"We felt we had our victim's identity so we had the body sent to the medical examiner's office for an autopsy. We had also found the bloody letter opener used to kill the man. We later had it checked by that new fingerprint process, but the blood smears on the handle obscured any fingerprints.

"Several hours later, when Simon Rhoads had finally become sober, we asked him why he had killed Paul Watts. He appeared shocked by our questions. He admitted he had been drinking with Watts the night before. He told us they had argued, but they had also reconciled and continued drinking. Rhoads said that he and Watts were friends and he would never hurt him."

Holmes interrupted. "So, Simon Rhoads never actually set eyes on the dead man in Battersea Park."

"That's right."

Sergeant Cummings became quiet. Now, with the benefit of hindsight, he was beginning to see where their initial investigation may have taken a wrong turn.

"In fact, he said that Watts had planned to leave that morning for America. But we never checked the ports because we thought we had the body of Paul Watts down in the morgue. Rhoads always denied he had killed anyone. But he could not explain why he was found in the park with a dead body, why his bloody letter opener was at the murder scene, or how his clothes had become covered in blood. Witnesses had come forward saying they had seen Rhoads and Watts together in the pub the night before, arguing, drinking, and then leaving. All Rhoads did was swear that he had not killed the man."

Sergeant Cummings then quietly concluded, "He continued to claim his innocence all the way to his execution."

We were all silent as we digested what we had just heard. Only Sergeant Cummings had worked on the original case, but the more I heard, the more I wanted to get to the bottom of this nefarious affair.

After another moment, Sergeant Cummings turned to Holmes. "However, I will say this. I believe, as you suggested Mr. Holmes, that we are about to uncover a horrible scheme whose intention was the death of Simon Rhoads, and now Paul Watts. I say that, Mr. Holmes, because of our discussion about how Watts' body was laid out this morning. That was exactly how the body of the man we found in Battersea Park was laid out. On his back, feet together, arms at his side."

"Right you are, Sergeant Cummings," Holmes said. "I've already started to form some theories concerning those similarities, which I will share in due course. Thank you for your summary. It will help us all as we begin to look through the documents we have here tonight."

Holmes paused a moment, then concluded, "We must all remember that we cannot undo a wrong execution, but we can try to expose an intentional miscarriage of justice."

To this we were all in agreement. After another moment, Holmes said, "Prepare yourselves, gentlemen. It is going to be a long and difficult night."

And so, we began our review of the original Simon Rhoads capital murder investigation and trial.

Chapter IX: An Assessment of the Rhoads Investigation

Four hours later, we all sat in our room, bleary eyed from so much reading and exhausted from the day's events. A cloud of pipe smoke had filled the room, so focused was our attention on the task before us. But I have to say that by the end of the night, we all had a much better view of the original case and investigation.

We each completed our readings about the same time, so Holmes called down to Mrs. Hudson for some tea. I opened the window to let some fresh air into the room and heard the whispered sounds of London late at night: the occasional clip-clop of a horse-drawn carriage; the far-away whistle of a constable; the distant, slurred baritone of a drunkard's lullaby to the night. As the bell of Big Ben struck eleven o'clock, fog began to settle over the dark streets bringing with it a chill to the air. It seemed that a cloak was being drawn around the city as if in an effort to guard her secrets. And here we were, mere men, attempting to unearth some of those secrets.

As Mrs. Hudson left after bringing the tea, muttering about the lateness of the hour, Holmes began to guide us through all we had just read.

"I can see several opportunities for the case to be investigated differently, but we must allow that we have the benefit of hindsight. And we also do not know to what extent forces outside Scotland Yard may have been involved in producing contrived evidence used to convict Simon Rhoads. I only say that because at this point, I don't see any mischief on the part of the Scotland Yard investigators. It appears that you, Sergeant Cummings, and Inspector Hall followed the evidence that was presented to you faithfully."

Having read the case notes of both the inspector and the sergeant, I had to agree that there didn't seem to be any malfeasance during the investigation. Every lead had been followed up; every hunch investigated; every witness cross-examined.

Holmes then turned to me.

"Watson, what can you tell us regarding the two autopsy reports?"

"Well," I began, "let me start with the similarities between the two autopsies. Both victims were stabbed from behind on the left side. In both cases the blade penetrated between the fourth and fifth rib, tearing through the left lung and the left ventricle of the heart. The upper arms of the victims had sustained the same type of bruising, although, the bruises on Paul Watts' arms from this morning were closer to his elbows, while the bruises on the Battersea Park victim were nearer his shoulders. There were also small abrasions across the throats of both victims, but these were not thought to be a contributing factor to either death."

"So, in your opinion, would it be correct to say that both men were killed in an identical fashion?" Holmes asked.

"I believe that to be the case."

This revelation spurred Inspector Gregson to ask, "So you're saying that whoever murdered our first victim in

Battersea Park eighteen months ago murdered Paul Watts early this morning?"

"It would appear so, Inspector," Holmes answered. "If you add the fact that both bodies were positioned the same, I don't believe that there is much doubt."

"And," Holmes continued, "I believe we can make some assumptions regarding the killers."

"More than one killer?" Inspector Gregson asked in astonishment.

"Just consider these points," Holmes said as he nodded in affirmation. "First, both victims were stabbed in the back, on the left side; second, both victims had bruising on their upper arms; and third, both victims had small abrasions across their throats. What do those facts suggest to you?"

"At least two killers!" Sergeant Cummings said excitedly.

"Right you are, Sergeant," Holmes confirmed. "One in front to hold the victims, and one behind, who wrapped his right arm around the victim's neck and struck the killing blow. And I'll wager that when we find the man who wielded the murder weapon, he will be left-handed."

The look on the inspector's face showed a man who had just had all that he had believed in suddenly taken from him and shown to be a fiction. Never had I gazed upon a more disheartened countenance.

"Were there any differences?" Holmes asked, turning back to me.

"There were several significant differences, but primarily with the bodies. In the autopsy today, the victim was estimated to be between thirty to thirty-five years old, well-nourished, and in reasonably good health. He measured five feet ten inches long and weighed twelve and a half stone. In the autopsy eighteen months ago, the victim was estimated to be between the ages of forty-five and fifty years old, poorly nourished, measured to be five feet five inches long, and weighed just over eleven stone. His skin was dark and rough, apparently from long exposure to the elements, and his hands were shown to have heavy calluses.

"He had several tattoos, including the heart tattoo that Sergeant Cummings mentioned. You'll recall that our victim from this morning had no tattoos."

"So, our victim from eighteen months ago bore no resemblance to the actual Paul Watts," Holmes stated emphatically. "No one could honestly mistake one body for the other."

Then Holmes went over to the table where we had placed the contents of the boxes. He rummaged around for a moment until he picked up a pair of shoes.

"These were the shoes that were found with the victim in Battersea Park. Observe that they are size ten. Yet the victim was smaller in stature and most likely wore a smaller shoe size; probably a size eight or nine. Also recall that the shoes were only found *with* the victim in Battersea Park, not actually on his feet."

Looking at all of us, Holmes continued. "I suggest that these shoes found with the Battersea Park victim would more likely fit the real Paul Watts. Let's compare them with the shoes Watts was wearing this morning."

Putting action to the word, Holmes checked the shoes that had been found on Watts, and indeed they matched the size and quality of the shoes found with the Battersea Park victim: size ten.

Holmes then reached over and removed the bag containing the ripped and bloody clothes of the Battersea Park victim and unfolded them on the table. Once he was done, he held them up.

"Gentlemen, look at these clothes found on the Battersea Park victim. They are much too large for someone who is five feet five inches tall. They would better fit our victim from this morning. I suggest that these clothes were intentionally ripped so as to hide the fact that they were the wrong size for the victim."

Turning to me, Holmes asked, "Watson, were there approximately the same number of wounds identified on the Battersea Park victim as there are rips in these clothes?"

"Now that you point it out, that seems to be the case," answered I. "There was the one fatal stab wound in the back, but there were a large number of additional superficial cuts and scratches all over the body."

"So, gentlemen, if the clothes had been ripped as part of a vicious attack, there would be many more deep wounds on the Battersea Park victim. Instead, we only have the one fatal wound and a number of minor wounds. I believe we can safely conclude that the clothes were deliberately torn to disguise the fact that the clothes did not fit the victim."

He then turned to our Scotland Yard companions. "It is at this point, gentlemen, that I believe someone was attempting to feed the investigation certain incorrect information in order to guide the police investigation to a desired conclusion. Someone intentionally provided the wrong identification."

Looking through the case notes he said, "The name of the man who identified the body as Paul Watts is Asa

Bloom. At the time, he gave his address as a boarding house on Liverpool Street. That will bear investigating."

We then moved on to a review of the case notes. Both Inspector Gregson and Sergeant Cummings had spent time reading the case notes and had had some quiet discussions.

"After reviewing the case notes," Inspector Gregson said, "it appeared that both Inspector Hall and Sergeant Cummings not only followed proper police procedures, but also followed where the evidence led them. Looking back now, the investigation seems to have been a solid one, yet we know that they came to the wrong conclusion."

"Ah, but again we have to remember," Holmes emphasized, "that we have the benefit of hindsight. We are in possession of several facts eighteen months after the incident, facts that the original investigation team did not, and could not, have known."

Gregson sighed as he nodded in agreement. "We will have to recheck *all* of the evidence and statements that both Inspector Hall and Sergeant Cummings received. In my opinion, any number of these statements could have been an attempt to steer the investigation."

"I concur, Inspector," Holmes said. "And we will have to carefully confirm the evidence without causing anyone to suspect that we are reinvestigating the initial murder case."

After a couple of moments, Holmes asked the two policemen, "What are your thoughts on the trial notes?"

"Well, according to the trial notes," Sergeant Cummings pointed out, "Simon Rhoads had a business partner, Mr. Basil Hart, and they co-owned Holtz Manufacturing, a small manufacturing company. Now, Hart testified that he and Rhoads had been in business together for five years and that they had a friendship. But Hart's testimony did more harm than good. Hart was one of the witnesses who stated he saw Rhoads and Watts drinking and arguing the night before the murder. He also stated that their argument had eventually come to blows, but later they appeared to have made amends and continued drinking until they finally left the pub together."

"As for Paul Watts himself," the inspector added, "Colin Dunn employed Watts at his accounting firm. He testified that he knew Watts well, but only knew Simon Rhoads from a business perspective. He, too, was in the pub with Basil Hart, and testified that he saw Rhoads and Watts argue and later leave together."

"I would really like to know what their argument was about," Holmes said to no one in particular. "I didn't see anything in the case notes explaining why Watts and Rhoads were arguing. I don't know if it's important, but it's something we definitely need to determine."

"As I recall from my reading," I added, "Mrs. Frances Rhoads, Simon Rhoads' wife, was called to the stand by the defence. She said she loved her husband and that he was gentle. But upon further examination by the prosecution, she admitted that her husband had been out all night on the night in question."

"Yes," Holmes said slowly as he stroked his chin. "And she made two damning statements in the courtroom. First, that she had given the fatal letter opener to her husband as a gift, and second, that he could be violent when he drank to excess."

We were all silent for several moments as we weighed the testimony we had just reviewed. All of the evidence, from the police investigation to the testimony in the courtroom, had pointed to Simon Rhoads as a man guilty of murder. And yet we knew this to not be true.

Holmes finally broke the silence. "We all must realize that we will have to check every statement made in that courtroom. Anyone who would be willing to plan a murder and have another man executed for it would have no hesitation about committing perjury. Right now, I'm not sure we can believe anything we have read in the trial notes."

I checked my watch and saw that it was getting late. Holmes must have seen my movement because he began to bring the evening to a close.

"Gentlemen, it is late and we are tired. There is not much more we can do here tonight. Tomorrow morning, Watson and I will go pay Mr. Asa Bloom a visit and try to get to the bottom of this identification business.

"Inspector, I'd like to ask that you and Sergeant Cummings find out everything you can about Simon Rhoads and Paul Watts. For instance, what was Rhoads' business? Is his partner, Mr. Hart, still in the business? Who were Rhoads' friends? Where is his wife now?"

"As for Watts," Holmes continued, "perhaps you can also interview someone at the local Alpine Club. Maybe you can locate someone who knew Paul Watts and his habits. We've learned he didn't have many friends, and he wasn't married, but was there perhaps a fiancée? We especially need to know who the friends were that he contacted prior to his return."

Holmes shook his head. "There is minimal information in the case files, and I'd like to know these facts. We only have a scant picture of him from his American business partner, who didn't really know him while he was in London.

"However," Holmes concluded, "find out what you can without alerting either Mr. Hart, Mr. Dunn, or anyone else. I don't think we are quite ready to make others aware of our investigation."

We were all agreed on our assignments.

Finally, Holmes rose from his seat and said, "Let's meet back here at Baker Street tomorrow at noon and we can assess where we stand. Good night, gentlemen."

And with that Inspector Gregson and Sergeant Cummings left for their own homes. I too, was ready to retire, but Holmes said he wanted to smoke one more pipe before going to bed. I left him sitting in his chair, smoking his pipe with his eyes closed.

Sleep came easily to me that night from the long day's efforts. But my dreams were filled with visions of bloody clothes, bloodstained pavement, and hanging men.

Part III:

Day 2 – Tuesday

Chapter X: The Search for Asa Bloom

It was an early morning that found Holmes and I up and out of our Baker Street residence the next day. The London streets were already bustling with pedestrians, lorries, and all manner of commerce as we made our way through the maze of boulevards and thoroughfares. The chill of the morning air had not yet succumbed to the warmth of the rising sun. As we passed Goswell Road on our way to Liverpool Street, light snow flurries, destined to melt within the hour, began to fall.

The address we were seeking brought us to a boarding house just down from Liverpool Street Station. The house was set back from the pavement a good fifteen feet, with stone stairs leading up to a wooden door with a large mullioned window set in the upper half. The wrought-iron railing on either side of the stairs needed a fresh coat of black paint, and there were several rusted areas that would eventually dislodge the entire assembly if not given proper attention. It was apparent from the outside that the building had two floors, with some additional attic space at the top.

With the cool spring air at our backs, we knocked on the door and awaited entry.

After a few moments, the door was opened by a small-boned woman whom I would estimate to have been possibly sixty-five or seventy years. Her grey hair was tied tightly in a bun, and her rheumy brown eyes peered at us from behind black-rimmed glasses. Her long, grey skirt and dark blouse hid her frame, but I would guess that she weighed no more than six and a half stone and stood little more than five feet. She pulled a lacey white shawl around her as she faced the brisk morning air to greet us.

"Yes? What can I do for you gentlemen? If you're seeking a room to rent, I have none available." Her voice, while soft, carried a stridency, possibly from having to call after children or more likely, given the state of the wrought-iron railing, a lazy husband.

"No, madam," Holmes began, "we are only seeking information. We are looking for someone whom we believe lives here. May we come in to discuss the matter?"

"Are you the police?" she asked.

"No, madam," Holmes said, his frustration mounting, "but we are working with the police. If you like, I can have Scotland Yard come around and interview you, as well as each of your tenants."

The woman considered this for some moments, then decided it might be better to have the discussion with us rather than involve the official police.

"Well, I suppose you better come in out of the cold," she sighed, and stood aside so that we could enter.

As we stepped inside, she closed the door behind us. We were standing in a wide corridor, a small chandelier hanging above our heads. To the right of the entryway was a smaller door, partially open, which led to a room. To the left was a closed door, which I assumed was one of the rented rooms, followed by another closed door further down the hallway. Steps leading to the upper floor were on the right, a red and gold runner ascending the stairway. A kitchen could be seen at the back of the house, the last remnant odours of the morning's meal still present in the air.

The old woman closed the door to the room behind her and said, "Come this way." She led us down the corridor at a slow pace. Her limp suggested the arthritis in her right hip was particularly bothersome due to the cold morning air. We walked past the stairway, our footfalls echoing loudly over the creaking of the old wooden floorboards, and turning right under the stairs, we went through an archway and into a small sitting room. There were several chairs along the wall and a small sofa in the middle of the room. The furniture appeared comfortable but somewhat tattered, having seen better days. A window looked out on an alley, and a small fireplace stood at one end of the room. The dining room was visible at the back of the long room which I assumed connected with the kitchen.

"Please sit down," she said as she sat in one of the chairs. Holmes and I sat on the sofa.

"What is your name, madam?" Holmes asked as I took out my notebook.

"I am Mrs. Alicia Hunt. I own this boarding house. It was left to me by my late husband, Ernst."

"How many tenants do you have, Mrs. Hunt?"

"I have six tenants. I have seven rooms, but only six tenants. I live in the first room by the front door. There are two other rooms on this floor and four additional rooms on the floor above."

"I see," Holmes said. Then, "Mrs. Hunt, we are interested in speaking with a tenant of yours by the name of Asa Bloom. Would you direct us to his room, please?"

Mrs. Hunt had a puzzled look on her face as she considered Holmes' request.

"There is no one by that name here," she finally stated.

"Well, he gave this as his address several months ago. Perhaps he left a forwarding address. Might we trouble you for that?"

"I'm sorry, sir, but there has never been anyone by the name of Asa Bloom living here, now or several months ago."

Holmes was silent as he took this information in. Then he asked, "Are you quite sure, Mrs. Hunt?"

"Yes, I am. I keep a register of payments for all of my tenants, and it goes back several years."

"Ah," Holmes brightened. "Perhaps you would allow us to look at the register, just to make sure."

"Why can't you just take my word for it, young man?" Mrs. Hunt indignantly asked.

"Well, the police will want some proof, and since we are here, perhaps you could let us look. Otherwise, we will need to bring Scotland Yard back to review your register."

Mrs. Hunt again considered Holmes' request and her options. Then with a heavy sigh she said, "Well, wait here a minute." She lifted her frail body from her seat and left the sitting room. We heard her slow, measured footsteps echo down the corridor. The sound of a door being opened was followed by a brief silence, before a door was closed again, and Mrs. Hunt's footsteps sounded once more in the corridor. Less than two minutes after she'd left, she returned, carrying a large, leather-bound book which she took over to the dining room table.

"Here. Come take a look," she called to us from the table.

We rose from our seats and approached the table. Mrs. Hunt opened the book for our inspection.

Holmes spent a few minutes looking through the entries. He checked the most recent month but found no one listed as Asa Bloom. He then checked the register for three months before and three months after September, 1894, and still there was no Asa Bloom listed. Holmes finally stepped back and closed the book.

"Satisfied?" Mrs. Hunt asked with some condescension.

"Perhaps I can describe the man. He presents himself as a gentleman. He is about six feet tall with a long, heavy beard, but his most distinctive feature is that the top of his right hand and his upper neck are a much lighter colour than the rest of his skin. Do you recall ever renting a room to, or perhaps seeing, a man of that description?"

I could see that the woman's patience was wearing thin, but to her credit, she gave some consideration to the question Holmes had posed to her. After several moments, she picked up the register we had been looking through.

"No, I'm sorry," she stated flatly. "I've not seen anyone such as you've described, and as you've seen, I've not rented a room to anyone by the name of Asa Bloom. Now I've answered your questions, and I've work to do, so I'll see you both out."

"Very well, madam," Holmes said and we followed her down the hallway to the front door. She opened the door, and Holmes turned to her and said, "Thank you, Mrs. Hunt, for your time. It would seem that we have been set upon a wild goose chase. Good day."

We walked down the steps to the pavement as Mrs. Hunt closed the boarding house door. In short order we had a cab and were on our way to Baker Street, empty handed.

Holmes was quiet on the ride back to Baker Street, no doubt contemplating our next steps in identifying the elusive Asa Bloom, if that was in fact the man's name. As I considered the matter, it occurred to me the answer could simply be that the man's address was copied down incorrectly. If that were the case, perhaps Sergeant Cummings' memory could be prodded to recall the correct address.

What concerned me more was the possibility that someone had intentionally provided the wrong name and address because they had deliberately provided the wrong identity for the Battersea Park victim. This would again support Holmes' view of some maleficence by dark forces driving events in this affair.

# # #

It was late morning as we travelled back to Baker Street. Partway during our journey, Holmes requested the cabman make a brief stop at a telegram office. As he exited the cab, he told me he needed to send off a message and he would be just a few moments. Shortly, he returned, and we resumed our travels. When I enquired as to the message, he mumbled something about another possible line of enquiry and then would say no more.

Once we were out of the cab at our Baker Street address, we were about to enter our residence when Holmes touched my arm and said, "Just a moment, Watson." He quickly walked down to the corner, and there spoke to a young lad wearing tattered clothes and a hat two sizes too large. Holmes handed the lad something before the lad ran off, after which Holmes rejoined me at our door.

Upon entering, Holmes bounded up the stairs to our rooms. I ascended at a slower pace and when I entered, I saw that Holmes had gone straight for the investigation case notebooks. As I sat in my chair contemplating our interview with Mrs. Hunt, he spent some time perusing the statement of Asa Bloom, turning the notebook pages back and forth as he attempted to get a complete picture of the interview. Finally, he put the notebook on his knee as he sat in his chair, looking vacantly into the fireplace.

"Reading this statement," he began, "it would seem that anyone could have presented themselves at the scene, looked at the body, and said that it was that of Paul Watts. This Asa Bloom fellow even used the presence of the tattoo on the body's left arm as confirmation of the identity, but we know that the real Paul Watts had no tattoo."

"But in defence of the police, they found an Alpine Club card on the body with Paul Watts' name on it," said I.

"That card could have been placed on anyone. And since our Mr. Bloom has been shown to have provided a false address, it stands to reason that the name is also false. All of this begs the question, why did he present himself as a witness, and why did he make an obviously incorrect identification?" With a frustrated shake of his head he concluded, "We *must* find this Asa Bloom. I believe if we can find him, he will lead us to the people behind this torrid affair. The entire case hinges on this single point!"

We were silent for some minutes, each contemplating the many varied aspects of this complicated case. Then Holmes looked again at the investigation case notes and finally said, "Reading this description, it would seem that Asa Bloom suffers from some form of depigmentation on his right hand and upper neck. Perhaps vitiligo, which can sometimes be confused with leprosy. If that's the case, I might imagine that he has spent the better part of his life on the fringes of society, finding whatever work came to hand. He most likely moved in the less desirable social circles."

We were silent a few moments more, until we heard a ring at the door followed by the quick steps of someone ascending the stairs. Shortly, there was a knock on the door. I rose to answer and found the young lad Wiggins standing on the landing.

"'ello Dr. Watson," he said smartly.

Before I could respond, Holmes had come to the door.

"Wiggins!" Holmes said excitedly. "Have you brought the others with you?"

"I 'ave, Mr. 'olmes," he said proudly. "They are outside waiting for us, as you instructed."

"Excellent!" Holmes said. "Come with me." We all went down the stairs and out the door to the pavement, with Holmes leading the way.

Once outside, we encountered the rest of the Baker Street Irregulars, as Holmes liked to call them. They were a group of young, ragged street urchins that Holmes employed from time to time to run errands. The boys were between the ages of eight and fifteen, dressed in ill-fitting clothes. Because they lived on the streets of London, no one took any notice of them, so they could move in areas where the official police would be unwelcome. And by going unnoticed, they could observe the goings on in the seamier parts of London without drawing attention to themselves.

"Listen closely," Holmes said to the boys after he had their attention. "I'm looking for a man, and it is very important that I find him. He is about six feet tall and has a long, heavy beard. Now, his most distinctive feature is that the top of his right hand and his upper neck are a much lighter colour than the rest of his skin. I expect him to likely be a day labourer, so you will want to check the docks and alleyways of East London."

"Aye," Wiggins interrupted, "and 'ave a look at the flop 'ouses and outside the charity 'ouses and opium dens."

"Precisely!" Holmes agreed. "I have a shilling for each of you, and a guinea for the boy who finds him." Holmes began to hand out coins to each boy, and as each received his, he was off on his mission to find our quarry.

After each of the boys had received their payment and left, Holmes and I returned to our rooms. I must say that I was doubtful of the success Holmes might obtain from his use of the boys in our search. However, they had proven successful in prior cases, and Holmes was counting on their ability to find our target.

Once we were back in our rooms, Holmes said, "I hope that Inspector Gregson and Sergeant Cummings are not too delayed in returning. There is still much we have to investigate."

We resumed our seats to wait, but not until after we had each retrieved one of the investigation notebooks. For several minutes we both read and reviewed the data, but neither of us could derive any further clues from the notes.

After returning the notebooks to the evidence box, Holmes began to pace about the room. Like a restless animal in a cage, Holmes continually moved, occasionally stopping to glance out the window before resuming his pacing. I recognised anxious energy when I saw it and knew that for Holmes it could not be pent up, but had to be expressed in some manner.

I, too, found myself dealing with some impatience, driven by a most uneasy feeling. It began to seem that we were approaching a turning point in our investigations. I went over and re-examined the shredded clothing that had been found on the Battersea Park victim. I could not help but wonder what kind of mind could concoct such a plan to misdirect the police and drive the investigation to the tragic execution of an innocent man.

Chapter XI: Rhoads' Business

Finally, not too many minutes later, there was a knock at the door. Since we were expecting the return of both Inspector Gregson and Sergeant Cummings, we were surprised to find only Gregson standing on the landing.

"Ah, Inspector. Come in," Holmes greeted, stepping aside to allow the inspector entry. "Sergeant Cummings did not accompany you?"

"After we finished our enquiries, I sent Sergeant Cummings to Scotland Yard," the inspector replied as he entered and removed his coat and hat. "As of this morning, I had not yet received a response from Inspector Hall to my message from yesterday. I asked Sergeant Cummings to go to Scotland Yard and check in the event that a response had been directed to me there. I expect him to rejoin us shortly."

"Very well," Holmes said. "We definitely need to speak with the inspector. Now, were you successful in finding out anything about either of our two victims?" It seemed that Holmes had concluded that Simon Rhoads had also been a victim of foul play.

"Aye, we were," Gregson said, smiling.

"Excellent!" Holmes enthused. "Pray, take a seat and enlighten us."

I was looking forward to hearing what had been discovered about Rhoads, his family and friends, as well as whatever had been uncovered about Paul Watts.

The inspector sat in one of the available chairs and took out his notebook. I, too, opened my notebook so as to keep a record of their findings.

"Well," Gregson began, "we know that Rhoads was co-owner of Holtz Manufacturing. It's a small company located near Petticoat Lane Market. They manufacture the wooden parts of a loom such as..." the inspector paused to focus closely on his notes, then continued, "the warp beam, sley, reed cap, shuttle, beaters, heald shafts, and take-up roll, as well as the leather picker. The parts are then purchased by various loom makers, who manufacture the metal framework of the loom. The loom makers then assemble all the parts together and sell the completed product. It seems to be a quite lucrative endeavour."

After a brief pause, he continued. "We felt that the best way to find out about Simon Rhoads and his business without alerting his business partner, Basil Hart, was to speak with their competitor. It turns out there is only one other company, located a few blocks away from Holtz Manufacturing, called Simmons Manufacturing. It is owned by Hadiyas Simmons, an older gentleman, I would say about sixty-five, but very fit and energetic. He comes across as a focused and intense businessman with his sharp grey eyes and firm handshake. I would also think that he at one time was quite a brawler. He has a crooked nose that appears to have healed after being broken many years ago. At first, he said he did not have time to speak with us, but when we said we were from the tax office and were conducting some routine enquiries into Holtz Manufacturing, he had us come into his office."

"So, Holtz Manufacturing has remained in business?" Holmes asked.

"Oh yes," the inspector said. "And Basil Hart runs the entire business. Now, we were told all of this by Mr. Simmons. He heard it from his lumber suppliers. He uses many of the same suppliers that Holtz Manufacturing uses, so he was kept abreast of the troubles Holtz was facing.

"It seems that the business was close to going bankrupt before Rhoads was put on trial. The lumber companies were reluctant to sell wood to Holtz for fear of not being paid. Even the companies that serviced the Holtz machines were suspending their services until some past-due bills were addressed. But it seems things turned around abruptly eighteen months ago. There was an inflow of capital, and the word is it came from Colin Dunn, the man who owns the accounting firm which employed Paul Watts part time. Anyway, the bills that were in arrears were all paid and since then there has not been a problem."

"You got all this information from his competitor, Mr. Simmons?"

"Aye, but until we can speak with Basil Hart, we will not be able to find out why the bills were paid by Dunn."

"I believe we will find out everything about that shortly. What about Rhoads' wife? Where is she now?"

"Well," Inspector Gregson said as he scratched his head, "that is something else Mr. Simmons seemed to know a great deal about. And I have to say I would not have expected where she ended up. Her family's name is Hillsdale, from the Hillsdales of Essex. She was Miss Frances Hillsdale prior to her marriage to Simon Rhoads. She and Rhoads were married four years ago. They never had any children and lived in a house on the west side of London.

"Simmons says she is still an extremely stunning woman and he would have pursued her himself after Rhoads' execution if he were twenty years younger. But a year after Simon Rhoads was hanged for the murder of Paul Watts, Mrs. Simon Rhoads became Mrs. Colin Dunn."

"Ah! Her marriage to Mr. Dunn is significant," Holmes stated.

"Aye. Since Mr. Dunn's firm did the bookkeeping for Holtz Manufacturing, that is how Rhoads met Watts. Watts would come to the business once a week and update the books as needed. It's been said that Mr. Dunn was also a frequent visitor to Holtz Manufacturing, so he also knew Simon Rhoads, *and* Mrs. Rhoads would do filing at the office from time to time. According to Mr. Simmons, he heard that Dunn made a point of being at Holtz Manufacturing whenever Mrs. Rhoads was working."

"So, it would seem that Dunn, Watts, Hart, Rhoads, and Rhoads' wife all knew each other," Holmes concluded.

"It would seem so," Gregson confirmed. "And I also recall reading in the trial notes that Mr. Dunn and Mr. Hart were two of the witnesses in the pub who testified that Rhoads and Watts had quarrelled that night."

"I find it very interesting that the former Mrs. Rhoads is now Mrs. Dunn," added I, looking over the notes I had taken.

"Yes," Holmes agreed, "but what is more interesting to me is that not one of these people, when called into court in Rhoads' defence, provided anything but a minimal characterisation of the man. Nor did they remain in court during the trial in support of Rhoads."

After a few moments, Inspector Gregson asked, "What did Asa Bloom have to say for himself?"

"It would seem," Holmes replied with some frustration, "that whoever identified the Battersea Park victim provided a false name and address to Sergeant Cummings. If we are going to locate him, we will have to hope that he is still in London."

We briefly discussed the significance of the mysterious Asa Bloom, as well as what the two Scotland Yard detectives had discovered. However, in short order speculation began to take over the conversation.

I could see that Holmes was becoming frustrated, as he was loathe to speculate without data or facts and we were still in need of both before any solid conclusions could be developed. Finally, he could take no more.

"Gentlemen, we can sit here and speculate all day to no avail. We must continue to seek our answers by questioning all of the parties involved. I believe I know what our next steps should be."

We waited for Holmes' direction. But before he could make his next statement, we heard a commotion downstairs as the door to the street was opened and loud voices preceded footsteps ascending the stairs to our rooms. One was an angry voice that was unfamiliar to Holmes and myself, but the other was the voice of Sergeant Cummings.

Inspector Gregson simply said, "Ah. It seems that instead of returning with a message from Inspector Jack Hall, Sergeant Cummings has returned with the man himself."

I had been anxious to hear what information Inspector Hall could add to our investigation. Perhaps he had some ideas he had not recorded in his notebook. Or perhaps he had developed some other theories all these eighteen months after the case was closed. But more likely, he had not thought of the case at all, and his ire was up that anyone was now looking into it.

In any event, it seemed that now we might get whatever information Inspector Hall could provide first hand.

Chapter XII: The Reminiscences of Inspector Hall

The voices continued to carry on, almost to shouts, as they ascended the stairs. It was apparent that Inspector Hall was none too pleased about being brought to Baker Street.

"I've never heard of Scotland Yard working with an amateur detective!" Inspector Hall shouted, his voice dripping with disdain. "No professional policeman would even consider it!"

"Sir," Sergeant Cummings said as they reached our door, "I believe you'll find this was the right course of action."

"I very much doubt it!"

It was at this point that Holmes opened the door. There on the landing stood Sergeant Cummings with a short, compact man who stood approximately five feet six inches tall and appeared to be about sixty years old. His close-cropped beard and hair had gone to grey, and his green eyes flashed in anger. He was dressed in a black suit, white shirt, and boots. His hat and coat were stylish but a bit out of date. Although he did not remember me, I recognised the inspector from the Rhoads execution we had both attended. That memory caused a brief wave of nausea to sweep over me.

As both men entered, Inspector Hall took a moment to look at each person in the room. His eyes briefly swept over Holmes and myself until they landed on Inspector Gregson.

"Inspector Hall, it is a pleasure to meet you," Holmes said, extending his hand.

The former inspector ignored the hand and walked over to Gregson.

"Tobias! I received your message yesterday, and as it happened, I was coming to London today for some business. After my business was completed, I went looking for you at Scotland Yard. No one there seemed to know where you were or what case you were working on. I only came upon Sergeant Cummings here as I was leaving to return home.

"Now, what is this nonsense Sergeant Cummings has been telling me? Partnering with an *amateur* detective! What has happened to the Yard since I left?"

He turned to face Holmes and myself.

"I've heard of Mr. Sherlock Holmes and Dr. Watson," he said as he looked us up and down. "Read of some of their exploits. A lot of nonsense and guesswork, if you ask me. *Real* detective work requires facts and evidence! Not fanciful imagination." The contempt could not be any clearcr.

"Jack!" Inspector Gregson said in a raised voice, placing a hand on Inspector Hall's shoulder. "This is an important case and you need to hear what we have discovered so you can, hopefully, provide us with some assistance."

Inspector Hall turned towards Inspector Gregson and began to respond, but Inspector Gregson raised a hand and continued sharply.

"Mr. Holmes and Dr. Watson are working on this case with us at the request of both the assistant commissioner and commissioner of Scotland Yard, as well as the Home Secretary. You would do well to listen and provide whatever assistance you can. Even though you no longer work for Scotland Yard, you are still an Englishman, and you have a vested interest in this case and its resolution."

Inspector Hall stood quietly for a few moments, contemplating the words he had just heard. Finally, he turned and faced Holmes.

"Very well," he said with a sigh. "Let's hear about this case that Scotland Yard cannot solve without your assistance. All the way over here from the Yard, Sergeant Cummings refused to reveal any details to me."

"He was right to do so, Inspector Hall," Holmes said as he closed the door. "Pray, take a seat and we may begin."

Inspector Hall and Sergeant Cummings removed their hats and coats and took a seat, as did the rest of us. The tense air in the room dissipated somewhat after everyone sat, but it was still evident that Inspector Hall was sceptical and remained to be convinced that this matter required the assistance of someone outside Scotland Yard.

"As you can see, Inspector Hall," Holmes said as he waved his hand across the room, "we have a number of items from Scotland Yard here. Among them is the evidence box of the Simon Rhoads murder case, a case in which you played a major part in investigating."

"Aye," Inspector Hall agreed with a nod of his head. "Both Sergeant Cummings and I investigated that case. We got a solid conviction and the man was executed, as prescribed by law."

"And the man you convicted, Simon Rhoads, was sentenced to hang for the murder of Paul Watts," Holmes stated.

With an impatient sigh, Inspector Hall said, "So do we need an amateur detective to restate what has already taken place?"

"Jack," Inspector Gregson said softly, "Paul Watts was found murdered early yesterday morning after departing a ship that had just arrived from America. He had been abroad for eighteen months. He wasn't murdered by Simon Rhoads."

There was a moment of stunned silence from Inspector Hall, but it was quickly replaced with a boisterous laugh as he turned to Inspector Gregson. "Is this some kind of joke, Tobias? Of course he was murdered by Simon Rhoads. I don't know what you found yesterday morning but you are seriously mistaken, sir!"

"Inspector Hall," Sergeant Cummings interjected, "I personally verified our victim's identity yesterday morning through the passport office, tax office, and with his American business partner. There were only three Paul Watts in London; two are still here and alive, but the third emigrated to America the morning of the 13th of September, 1894. That's the very day we found a body in Battersea Park, whom a man from the crowd identified as Paul Watts."

"So far," Inspector Gregson added, "we have been unable to locate that man."

As Inspector Hall listened, Holmes and Inspector Gregson started to review all of the evidence that had been uncovered concerning the murder from yesterday morning and the Simon Rhoads conviction.

"Inspector Hall," Holmes began, "the murder weapon was a letter opener that Rhoads' wife gave him as a gift. Where did he keep it?"

"He said he kept it in his office."

"Locked away or on his desk?"

"Well, he said he kept it on his desk to remind him of his wife."

"So, anyone could have taken that letter opener from his office?" Holmes asked.

"Aye, they could have. But who would?"

"The perpetrators of this crime, of course," Holmes replied simply.

After a moment, Holmes continued.

"Now let's talk about the clothes that were found on the Battersea Park victim. We have them here," Holmes said as he walked over to the table upon which sat the evidence boxes. After rummaging around for a moment, he removed the bag containing the murder weapon, the bag with Simon Rhoads' clothes inside, and the investigation notebooks. Finally, he extracted the torn clothes of the victim.

"These are the clothes that were found on your Battersea Park victim. Now we know that the victim was only five feet five inches tall, as stated in the autopsy report. Yet look at how long these trousers are, and the sleeves of this jacket. Even though they are badly torn we can see that they would be much too large for a man of that stature. You yourself, Inspector Hall, are what, perhaps five feet six to seven inches tall? Come see if these clothes are even a close fit for your physique."

To the former inspector's credit, he rose from his chair, stood next to Holmes, and reached out to hold the tattered trousers next to himself. They were obviously too large. Holmes then removed the shoes from the evidence box.

"Here are the shoes that were found with the victim. You'll recall that they were found *near* the body, not actually on his feet. These shoes are also too large to belong to the victim. You have only to observe your own feet to see that they would be too large for you as well."

Inspector Hall was silent as he looked closely at the shoes, even placing his own shoes next to them to verify the discrepancy. After a few moments, the former inspector began to return to his seat, but then whirled around to face Holmes.

"Those are interesting points, Mr. Holmes. But there is one thing you are forgetting: the body! There were no other murders reported that day, nor were there any missing people similar to the victim's age on the day we found the corpse. If the body was not that of Paul Watts, who was it, and where did it come from?

"And his hands," Inspector Hall continued, trying to hold on to his scepticism. "They were extremely rough and calloused. We attributed that to his mountaineering adventures."

Holmes shook his head.

"Inspector, the man whose body you found in Battersea Park was most likely a day labourer of some kind. His physical condition, and especially his hands, indicated as much. He probably drifted from one manual job to the next, sleeping rough when there was no money at hand. He was someone who lived on the fringes of society and so would most likely not be missed.

"But I believe we will eventually find out who the man is. And when we do, it will help answer how this atrocity was accomplished. The reason I hold that belief is because both men, the Battersea Park victim from eighteen months ago and Paul Watts from yesterday morning, knew and trusted their killers. It doesn't appear that either man fought their murderers. When we find out who both of these men knew, I believe we will be within arm's reach of our murderers."

Both men were silent for a few moments. Looking downcast, Inspector Hall returned to his seat.

"In reviewing the autopsy reports for both murders," Inspector Gregson added, "we have the fact that both the Battersea Park victim and our victim from yesterday were killed in the exact same way: by *two* people. The bruising on their upper arms and the fatal wound in the back indicate as much. We believe that the people who killed your victim in Battersea Park eighteen months ago killed Paul Watts yesterday morning."

Inspector Hall, looking down at the carpet beneath his feet, slowly began to shake his head. "No, no, no!" he defiantly stated. With his finger pointed at Holmes, he made his final, best argument. "We know that Paul Watts was in the pub with Simon Rhoads the night before he was killed. Rhoads admitted he had been drinking with Watts. Colin Dunn, who employed Watts and that fellow..."

Inspector Hall paused a moment, trying to think back to the principles of the case.

"Hart!" he finally exclaimed. "Basil Hart, who had hired Watts to keep the company's books. They all knew

Paul Watts and testified that he was there in the pub drinking and arguing with Simon Rhoads. Even the publican, who also knew Watts, said he was there. Are you suggesting that all these people, including Simon Rhoads himself, conspired to deceive Scotland Yard about Watts being at the pub that night?"

"No, Inspector," replied Holmes calmly, "I fully believe that Paul Watts was in that pub, drinking and arguing with Simon Rhoads as the other witnesses testified. I also fully believe that Paul Watts left the pub with Simon Rhoads as the other witnesses stated. However, no one could testify as to what exactly happened *after* Paul Watts and Simon Rhoads walked out of that pub and into the night."

"So, Mr. Holmes," Inspector Hall asked, folding his arms, his voice holding on to its last shred of confidence, "what do you believe happened after they walked out of that pub?"

"Oh, I know what happened," Holmes replied calmly. "Once they were outside, Paul Watts left to board the ship he had booked passage on to America. It was due to leave in the early morning hours. Simon Rhoads, drunk and in no state to make the journey home to his wife, went over to Battersea Park, laid down under an oak tree and went to sleep. It was a drunken sleep that he did not awaken from until almost noon the following day when he was being held in jail.

"It was at this point, that two people brought a man dressed in clothes that once belonged to Paul Watts to Battersea Park and murdered him using Simon Rhoads' letter opener. The victim's blood was then spread all over Simon Rhoads' clothes, and the dead victim's clothes were torn to disguise the fact that they did not fit him. Then they left the park, expecting their grisly work to be discovered in the morning.

"When it was discovered, someone, possibly one of the murderers themselves, was present at the park as the police were looking over the crime so as to falsely identify the body as Paul Watts, while the real Paul Watts was on a ship to America."

Seeing that Inspector Hall still held on to a fragment of disbelief, Holmes continued. "The man who identified the body as Paul Watts said he recognised the tattoo on the victim's left arm. Paul Watts had no tattoos. None at all."

Inspector Hall was silent as he considered what Holmes had revealed. Then he said, "Well, it would have to have been an extremely well-planned effort to get Scotland Yard to convict a man for the murder of someone still alive."

"Not really. There are only two things that could have spoiled the plot. First, someone who actually knew Paul Watts would have had to formally identify the body; or second, Scotland Yard would have had to check the departure logs for ships departing for America, where you would have found that Paul Watts had been on one of those ships. Sergeant Cummings did just that as he was trying to verify the identity of yesterday morning's victim."

Holmes paused a moment before he concluded.

"You didn't check the ship departure logs because normally there would be no reason to do so. But you also didn't have anyone else formally identify the body because you believed you already had your victim's identity based on the statements from a man in the crowd. Mr. Asa Bloom never showed up again in your case notes. Did you or Sergeant Cummings ever speak to him again during the investigation or trial?"

"No," Inspector Hall said quietly. "I meant to look for him, but I became involved in the prosecution and never had time."

The colour seemed to have drained out of Inspector Hall's face. He sat, staring vacantly, but not seeing anything. After a moment, he turned to Inspector Gregson.

"Tobias, does what he is saying hold true to what you have found so far? Was Paul Watts not the victim that Simon Rhoads was convicted of murdering?"

"I'm afraid it does, Jack. From what we have found so far, there was a concerted effort to feed your investigation evidence that Simon Rhoads murdered Paul Watts even though it was known, by the people we are now seeking, that Paul Watts was on his way to America."

Inspector Gregson paused a moment, then concluded, "We are on the trail of these scoundrels, and we believe we are getting closer."

"But that will not right the serious wrong that I have caused," Inspector Hall said quietly, almost to himself.

"No, it will not," Inspector Gregson agreed.

We were all silent for several moments to allow Inspector Hall to absorb the information he had just received. I can say with certainty that Holmes took no pleasure in showing the former inspector where his investigation had gone awry.

For me, it was difficult to watch this proud man who had started the day confident in his view of himself and the world, suddenly discover that his last efforts as a Scotland Yard inspector had resulted in a fatal error. He appeared defeated. This was a man who identified with his life's labours; it was his essence. In his eyes, any flaw uncovered in his work would be a flaw in himself. Well here, a tremendous flaw had been revealed, with the gravest of consequences as the result. As I watched, the man almost seemed to become physically smaller before my eyes.

Finally, Holmes asked, "One question I have not been able to find in either your case notes or those of Sergeant Cummings. Do you know what Paul Watts and Simon Rhoads were arguing about when they were drinking in the pub?"

The former inspector was staring across the room and had not appeared to have heard Holmes' question. He did not respond until Inspector Gregson placed a gentle hand upon his shoulder.

"Oh, yes," the former inspector finally replied with a vacant stare. "Watts was telling Rhoads that because Holtz Manufacturing was in such dire financial distress, he and Basil Hart had two options before them. First, they could simply declare bankruptcy and close the business; or Watts' employer, Colin Dunn, would be willing to invest enough money to relieve the financial distress in exchange for becoming a controlling partner in the business. Rhoads would not accept either option. That is what Rhoads said they were arguing about during one of my interviews."

"Thank you, Inspector," Holmes said as he rose from his seat. "That is most helpful."

The rest of us also rose from our seats, however, Inspector Hall remained seated, staring off into the distance and seemingly unaware we had all stood.

Holmes motioned to Inspector Gregson and Sergeant Cummings as they retrieved their coats and hats. "Perhaps you both could accompany Inspector Hall to the train station and see that he gets on the train back to his wife. He seems shocked and disoriented at the moment and may need some assistance returning home."

"Aye, we'll be glad to help him," Inspector Gregson said as he looked at the poor man. "He was a good investigator; one of the best, regardless of how this case turns out."

Then he and Sergeant Cummings got Inspector Hall out of his seat and helped him put on his coat and hat. As they were going out the door, Inspector Gregson turned to us.

"After we put Inspector Hall on the train, Sergeant Cummings and I will travel to the Alpine Club and obtain what information we can regarding Paul Watts, his friends, and associates."

"Very well, Inspector," Holmes said quietly, "that will be helpful."

Inspector Gregson turned and followed his colleagues. In a few moments they were down the stairs and out onto the pavement to hail a cab for the train station.

Holmes and I were silent after the others had left, putting away the items of evidence that had been removed from their boxes during our discussion. As we worked, I continued replaying our conversation with Inspector Hall over and over in my head.

While carrying out the deception seemed simple enough, it appeared to me that there had to be a significant level of forward planning involved. These perpetrators had to know that Paul Watts was going out of the country; they had to get their hands on Paul Watts' clothes; they also had to get their hands on Simon Rhoads' letter opener; and most difficult of all, they had to get their hands on someone they could kill who would not be missed. The level of long-range preparation seemed extraordinary to my mind.

As we completed our efforts, Holmes finally turned to me.

"Watson, I believe it is time that we reveal to the principals of this matter that we are looking into their affairs. You and I will go speak with Mr. Basil Hart at Holtz Manufacturing this afternoon. Let us see what we can find out. Why did he not provide support at the trial or attempt to assist his friend and business partner more? Were their relations cordial? We know that the business was in financial difficulty at the time; how were those difficulties resolved? Did Mr. Hart agree to the offer from Mr. Dunn? And how is the business faring now?"

I thought a moment, then I asked a question that had been weighing on my mind for some time now.

"Holmes, he will want to know why we are looking into this affair some eighteen months after the matter was closed. What reason should we give?"

After a moment's thought, Holmes answered. "We'll simply tell him that some distant relatives of Paul Watts, with connections to the authorities in Scotland Yard, have requested a better understanding of the life and death of Paul Watts." Holmes paused a moment, then added, "We will make it seem like a minor assignment that we have been given so that official police resources are not being tied up on the enquiry. We are simply attempting to satisfy the whims of a superior at Scotland Yard."

That seemed a plausible enough story that should satisfy Mr. Hart's curiosity. As I considered Holmes' comments, Holmes checked his pocket watch, then reached for his coat, hat, and walking stick.

"Let us be on our way. I want to meet this Mr. Hart during business hours so I can observe how the establishment is faring. Come along, Watson."

After I gathered my hat, coat, and walking stick, we went outside and hailed a cab for our brief journey to Holtz Manufacturing. As we rode, I was wrestling with whether or not we could uncover the sinister powers behind this affair. It seemed to me that a great force of evil would be necessary to manipulate a police investigation and obtain a desired trial verdict. And yet that appeared to be exactly what had happened. I began to wonder if even my good friend Sherlock Holmes, whose skills I had witnessed on many occasions, would be up to the task of resolving this case.

Chapter XIII: Basil Hart

Holtz Manufacturing was located on the edge of London's business district, near Petticoat Lane Market. Looking at the building from the outside one could just as easily mistake it for one of those large department stores that seemed to be occupying every thoroughfare. It was a large, red-brick building that stretched across one third of the block, with windows that ran along the front of each of the three floors. There was a front door placed at the centre of the building, which gave access to the company's offices on the ground floor. An alleyway to the right of the building led to the rear and came out onto a wide backstreet. This was where all deliveries arrived and shipments departed.

Holmes and I entered through the front door and found ourselves in a large, open office area with desks arranged in rows. Some of the desks were lined up along the windows, but most were simply set up in a grid pattern filling the office space. The enclosed space would have been stifling hot, except that several of the windows throughout the office were open about six inches. The constant sound of a thriving city made its way through the open windows.

Each desk had a young man or woman working at a typewriter or making journal entries into large, leather-bound books. Filing cabinets were spaced along the left and right-hand walls. Every so often one of the office workers rose to retrieve or deposit some paper or large book into one of the file drawers. All of the workers seemed focused on their tasks, and no one seemed to take any notice of us as we closed the door behind us. It was apparent to me that this business was thriving.

I observed that along the back wall of the room were several doors that led, I assumed, to the offices of the various managers, as well as out to the manufacturing area. There was a single desk in front of the last door on the right, occupied by a smartly dressed woman whom I would guess was no more than thirty-five years of age. Her brown hair was cut short, and the collar of her high-necked blouse was clasped by a turquoise broach. She looked up as we entered. Her green eyes flashed as they took in our presence by the door, and the frown on her mouth indicated that we had become an interruption she did not wish to tolerate. It was apparent from her bearing that, in this room at least, she was in charge.

Holmes and I made our way to her desk to introduce ourselves. As we wove our way through the maze of desks no one took any notice of our passing, so intent were they upon their tasks. When we reached the lady's desk at the back of the room, Holmes made the introductions.

"We apologize for the intrusion," he began quietly. "I am Sherlock Holmes. This is Dr. Watson. We have an urgent matter that we wish to discuss with Mr. Basil Hart. Would you be so kind as to direct us to where we may find him?"

The woman carefully looked us both up and down. I noticed that there was a name plaque on the desk that read "Lola Peters." I doubted anyone ever referred to the woman as "Lola."

"Mr. Holmes, what is this in reference to?" Miss Peters asked after a few moments' pause. She had folded her arms across her chest, and the scowl on her face told us our reason had better measure up to her expectations or we would leave empty-handed.

But Holmes was having none of it. "It is a personal matter with Mr. Hart. We would prefer to keep this a 'routine' visit, but I can have fifteen Scotland Yard officers here within the hour, if you believe that would be Mr. Hart's preference."

This caused Miss Peters to reconsider her position for a moment. I am sure that neither she, nor Basil Hart, wanted a group of Scotland Yard officers traipsing around the business.

"Very well," she finally said with a scowl. "Please wait here a moment. I'll get someone to take you back to the shipping dock. Mr. Hart is verifying some incoming inventory."

She turned and walked over to one of the office doors and stepped inside, closing the door behind her. We stood there quietly and waited while the sounds of commerce on the street outside continued to waft through the open windows.

After some moments, Miss Peters emerged from the office she had entered, followed by the largest man I believe I had ever set eyes upon. He stood at least six feet seven inches tall and must have weighed a solid twenty-five stone. His arms, neck, and legs seemed as thick as tree trunks, and his barrel chest could barely be contained by the suit jacket he wore. His shoes appeared to be a size fourteen. His hair was dark black and grew down to his shoulders. I could not help but notice small flecks of sawdust scattered about in his hair and on his shoulders. He had a heavy black moustache, and eyes that peered out from under heavy eyebrows. A small, brown mole had established itself on the bridge of his nose by his right eye. There was also what appeared to be a recent scratch down his left cheek. If I were to see this man out on the street, I would speculate that he had been a strong man in a circus at one time. Both Holmes and I stood dumbstruck as the pair approached.

Miss Peters, amused by our reaction upon seeing the behemoth, made the introductions.

"Gentlemen, this is Mr. Cahn. He will take you to the warehouse to see Mr. Hart." Then turning to the brute, she gave a curt nod with her head towards the centre door.

Our guide turned and began to lumber towards the indicated door. We were compelled to follow, however, I kept a firm grip on my walking stick, even though it probably would not have provided an adequate level of assistance if the need had arisen. We were led down a short hallway before we emerged into an enormous warehouse.

Upon entering, the odours of burnt wood and coal filled our nostrils. The sounds of machines driven by steam were almost deafening, and the heat from the coal fires required that two of the warehouse doors remain raised. On the left side from where we stood were stacks of lumber, cordage, cartons of thread, and the like. There was also an area for spare machine parts, drills, and sharpeners, all stacked on shelves from floor to ceiling. Located on the right side of the warehouse were men and machines that took the raw lumber and cut, shaped, or bored into the wood in order to fashion the implements that were to be sold to the loom manufacturers. Those items were then sent to a packing station where they were packaged, inventoried, and crated for shipment.

We took a few steps into the warehouse until finally our guide stopped and pointed to a man standing next to shelves of lumber. Without another word, he turned around and went back the way we had come. Holmes and I looked at one another and then made our way over to the man working by the shelves.

As we approached, the man wrote on a piece of paper he held, looking first up at something on the shelves, then down at his notations. He seemed quite engrossed in his work. When we were about ten feet away, he glanced at us briefly, then went back to his task. We finally came up to the man and as we did, he appeared to sign something, and then looked up to give us his full attention.

He appeared to be a man of rather slight build, who stood perhaps five feet eight inches tall. His hair, beard, and moustache were black with flecks of grey peppered throughout. He presented a nervous energy, always fidgeting with his papers, his pencil, or his shirt sleeves. I got the impression that his was a wiry physique, but also that he was perhaps stronger than he appeared.

"Now I'm not going to pay any more than we agreed last month for this lumber," he said to us as he tapped his pencil on a piece of paper. "We had a contract, regardless of whether your delivery expenses increased." He then shook his head and concluded. "We will discuss any increases next month." And with that, he turned and began to walk off.

"Mr. Hart, if you please," Holmes called after him. "I'm afraid you have us confused with someone else."

Hart stopped, turned, and walked back to where we were standing. His expression was one of exasperation, as if he were too busy to be bothered with anything other than whatever tasks he was doing.

"We are here," Holmes continued, "to discuss another matter that I believe you have an interest in."

"Please forgive me. I thought you were here regarding a shipment we received last week. You can make an appointment with my secretary, Miss Peters. Please do so. I am needed over at the boring machines." Mr. Hart again turned and began to walk towards the other side of the warehouse.

"It concerns a man by the name of Paul Watts," Holmes called out. "I believe you knew him."

At the mention of the name, Basil Hart stopped and stood stock-still. It was a moment before he turned to face us, and when he did, he remained where he was, carefully looking us over as if to permanently fix our features in his mind. Finally, he approached us, slowly, almost cautiously.

"That's a name I haven't heard in quite some time. Exactly what is your interest in him?"

"Well," Holmes replied, "my name is Sherlock Holmes, and this is my friend Dr. Watson. We have been tasked by Scotland Yard to collect some details about Paul Watts' life and death. It seems some very distant relatives have just learned of his passing and they contacted a friend of theirs, a senior member of Scotland Yard. Scotland Yard requested that we find out what we could for the family." Then in a conspiratorial manner, Holmes leaned forward and softly said, "They don't want to involve 'actual' police resources on such a trivial errand just to placate some distant family relatives. So, we've been asked to collect some information, you understand."

Nodding, Hart said, "Of course. I understand. Let's go talk in my office. It will be quieter in there."

"Splendid! Lead the way," said Holmes, and we followed Basil Hart back through the short corridor through which we had come and into the general office area. Once there, we went into the office behind Miss Peters' desk. Basil Hart closed the door and waved us both to chairs positioned in front of a desk.

The office was about twelve feet by fourteen feet in measurement, with grey carpet on the floor. Behind Basil Hart's desk and chair, there was a large window that looked out over the alleyway. A small book shelf sat under the window, holding leather binders and notebooks. On the wall behind our seats hung a painting of a rural landscape. Two large filing cabinets stood along each of the other two walls.

The desk stood in the middle of the room. The ink blotter was somewhat askew and covered with papers, presumably placed there by Miss Peters. Several pencils rested haphazardly beside the blotter. A small desk lamp anchored one corner of the desk, while some papers protruded from a tray sitting on the opposite corner. As Basil Hart passed the tray, he quickly took the papers and straightened out the small mess, placing the papers back in the tray before taking his seat behind the desk. The entire space gave the impression that its occupant was all business. That notion was supported with the presence of Miss Peters just outside the door.

Once we were seated, however, Basil Hart continued to straighten pencils, stack papers, and centre the ink blotter, finally aligning it with the bottom edge of the desk. It was some moments until he had arranged everything to his liking.

I wondered if Miss Peters took some indecent pleasure from intentionally leaving papers in disarray and moving the desk blotter, knowing of Basil Hart's predilection for neatness. It was idle speculation on my part, but given my brief assessment of her personality, I would not have been surprised.

Once he finished, he said, "All right, how can I help you?"

"We understand that Paul Watts worked here for you, is that right?" asked Holmes. He had purposely misspoken to give the impression that we were not very knowledgeable about the man.

"Well," Basil Hart began, "Paul Watts actually worked for Colin Dunn. He owns an accounting service, and he employed Mr. Watts. Mr. Watts did come here weekly to manage the business' books, but my dealings were mainly with Mr. Dunn."

"Oh, I see," Holmes said, nodding. "Then perhaps we can speak with whomever he worked with here, if not you. We're trying to get a sense of what his life was like and what his interests were...for his family, you understand. So far, we seem to have learned that he only liked accounting and mountaineering."

Hart was quiet for several moments, not quite sure what we knew or how to explain who Watts had worked with.

"Well," he finally said, "when he was working here, he primarily worked with my former business partner, Simon Rhoads. Is that name familiar to you?"

"Yes, I am afraid it is," Holmes said with a look of concern on his face. "I understand that he was the man who murdered Paul. How did you get along with Mr. Rhoads? Was this Rhoads fellow normally a violent person?"

"No, he wasn't normally prone to violence, and we were on reasonably good terms."

"Then can you help us to understand what caused the conflict between the two men?"

"Well, at the time, our business was having financial difficulties. It was a matter of cash flow, but it impacted some of our vendors. I am not sure, but I had always assumed that Rhoads became angry with Watts because Watts may have thought that the financial issues the company was experiencing were down to Rhoads' actions."

"And how were the financial issues resolved?" asked I.

Basil Hart hesitated, not sure if he was going to answer, but he decided to press onward.

"Well, after Simon's...death, I became sole owner of the business. I was able to get a loan from Colin Dunn, the man who owns the accounting company we use, and pay off all of the debt."

"Well, it was certainly fortunate Mr. Dunn was willing to provide such an influx of cash. So, you both are in the business together?"

"Oh yes, he owns a portion of the business now. In fact, there was an article in *The Strand Magazine*, a few months after Simon's death, featuring Holtz Manufacturing and several other businesses in London. It was quite exciting."

Hart paused a moment before continuing. "But I am paying the loan back and will become the sole proprietor in several months. Colin Dunn and I have also grown quite close. We have travelled to several countries over the past few months: France, Spain, Italy. And I am a frequent guest at his house."

"Ah, regretfully, I don't get over to the continent often enough," Holmes stated. I have to admit I was surprised by the comment but kept my face neutral.

"Oh, it's wonderful. We try to go in the late spring or early summer."

"Yes, I believe the last time Dr. Watson and I were over in Spain was June of '94. We spent some time near the Pyrenees."

"Ah, we were there about that same time. What a coincidence."

"Yes, isn't it. Pray tell me, did Paul and this Rhoads fellow get along together? Were they on friendly terms?"

"They seemed friendly enough. Theirs was primarily a business relationship, but they would occasionally go to a pub together."

"You know," Basil Hart continued, "Paul had intended to emigrate to America the very day he died. He was going to start a business there. Both Colin Dunn and I had helped him dispose of his clothes and possessions to charity."

"Ah, did Paul have a favourite charity? Perhaps his family might make a special donation in his name?"

"Well, the Randall House is a particularly good organisation, and they are always happy to receive any donations. I believe most of Paul's possessions went there."

Holmes was quiet for a moment, then he said sympathetically, "With this Rhoads fellow being your business partner, the trial could not have been easy for you. I imagine it was difficult sitting through the proceedings."

"It was. I liked the man, but he was not a close friend. I made an effort to only attend when I was called as a witness. In all honesty, I could not say he was a calm person when he drank to excess."

"Oh! You had to be a witness *against* your business partner?"

Hart paused a moment, then nodded.

"Yes. In fact, both Colin Dunn and I had to testify that we were at the Fox and Goose pub the night before Watts was... killed. We saw him and Rhoads sitting together, drinking, and in animated conversation. That discussion broke out into an argument and both men had to be restrained. Once tensions abated, they resumed their seats and continued drinking until they left together."

Holmes was silent for a few moments as he digested what he had just heard. Then he asked a question.

"And what of Mrs. Rhoads? How has she fared these many months?"

No sooner had Holmes made the enquiry then the expression on Hart's face showed it was a question too far. As I watched, the man seemed to replay the entire conversation over in his mind. At some point he realized the wide breadth of the questions and that he may have said too much.

Suddenly rising from his chair, he shouted, "Sir! I fail to see how Mrs. Rhoads' status could be of any interest to the family of Paul Watts. That also applies to my company's financial status. Why are you asking these questions now? That was a hurtful period best left forgotten! Now I am a busy man so I think our time is up. I'll have Mr. Cahn show you both out. Good day!"

Basil Hart quickly went to the office door and as we stood, we heard him call to someone. We emerged from his office to find Mr. Cahn, dwarfing Basil Hart and Miss Peters, who were standing next to him.

"Don't trouble yourselves," Holmes said calmly as we began to leave, "we know the way out. Good day to you."

We weaved our way through the grid pattern of desks and workers until we reached the door. I could almost feel their eyes boring into our backs. Before we stepped out onto the pavement, I happened to look back and saw Basil Hart, Miss Peters, and that Cahn fellow closely watching our departure. I was much relieved to be outside and out of that office.

Holmes hailed a cab, and in moments we were off to Baker Street. Initially we were quiet, but after a few moments, Holmes turned to look at me.

"Well, that was interesting. Eh, Watson?"

"I don't believe I shall forget that Cahn fellow for some time. He is certainly intimidating."

"Oh," Holmes scoffed, "he's not so intimidating. He just thinks he's menacing because he's big and strong. And that is his weakness. He is over-confident in his abilities."

"Well, I *am* confident in his abilities. He could crush either one of us quite easily."

We rode in silence for another few moments, then I asked, "Did you learn anything from our visit? We have just partially revealed ourselves to Basil Hart. He now knows someone is looking into the affairs of Paul Watts. I hope our visit was worthwhile."

"Oh, very much so, Watson. We have at least discovered that Basil Hart is not an honest man. Do you recall his explanation for why Watts and Rhoads were arguing in the pub? He said that Watts had accused Rhoads of accounting improprieties that led to the financial distress of Holtz Manufacturing. We know from our conversation with Inspector Hall that Watts and Rhoads were actually discussing the possibility of Colin Dunn purchasing a controlling interest in the business to stave off certain bankruptcy; an option Simon Rhoads would not tolerate. Why would Basil Hart lie about that conversation, unless it was to further sully the name of Simon Rhoads?

"Yes," he continued, "we learned a great deal that we didn't know before. In fact, I want to make a quick stop." And with that Holmes called up to the cabman to pull over to the curb. Once we were stopped, Holmes exited the cab, telling me he would be back shortly.

As I waited for Holmes' return, I tried to replay our conversation with Basil Hart, even looking through my notes. But I didn't see that we had learned very much at all.

I put my notebook away as Holmes returned to our carriage. Once he told the cabman to drive on and we were under way again, he turned to me.

"I've just sent a telegram to Mr. and Mrs. Colin Dunn, requesting that we may visit them tomorrow morning. I was brief on our purpose but said we were assisting some family members of Paul Watts. I imagine that even now Basil Hart is in communication with Mr. and Mrs. Dunn to tell them about our visit. So, I am sure they will accept our request, if for no other reason than to gauge what we know."

"And what do we know?" I asked somewhat doubtfully.

"Oh, a great deal, I think," Holmes replied, and he was silent for the remainder of our journey.

Chapter XIV: Inspector Lestrade Brings a Case

It was midafternoon when we arrived back to Baker Street. We asked Mrs. Hudson to make some sandwiches and then went up to our rooms. Once there we removed our coats and hats and cleared the table.

A few minutes later Mrs. Hudson brought up sandwiches and tea, setting them on the table. It was evident that she had made a special effort as there were a variety of meats and pastries.

"Just put those down anywhere, Mrs. Hudson. Thank you," Holmes said distractedly. With a "harrumph" Mrs. Hudson set the tray down and went out the door. I went after her and caught her on the landing.

"Mrs. Hudson, we really do appreciate the food and tea. I know we have been asking a great deal from you of late, beyond what we usually do, and you have been more than kind. Holmes doesn't always show it, but he is grateful as well."

"Oh, Dr. Watson," Mrs. Hudson blushed. "I know you men are working on something serious. When there are Scotland Yard folks about at all hours of the day and night, it must be important. I'm glad I can help." She put her hand on mine. "But thank you for saying so." Then she went downstairs.

I turned back to our room and closed the door behind me. I found Holmes perusing some documents. I wandered over to see what he was looking at.

"Where did you go, Watson?" Holmes asked distractedly. He was examining the two autopsy reports closely.

"I went to thank Mrs. Hudson for making these meals we have been eating. You know, it would not hurt you to thank her once in a while yourself."

"Yes, I will," he replied absently, never taking his eyes off the papers.

Moments later, we heard the street door open and the unexpected voice of Inspector Lestrade as he enquired of Mrs. Hudson as to our presence. With his steps ascending the stairs to our rooms, Holmes and I quickly placed the Scotland Yard evidence boxes behind the couch, throwing a blanket over them. By the time we finished, there was a knock on the door.

"Who is it?" I queried in order to give us a few additional moments to ensure all was hidden.

"Inspector Lestrade, Dr. Watson. May I come in?"

Seeing everything was in order, Holmes gave a nod and I moved to the door and opened it.

"Certainly, Inspector, it's a pleasure to see you."

"And you, Doctor," he replied with a handshake. Looking past me, he finally saw Holmes.

"Ah, Mr. Holmes. I'm glad to see that you're in," he said as Holmes came up and shook hands.

"Hello, Lestrade. Come in and have a seat," Holmes invited as I closed the door.

As Inspector Lestrade folded his lean figure into a chair, I studied the look of the man. His eyes seemed to have lost their lustre, as if they had seen too much recently and cared to see no more. His face was drawn and his hair seemed dishevelled as he removed his hat and placed it in his lap.

Holmes and I moved to sit across from him, and as we did, I confirmed that Lestrade could not see the blanketed mass behind the sofa. Once I was settled, I took out my notebook.

"Would you care for a sandwich?" Holmes asked, waving at the plate on the table.

"Oh, no thank you, Mr. Holmes," Lestrade declined.

"Then what brings you here, Inspector?"

"I have an unusual case that I thought might be of interest to you. So far, this case has plagued me with three similar murders over four months, and I must admit I have not made the progress I would like."

"Four months, eh? Pray, tell me about the case. But I must warn you that I am currently engaged in another matter at the moment."

"Very well. The body of a man, a day labourer, was found two nights ago in an alley behind Charing Cross Hospital. He wasn't stabbed or shot, but appeared to have been crushed to death."

Lestrade paused a moment as he scratched his head, then he continued.

"The medical examiner said the man actually died from suffocation. But the odd thing is, his ribs and his spine were broken as if the life were squeezed right out of him. It would take an unusually strong man to squeeze someone to death in that fashion. I asked the medical examiner if there was some kind of machine that could inflict those injuries and he said the only machines he knew of that could crush a man would also mangle the body. This man's body wasn't mangled."

The inspector shook his head slowly and continued.

"The thing is, this is the third such murder over the past four months. All of the victims have been itinerant seamen or day labourers and they have all been killed in the same manner."

Holmes was silent for a moment, then asked, "Were there any other injuries?"

"Aye. You could tell by their faces that they had each suffered a severe beating. And there were scrapes on their knees as if they'd been dragged someplace."

As he listened to Inspector Lestrade describe the murder victims, I could see that Holmes had a worried expression on his face. His next question told me why.

"Could any of the victims have been attacked due to some handicap, impediment, or other distinguishing marks they possessed, such as skin discolouration or facial disfigurements of some kind? You know ruffians will sometimes target people for their appearance."

"No, these all appeared to be able-bodied men, no unusual deformities or markings other than tattoos. And it was also obvious that they were all rather poor, so robbery as a motive was out of the question."

As Lestrade answered, Holmes glanced briefly at me, and I knew what he had actually been asking. Fortunately, it seemed that our missing Asa Bloom had not been one of

Lestrade's three victims. At least that avenue of investigation remained open to us.

Holmes then focused back on Inspector Lestrade and continued his questioning.

"Were you able to identify any of the men?"

"Well," Inspector Lestrade nodded, "we were never able to identify the first murder victim by name. Only that he had red hair and was missing the thumb on his right hand. These day labourers aren't too keen to speak to the police. But we finally found out the second victim's name was Liam Norwell. He was known to a couple of the charity houses."

"And your latest victim?"

"Ah, we know a bit more about him. His name was Roy Hallis. He worked odd jobs as a carpenter's helper, a day labourer, sometime seaman, whatever job came to hand. Since he held assorted jobs, he normally stayed at the various charity houses throughout London. He had a partial stub from a meal ticket in his pocket, but the name of the charity house had been torn off. That's how we discovered his name, by asking around at the charity houses."

Holmes glanced quickly at me before he enquired.

"Who identified the body?"

"Well, two people identified him," Inspector Lestrade responded. "I had Constable Rance, who was on patrol around that location, go to three of the charity houses in the area with the man's description to see if anyone knew him. I went to the two remaining houses. When I spoke to the manager of the Galloway House, a man by the name of Keenan Talbot, he said he recognised the description. When I brought him to the medical examiner's office to see the body, Constable Rance was already there with the manager of the Howard House who had already provided an identification. I thought that since we were already there, I'd have this Mr. Talbot identify him as well, which he did."

"Where was the last charity house he stayed?"

"Talbot recognised the meal ticket stub as belonging to a place called the Randall House. It's a charity house that caters mostly to men who are looking for employment or are willing to perform work duties around the area in exchange for a meal and a place to sleep."

"I presume you have spoken to the people at the Randall House?"

"Aye, I have. They remember him being there several nights ago, but after that, no one had seen him. That isn't too unusual. When these men take on a job, they can disappear for weeks at a time, and no one sees them until they turn up again."

"Did anyone at the Randall House recognise either of your first two victims?"

"They said the descriptions of both men sounded familiar, but they see a lot of men coming through their doors, so they couldn't be sure."

Once more, Holmes was silent a moment. Then, "How was the body of the latest victim positioned?"

"Well, that's another thing that has me baffled. The bloke was sitting upright, with his back against the wall of the hospital, his hands on his lap. I think he was placed there. He certainly couldn't have gotten there by himself. His spinal injuries were too severe."

"Were the other two victims positioned similarly?"

"Now that you mention it, the second one was sitting up against a fence post, but the first one was laid out flat on the ground. And they all had the same types of injuries: they had been beaten, dragged, and crushed."

Inspector Lestrade was silent for a few more moments as he searched his memory for any other similarities between the murders. Suddenly, his eyes got big and he snapped his fingers.

"There was one other thing the medical examiner said. All three men had bits of sawdust on their clothes. We've been checking all the local lumber yards, but they say they have never seen or employed any of the victims."

Holmes was quiet for a few moments as he considered what Lestrade had told him. Then with a sigh he rose from his seat.

"The case is interesting to me, Inspector, but as I said I am currently engaged in another affair. However, I will look into the case as time permits. But I cannot promise anything."

"That's fine, Mr. Holmes," Lestrade said, also rising. "If you can take a look, possibly point me in the right direction, I can take it from there."

"I'll do what I can," Holmes said as he walked Lestrade to the door. After good-byes were exchanged, Inspector Lestrade left and Holmes closed the door.

Holmes stood still for a full minute at the door after Lestrade had departed. Finally, he walked over to the table and sat.

"Well, that's interesting. Inspector Lestrade may have inadvertently brought us a clue."

"What clue was that, Holmes?"

"The man who was killed was staying at the Randall House. That charity house has come up in our investigation just today. You may recall Basil Hart said that he and Colin Dunn assisted Paul Watts as he donated belongings, and that the majority of Watts' possessions went to that specific charity. It serves the lower echelon of society. If you recall, our Battersea Park victim would have been a likely client of that charity, as most probably was the elusive Asa Bloom. And now Inspector Lestrade's victim has been found to be a resident of that charity house. It may bear visiting before this case is over."

Holmes paused a moment, then continued. "I highly doubt that Lestrade's victim, Roy Hallis, would have been of much interest to a common thief. But the fact that he was beaten prior to being killed suggests that someone wanted to obtain some information. What could they have wanted to know, and why did they believe Roy Hallis had the answers? Perhaps he and the Battersea Park victim knew each other."

# # #

As I considered these possibilities, we heard steps ascending the stairs to our rooms. Holmes went over and opened the door to find Inspector Gregson and Sergeant Cummings standing on the landing.

"Come in, gentlemen," said he. "We had just returned when Inspector Lestrade came to our door seeking assistance with a case."

"Aye," Gregson said as he and Sergeant Cummings entered and removed their coats and hats. "We saw him enter from the street just as we ourselves were approaching. We decided to wait outside until we saw him depart."

"That was wise," Holmes said, then he waved to the table. "There are sandwiches and tea. Help yourselves."

Both men were ravenous, and grateful for the nourishment. Holmes and I joined them.

While we ate, Holmes asked, "How was Inspector Hall? Were you able to get him on the train back to his home?"

"Yes, we got him onto the train, but he was in a bad way," Inspector Gregson said. "I believe this case is worrying him. All he could talk about was how they had been thorough in their investigation. But every time he said that, he then pointed out one of the details that we uncovered and stated that he had failed as an investigator."

"I've never seen him so despondent," Sergeant Cummings added between bites. "Once he was on the train and seated, he just seemed to look off into the distance without actually seeing anything."

"Aye. Sergeant Cummings and I went back to Scotland Yard after the train station. Our main purpose was to check for any messages, but we also kept an ear out for anyone asking about what we might be working on. Several folks asked if Inspector Hall had found us, and we confirmed that he had. But no one seemed to have any idea that we were working on anything special."

"And we need to keep it that way," Holmes said as he completed his meal. Inspector Gregson and Sergeant Cummings nodded their agreement.

When the two Scotland Yard detectives finished their meal, Inspector Gregson said, "After we finished at Scotland

Yard, we went over to the Alpine Club to learn about Paul Watts. Since Sergeant Cummings here is closer in age to Watts, he went in posing as a friend who had just come back to London."

Turning to Sergeant Cummings, the inspector said, "Tell them what you found out."

"Very well," Sergeant Cummings said as he straightened in his chair. "I went to the reception desk and asked if they could put me in touch with Paul Watts. I told them that I was an old friend who had been living in Australia for the past several years and had just come back to London. The young man at the desk said he would look the name up in their directory. But an older gentleman who had overheard our conversation came over and told us that Paul Watts had died. Apparently, the young man had not been working at the Alpine Club at the time of Watts' death.

"The older bloke took me aside and we sat in a couple of chairs in the reception area. He told me that Paul Watts had been murdered, to which upon hearing, I of course, acted surprised and distressed. He said the man who had killed Paul had been hanged.

"He then looked at me carefully and said, 'I don't recall Paul Watts having very many friends. In fact, I only know of one friend he had and that was Jeremy Bales, and he died almost two years ago. I knew Watts to be a bit standoffish, and he kept to himself. How did you get along with him?'

"I said, 'We had known each other since school. We had remained in contact while I was living in Australia, but Paul's letters stopped several months ago. I was hoping to find that he had married or something.'

"He replied, 'No, he didn't marry. I would occasionally see him in a pub, sometimes by himself, and sometimes in the company of a business associate or young woman. But never for any length of time.'"

Sergeant Cummings paused before concluding, "This man recounted how upset Watts had been with the death of his friend Bales, and he thought that single event had soured Watts on mountaineering *and* his life in London. He said that soon after his friend's death, Watts decided to emigrate to America, but was killed before he left. After that, there didn't seem to be very much more he could add."

Once Sergeant Cummings had finished speaking, we cleared the plates away. After settling down with a fresh cup of tea, Holmes summarised our visit with Basil Hart. Inspector Gregson and Sergeant Cummings listened intently, asking an occasional question. Once they were up to date, Holmes made a suggestion that I have to say surprised me.

"Gentlemen, let us rest for the evening. We have a lot to consider and we must be fresh and at our best, as we are due to provide Mycroft and the others an update on our progress tomorrow evening.

"However, Inspector Gregson, I'd like to ask that you and Sergeant Cummings further investigate Simon Rhoads' will, his finances, and perhaps any insurance he may have had. Perhaps you can speak with his solicitor. We need to know everyone who benefited from Rhoads' death other than Basil Hart."

"Aye, we can do that," Inspector Gregson said, Sergeant Cummings nodding in agreement. "We will also see that Chris Ross departs on his ship to America tomorrow evening as he has planned."

"Excellent. Watson and I will go see Mr. and Mrs. Dunn tomorrow morning. I've sent a telegram requesting an audience, and I suspect that they will want to see us to discover what we know and what we may be seeking.

"I am especially curious to find out," Holmes concluded, "how the widow of an executed man became the wife of a friend who neglected to vouch for him in court."

# # #

Not too many minutes later, Inspector Gregson and Sergeant Cummings left Baker Street for their own homes. It was almost early evening and I for one was exasperated from our investigation. It seemed that we had been on this case for days, but it had only been just over twenty-four hours.

"Holmes," said I with some frustration, "everything about this matter is going round and round in my brain. I have to clear my head of the matter. I feel I must do something other than mull over the facts of this confounded case. I'm going to my club for a change of scene. Would you care to join me?"

"Thank you, old fellow, but I have something I want to do and tonight is a good night for it."

He paused a moment, then added, "If I am not back when you return, don't worry. I should not be too much delayed." And with that, Holmes rose from his seat and went to his room.

So, I retrieved my coat, hat, and walking stick, and made my way to my club. I have to say that I very much needed a diversion from this affair and welcomed the chance to speak to friends and former comrades about anything other than murders and investigations.

Upon my arrival I immediately found my old colleague Withers, whom I had worked with at Barts for a time. After catching up, we each got a lager and sat down to play a couple of games of Cribbage. Afterwards, we became involved in an exciting game of Whist. Withers and I lost the first game but took the last two games, claiming two Honours in the final game. I must say the time spent was a welcome distraction, and as I left the club to start my journey back home, I felt both refreshed and restored.

When I got back to Baker Street, three hours had elapsed and Holmes had not yet returned. Even though he had told me not to worry, I was concerned that he might have got himself into a dangerous situation. I changed into my nightshirt, poured myself a whisky, and after placing my revolver on the side table, I sat in my chair to await his return.

I must have drifted off to sleep because I dreamt of circus tents and high-wire walkers. I was at the top of the platform about to begin to walk across the wire as the smell of sawdust and elephants assailed my senses. From my high vantage point, I observed a large man below bending metal bars, his face grimacing and his arms shaking from the enormous pressure he exerted. Keeping my eyes on the strong man, I stepped off the platform, missing the wire with my foot.

As I was falling towards the net in my dreams, I was suddenly shaken awake. My eyes flew open, and I saw before me the haggard face of a man with stringy hair, looking closely at me from under a floppy hat. I flailed my arms to wave the creature away. Reaching for my pocket to retrieve my gun, I realised I was wearing my nightshirt and had placed my service revolver on the table beside the chair. After grasping the gun, I tried to stand.

"Easy, Watson! Easy old fellow. It's just me." I recognised that chuckling voice as Holmes, but the face and the clothes were those of a vagabond. It took me a few moments, but as I looked closer, I began to see through the painted face, the false black tooth, and the well-worn hat.

It was indeed Holmes in disguise.

"Holmes! Why on earth are you in such a get up? I could have shot you!"

"I've been doing some quiet investigating on Inspector Lestrade's case," he said. Smiling to himself, he went and drew a bowl of water and carried it over to the table, where he sat. He removed his hat and wig, and then began to remove his makeup.

"Well, where did you go?" asked I, now fully awake, my heart still racing.

"I went to a pub called the Pelican a few doors down from the Randall House charity. I thought the best place to find residents of the Randall House was at the closest pub. I felt I would have a better chance of getting people to speak with me if I went alone and in disguise."

"And did they talk with you?"

"Yes, they did. I presented myself as Derek Hallis, a cousin of Roy Hallis, Inspector Lestrade's latest murder victim, although I didn't tell anyone he was dead. I let it be known that I was seeking friends of Roy Hallis. After buying a few drinks, I found three men who were willing to talk with me.

"I told them that Roy had mentioned to me there was plenty of work about if you were willing to take on jobs of any kind. These men told me that there was work if you wanted it, but to be careful which jobs I took, especially the jobs I might be offered from some of the volunteers at the Randall House. They told me that there were two particular gentlemen who would offer good money for odd jobs."

Holmes was quiet as he scrubbed some of the darkening stain from his face and hands. Then he continued.

"They told me that if those volunteers offered me a job, I'd be better off going somewhere else; the men were dangerous. These men always offered a lot of money, too much for what they asked you to do. And sometimes people were never seen again. The two gentlemen often have a big brute with them. He's huge and has a mole on the bridge of his nose by his right eye."

"Cahn!" I said excitedly.

"I suspect so, but we don't have any evidence that he is involved in the death of Hallis; at least not yet, although that scratch on his face appeared recent. We also still don't know who these gentlemen are, but I have my suspicions."

As Holmes continued removing his makeup he said, "And based on a premonition, I mentioned something else, just to see what kind of a reaction I would get. I said that Roy Hallis had told me about a friend of his who had some discolouration on the top of his right hand and on his upper neck. I asked them if they knew who he was or where I could find him. They looked at me suspiciously at first, but after a few more drinks, they said they recognised the description; however, they had not seen him for several months. I asked them what specific types of jobs he tried to get and they said they didn't know, but that he and another man would usually get jobs together. I asked them who this other friend was and they said he was a rather short man with a heart tattoo on his left arm."

"The man who was found in Battersea Park!" I exclaimed.

"Yes. They said they had not seen either man for at least a year, maybe two. They didn't know their names, or they wouldn't tell me. But this is important, Watson. We now know that the man who identified the body in Battersea Park knew the body was not Paul Watts, but was instead his own friend. He may very well be in hiding, and that is why we are unable to locate him. And we also know that they both would frequent the Randall House. That's a good deal more then we knew before."

When Holmes finally finished taking off his disguise he said, "Well, I think it's time we retire. We have a big day tomorrow and we need to rest."

"I'm just glad you're back safe. It was dangerous to go out by yourself at night to such a rough place."

"Yes, I'm glad to be back, too."

As I got ready for bed, I prepared a sleeping draught for myself and offered the same to Holmes. He declined my offer, saying he was going to quickly reread Dunn's court testimony before retiring. So, I bade him goodnight and went to bed.

All night I dreamed of a circus strong man carrying someone up the gallows steps under one arm towards a hangman's noose at the top. But the steps never seemed to end, they simply continued to ascend towards the gallows. In the morning, after awakening, I realized I had experienced a most unpleasant night and had not rested at all.

Part IV:

Wednesday - Day 3

Chapter XV: Mr. and Mrs. Dunn

Emerging from my room the next morning, I found Holmes sitting stoically in his chair, gazing into the unlit fireplace. I suspected he had gotten very little sleep. I also noticed that the nervous energy he often displayed when challenged by a case was absent.

Perhaps it was the result of a restless night, for I myself was engulfed in a feeling of lassitude coupled with a desire to abandon our enquiries and restore our normal routines. As I look back on that moment now, I often wonder if our moods that morning were the result of a certain dread about this affair; perhaps a weariness from our aggressive pursuit of the case beginning that afternoon at the Diogenes Club; or maybe we both felt some sinister premonition of what was to come over the next few days.

As we were finishing our breakfast, we received word that Mr. and Mrs. Dunn would grant us an audience in their home at eleven o'clock. The address showed the house to be located off the King's Road near Chelsea Manor Gardens. At about ten thirty we collected our hats, coats, and walking sticks and went down to the street to hail a cab, and in moments we were on our way. We rode in silence for the first few minutes, but then Holmes turned to face me.

"Watson, we may have shown too much of our hand yesterday when speaking with Basil Hart. I am sure that he has forewarned Mr. and Mrs. Dunn concerning our meeting. Without any hard evidence, we have no way of knowing whether any of these people are involved in this affair or are simply guilty of nothing more than being in the same social circle as Rhoads and Watts. I feel we must tread carefully."

I shared Holmes' trepidation. Not knowing whether these people were directly involved or not was hindering our ability to ask pertinent, straightforward questions. An additional impediment was the fact that we could not reveal that we knew the real Paul Watts had been killed on Monday last. As we interviewed the various participants, it might appear that we were accusing them of malfeasance when they were actually suffering through one of the worse periods of their lives.

When we arrived, it was evident that Colin Dunn had achieved considerable success. The home was two stories tall, with an attic. Three flagstone steps led up to a large, covered porch housing a set of massive wooden front doors. On either side of the porch stood two tall, mullioned windows that looked out onto the front drive of the brick house. Second story windows were located above each of the ground-floor windows and a large stained-glass windowpane was centred above the porch over the front door. Well-kept bushes had been planted below the front windows, with several flower beds placed next to the shrubbery.

As we alighted from the carriage, Holmes told the cabman to wait. We strode up the three flagstone steps and knocked on the front doors. After a few moments, a plump woman of about fifty-five opened the door. Her hair was pulled back tightly and she wore an apron over a plain cotton dress. Holmes made the introductions.

"Sherlock Holmes and Dr. Watson to see Mr. And Mrs. Dunn. I believe we are expected."

"Please wait here a moment," she said, then she closed the door to us. While we waited, I gazed up above our heads and saw a large carriage light centred in the porch ceiling and two additional sconce gas lamps on either side of the doors.

In just a few moments, the woman returned, opened the door, and bade us to enter. We passed through the large doors and found ourselves inside a grand circular entryway, about forty feet in diameter. As we were removing our coats and hats, I took the opportunity to survey our surroundings. We were standing on a marble floor that was inlaid with tiles that provided what appeared to be some type of Greek design. There was a large, round table in the middle of the entryway approximately twenty feet from the front doors. A grand, glass chandelier hung above the table, the glass twinkling a rainbow of colours as light cascaded through the stained-glass windowpane over the door. A vase of fresh flowers stood in the centre of the table, which indicated to me there must be a greenhouse somewhere on the grounds.

Just to the right of the front entrance was a set of opened double doors that gave way to a large dining room containing a grand table and chairs. A large buffet stood along one wall and a fireplace was set in the far wall at the end of the table.

Further into the entryway, past the dining room doors, was a grand staircase leading to the upstairs. I imagined that beyond the staircase was the kitchen and servant's entrance.

Just to the left of the entrance was another set of double doors, which were closed. The entire space conveyed an aura of grandeur.

Placing her hand on the table at the centre of the entryway, the woman said, "Please place your things here, and I will take you to them."

Once we had put everything on the table, she led us to the closed double doors on the left. She placed both hands on the knobs and opened the doors to a large, carpeted room.

"Mr. Holmes and Dr. Watson," she said and stepped aside so that we might enter.

The room was about twenty feet by thirty feet with bookcases filling the wall directly opposite the doors we had just entered. In front of the bookcases stood a large, mahogany desk, with one chair behind the desk and two chairs positioned in front. On the desk was a small lamp, along with folders and papers. An ink blotter sat in the middle.

A large fireplace with a massive, carved mantle stood on the wall to the right from where we were standing. The pleasant odour of burning wood filled the room and glowing embers from the morning fire were still evident in the grate. Small paintings hung on either side of the fireplace.

To the left were the two tall, mullioned windows that looked out onto the front drive. They ran from the floor to the ceiling, with sheer curtains held back by silk tie-back ropes. Between the windows stood a smaller round table with two chairs.

I noted all these details afterward, because as we entered, my attention was immediately drawn to the figure standing in front of the farthest window. Seeing only her profile at first, I was taken by the erect posture and confident stature. Once she turned fully towards us, the woman's alluring features came dramatically into view.

Her dark hair fell generously over her shoulders and her soft skin appeared flawless, possessing a slight rose-coloured hue. I placed her age to be no more than twenty-four or twenty-five, seemingly too young to present such striking beauty. Her oval face lifted slightly as we entered, as if to focus her full attention on our presence. She had a small nose and bright green eyes that I suspected had witnessed more than their share of heartbreak. Yet she gave the impression of a strong woman who was not intimidated by the affairs of men. She wore an attractive dress that had been tailored to flatter her figure and as she turned towards us, she placed her delicate hands upon the back of the nearest chair, her eyes never leaving us. If this was the former Mrs. Rhoads, as I suspected, she was indeed a stunning creature.

"Thank you, Haddie. That will be all," she said quietly in a voice that carried a sense of foreboding, coupled with a tremor of disquiet. Yet her eyes at that moment seemed to betray both a dreaded anticipation and welcomed relief. The housekeeper gave a slight nod and promptly left, closing the doors behind her.

At the desk sat a man, whom I presumed to be Colin Dunn, bent over some papers and occasionally writing some figures. He briefly raised a hand to us without looking up, indicating that he would only be another few moments as he continued to work.

I took this brief time to study the man. He appeared to be close to thirty-five years of age. His dark hair and beard had not begun to show any of the grey so often seen in men his age. When he glanced up, his eyes were dark, almost black. Then he focused them back on to the work papers before him, to the exclusion of all else. He wore a vest over a white shirt and collar, with sleeves rolled partway up his arms, and a lanyard cinched to his neck.

Once he had finished, he moved the papers over to one side of the desk and rose from his seat, giving his vest a slight downward tug. His height was about six feet and when he spoke, he hooked his thumbs inside his vest pockets.

"Gentlemen, I appreciate your patience. Please forgive me." As he said this he walked over to the woman by the windows, took her hand, and then turned back to us.

"My name is Colin Dunn, and this is my wife, Frances Dunn."

"I am Sherlock Holmes and this is my friend and colleague, Dr. Watson. We appreciate that you could make time to see us on such short notice."

"Please, sit," Colin Dunn said. He waved to the chairs in front of his desk. He held one of the chairs by the window for Mrs. Dunn, who sat and turned to face us. He then walked over to resume his own seat behind the desk.

"So, how may we be of assistance?" Colin Dunn asked after we were all seated.

Holmes provided the same fictitious tale he had given to Basil Hart. When he had finished, it seemed that both Mr. and Mrs. Dunn accepted the story.

"I see," Colin Dunn said. After a moment of silence he continued, "Well, we will do what we can to assist you, but as you can imagine, that period was a very difficult time for us, especially for my wife. Please keep your questions concise and relevant to Paul." It was apparent that Basil Hart had indeed related our discussions from the previous day to Colin Dunn.

"Of course," Holmes agreed. Then, "I understand that Paul worked for your accounting firm, Mr. Dunn."

"Yes, we had an arrangement that quite suited him. He would work for a few months every year and then leave on one of his Alpine Club expeditions, only to return a couple of months later, wanting to work again."

"Did he have any other interests; perhaps a lady friend?"

"No, he seemed most content working for my accounting firm and going on his various mountaineering excursions. Although, I must say that over the last several weeks before his departure, I did notice what seemed to be a lack of enthusiasm for the work he was doing. As if he no longer wished to focus his efforts totally on his duties. He seemed at all times to be distracted, morose. I believe a friend of his had recently passed away, and perhaps that was weighing on him."

Holmes paused a moment, then continued.

"Did Paul have any preferred charities?"

"Not that I am aware of. But when he was donating his possessions before his planned trip to America, Basil Hart and I assisted him. We are both supporters of the many charities around London, so several charities benefited from Paul's generosity."

"Not one charity in particular?"

"Well, looking back, I'd have to say most of Paul's clothes and furnishings were donated to the Randall House with the remainder going to the others."

"I see," Holmes said as he stroked his chin. He then turned to Mrs. Dunn. who was still seated in a chair by the window.

"Mrs. Dunn, had you ever met Paul?"

"Yes. I would sometimes assist with the filing in the office. On the days he came to Holtz Manufacturing to update the accounting books, if I was present, we would generally speak." Then after a moment's pause, she added, "But I believe his nature led him to be a quiet, private person."

Colin Dunn narrowed his eyes and said, "Frances is the former Mrs. Rhoads; however, I believe you already knew that."

"Yes," Holmes nodded. "I apologize for bringing this up again."

Mrs. Dunn continued with a pained expression on her face. "I have always regretted giving Simon the letter opener that was destined to become a murder weapon. I feel somewhat responsible for that horrible affair. I must also say that I suffer a pang of guilt for having to testify that when he drank to excess, Simon would sink into a rage and could be easily provoked."

At this, Colin Dunn rose from his seat behind the desk and went over to his wife, placing a comforting hand upon her shoulder.

Holmes then asked, "Did you, Mr. Dunn, know Mr. Rhoads very well? Did you perceive his violent nature? Was he a man that Paul would likely befriend?"

"I really only knew Simon from the times I would occasionally speak to him at Holtz Manufacturing. We never met socially."

"So, you were not called to court as a witness for his defence?"

"No. Nor did I believe that my presence would provide very much support to him during his trial."

Mrs. Dunn, gazing down at her hands, looked up and said, "I would have preferred to have been present in court to support Simon, but I was encouraged not to attend by Colin. He felt it would be too stressful for me to hear the testimony and face the newspapers."

She looked up at her husband, who gave her shoulder a supportive squeeze. She reached up and touched his hand.

"And he was right, of course," she continued. "Colin was so supportive and attentive during that terrible time that when it was over...the execution...I naturally turned to him for support and comfort. We were married a year later."

We were all silent for a few moments. We were discussing a period of time that would have been awful for everyone involved, and I could tell by their faces that this conversation was taking its toll.

"Well," Holmes said after a moment, "may I ask this please? Can you help us to understand what Paul's last hours in the pub were like?"

"I would say they were generally pleasant," Colin Dunn stated. "Both I and Basil Hart were in the pub that night. There was an argument between Simon and Paul that we helped break up. But they went back to drinking together and they left together."

"They left the pub together after their argument?"

"Yes. You see, Paul was due to leave the next morning for America. He had spent the past several weeks donating his clothes and furnishings."

"To the Randall House?" Holmes confirmed.

"Yes. When they left the pub, I assumed that Paul was going to board his ship to America. But when I heard that Paul had been found murdered, I thought that he and Simon must have had another argument outside the pub after they had left. I believe that was the police's theory, as well."

"Why weren't you called to identify the body?"

"I believe the police already had an identification. At least, I thought that to be the case at the time. At any rate, no one called upon me to identify Paul's body."

After a moment's pause, Colin Dunn's eyebrows furrowed and he asked, "Excuse me, but, is there some question about the identification now?"

"Yes," Mrs. Dunn added. "I'm confused as well. Why are you opening this matter back up again? We've spent the last few months trying to put this all behind us."

"I apologize, Mrs. Dunn," Holmes said.

But Colin Dunn was not satisfied. "I think we have answered all the questions regarding this matter that we are going to answer. You have caused us a great deal of stress, especially for my wife. I believe it is time for you to leave."

"As you wish," Holmes said as we rose from our seats. Colin Dunn went past us and opened the double doors that led out to the entryway.

"Thank you for seeing us," Holmes said looking at Mrs. Dunn. "I hope that we did not cause you too much distress."

Then turning to Colin Dunn, he said, "We can find our way out. Thank you."

We went out into the entryway and gathered our coats, hats, and walking sticks before exiting through the front doors. Colin Dunn watched us from the doors of his study, wearing a suspicious frown.

We got into our waiting cab and were shortly on our way back to Baker Street.

"What do you think, Watson?" Holmes queried as we rode down the street.

"I think we've just dredged up some very unpleasant memories, especially for Mrs. Dunn," answered I. With a sigh I added, "I hope it was worth it."

"Oh, I think so, old fellow. Did you notice anything about Colin Dunn as we were waiting for him to finish his paperwork?"

"Just that he seemed very busy and we were interrupting."

"He was writing with his left hand."

Suddenly, I recalled that Colin Dunn was indeed writing with his left hand.

"By Jove, Holmes! You're right. Do you believe he is our killer?"

"I don't know yet. But he is the first person in this quaint circle of friends who is left-handed. Both he and Basil Hart were known to Paul Watts. Perhaps they both were also known to our Battersea Park victim from the Randall House charity as well. Remember, both Basil Hart and Colin Dunn have mentioned their support for the various London charities. Perhaps they are actively involved with the Randall House charity. They have also stated that they were in the Fox and Goose pub at the same time Simon Rhoads and Paul Watts were there. So, we know they were at least in the vicinity of the murder sometime close to when it took place."

Holmes paused a moment, then said, "Perhaps someone at the Fox and Goose pub might still remember the events of that night."

"I doubt it. It was a long time ago."

"Maybe so, but it will not hurt to ask."

Holmes grasped his walking stick and rapped hard on the carriage ceiling.

"Cabman! Cabman!" Holmes called out.

A small trapdoor in the ceiling opened and the cabman looked down through the hole. "Aye?"

"Take us to the Fox and Goose pub near Battersea Park."

"Aye," the cabman called back and closed the trapdoor. Our direction was promptly altered and we were soon on our way to our new destination.

Chapter XVI: What the Publican Had to Say

We arrived at the Fox and Goose pub at the height of the lunch trade. With the cool and windy weather of late, everyone was inside, where the fire provided a welcomed warmth and the beer was in easy reach.

Once we were in the establishment, the noise and chaos of people crowded into a small space while trying to converse was deafening. We saw there were no empty tables available and no room to stand at the bar. Seeing that the publican and barmaids were hastily taking orders and serving, it was clear no one would be able to speak to us until after the lunch trade was over. So, we exited the pub.

Once outside, the noise level and temperature dropped considerably. Holmes quickly turned his attention to Battersea Park, which sat across the street. I followed his gaze and began to study the site of where this dreadful case had its beginnings.

Battersea Park covered approximately two hundred acres of what had once been marsh land that ran along the south shore of the Thames. When the wind was right, there was the slight odour of fish in the air, as well as the sounds of ship bells and the occasional horn. In the distance, teams of footballers could be seen on fields practising their skills in preparation for their upcoming games.

In the park directly across the street from the pub was a grassy area approximately forty yards deep and twenty yards wide. In the centre was a brick walkway that led from the street to a circular brick planter about twenty yards straight ahead. It was a simple memorial for a deceased councilman established by his family. The planter itself was only about three feet high and about ten feet in circumference. At the moment, it contained a bed of dirt and compost. In the spring and summer months, a variety of flowers were planted in the bed. A brick pathway surrounded the rock structure, with three benches placed evenly about the planter.

Surrounding the entire memorial area was a long hedgerow, standing about two feet tall. It began about ten yards on either side of the brick walkway and stretched into the park for about forty yards. Another hedgerow connected the two back ends.

Standing behind the back hedgerow was a large oak tree. It was under that tree that Simon Rhoads had been found with the body.

Holmes glanced at me, and then we both began to walk to the left side of the memorial until we came to the hedgerow. We then walked along the outside of the hedgerow until we reached the back, when we could finally make our way over to the oak tree. It stood about eight feet from the back of the hedgerow.

Once we arrived, I stared at the site.

There was, of course, no hope of finding any remaining evidence. However, I was overcome with a feeling of unease as I gazed at the place where this shocking case had begun. To know that evil had stood here, had been carried out here, caused a sense of disquiet to engulf me. The echoes of that experience at Newgate Prison suddenly overcame me. And I could not help but feel that I, and everyone who had participated in the execution of Simon

Rhoads, had been made a pawn in someone's evil plan. I felt used and victimised for having been made an unwitting party to someone's diabolical murder scheme.

"Look here, Watson," Holmes said, abruptly taking me out of my reverie.

"Yes, what is it?" I asked as I turned my focus to his pointing.

"This hedgerow has been cut back since the murder. Most likely it is cut back each year. But at the time of the murder, I recall that Sergeant Cummings said the hedgerow was easily five feet tall."

He pointed towards the pub and continued.

"At night, with the hedgerow at that height, anyone could come down to this tree unnoticed. And while they were here, no one would know that they were here unless someone walked up to them. I believe this is where the clothes the victim was wearing were ripped, after he was stabbed to death."

"Was this memorial here eighteen months ago?" asked I.

"Yes, it was established three years ago."

Holmes then walked slowly around the tree, keeping his eyes focused on the ground. He would stop occasionally, inspect a tree root with his lens, and then continue.

After a few minutes, he stood and looked out over the remainder of the park. There were fields and trees located throughout the park but this was the only tree standing by the hedgerow.

As we were standing, several large groups of people began to leave the pub. Holmes checked his pocket watch and then turned to me.

"I believe the majority of the lunch trade is leaving. Perhaps we can speak with the publican."

We retraced our steps back to the pub, and as the last of the people inside exited, we entered.

# # #

When we entered the establishment, it was evident that the lunchtime trade had been brisk. Plates and silverware were scattered about on the various tables, and empty glasses still littered the bar. The room itself appeared that it could hold perhaps sixty people, most sitting at tables. The air was thick with the odour of fried food and tobacco, accompanied by the smell of wood burning in the fireplace.

As we closed the door behind us, one of the barmaids passed by with her arms full of dirty plates, her fingers clasping empty glasses. A second barmaid was wiping down tables and straightening chairs. The publican was behind the bar, cleaning glasses and wiping the bar top.

We sat at one of the recently cleaned tables, and in a short while one of the barmaids came to take our order.

"Lunch is just finishing up so if you want something to eat you better order quickly," she said as she took out a pad of paper and pencil.

"We'd like to speak with the publican, if you please," Holmes said pleasantly.

She looked doubtfully at Holmes and said with a sly smile, "I'll see if he's available." She then walked over to the bar. As she spoke to the publican, they both looked over at us with suspicious eyes. I believe they were debating whether or not they should see what we wanted or just throw us out for impeding their clean-up efforts. Finally, with a sigh, the publican put down the glass he was cleaning and walked over to the table where we sat.

"What can I do for you gentlemen?" he asked, wiping his hands on a towel.

"Sir, we are seeking information regarding the murder that happened in the park across the street about eighteen months ago. It is a private matter, but we would be very thankful for any information you might provide." As Holmes said this, he placed two coins on the table. The publican eyed the offering, then pocketed the money and turned to one of the barmaids passing by.

"I'll be speaking with these gentlemen for a few minutes. Take a break and when I'm done, we can finish cleaning up."

"All right," she said, and after pouring herself a glass of water, she went over to one of the cleaned tables and sat.

The publican said, "I'll be right back." He strode over to the bar and drew three local lagers and brought them back to the table with a plate of bread and cheese.

"You can buy these, as well," he said as he placed the beverages in front of us. "The rest is on the house." After he sat, we toasted each other, had our first sip, and he began.

"The name's Hatch. Clint Hatch. I own this establishment."

"My name is Sherlock Holmes and this is Dr. Watson."

Mr. Hatch nodded to us both, then began his narration. "That murder happened quite a while ago and I wouldn't be truthful if I said I remembered everything from that night. But I'm not likely to forget when it was. It was bad for the bloke who got killed, but business was good for several weeks afterwards."

"Had you met Paul Watts, the man who was murdered, before?"

"Oh aye, both him and that Rhoads fellow had been in here several times before, together and alone."

"So, you knew Paul Watts by sight?"

"Aye, he was a regular customer."

Hatch took another sip of his drink and broke off a piece of bread.

"Am I correct that Watts and Rhoads got into an altercation that night?" Holmes queried.

"Aye, but to be honest it wasn't the fight that keeps it in my mind. We have fights break out at least once a week in this place. No, the fight wasn't unusual."

"Well, what was unusual about that night?"

"A few things. First off, Simon Rhoads, the man who killed Watts, had been in here drinking for a couple of hours before Watts arrived. Watts joined him when he came in.

"After a few drinks, Watts and Rhoads started arguing. They stood up and Rhoads struck Watts. A couple of other patrons separated the two." Hatch pointed over to the table where the barmaid was sitting. "They were sitting at that table. Anyway, after Watts and Rhoads were separated, everyone sat back down and continued drinking as if nothing had happened. After another half hour or so, Watts and Rhoads both got up and walked out together. No one saw them after that."

Holmes was silent a few moments. We each took a drink and then Holmes resumed his questions.

"Did you notice anyone by the name of Colin Dunn or Basil Hart in the pub that evening?"

The publican shook his head. "Those names are not familiar to me. But like I said, it's been a long time."

As the publican raised his glass for another sip, he stopped his arm midway. Then he placed his glass back onto the table.

"But now that you mention it, I believe the two men who stopped the fight knew both Rhoads and Watts. There was a third man with those two as well. He was a bit shorter as I recall. When the two gentlemen rose to separate Watts and Rhoads, the man at their table, the shorter one, remained seated. I couldn't say whether he knew Watts and Rhoads or not."

"Do you recall what that third man looked like?" Holmes asked the question nonchalantly, but I knew he was zeroing in on a key factor that might help solve this case.

"I don't recall too much. About the only thing I remember is that he seemed shorter than his companions and a bit older."

After another moment he added, "You know, I also seem to recall that his clothes appeared to be too large for him. As if he had bought them at a second-hand shop and took whatever was on hand."

Again, Holmes paused so as not to seem too anxious before asking, "Do you remember when the three of them left?"

"Oh, I couldn't say," Hatch said with a shake of his head as he took another drink. "People were coming and leaving all night long."

"But there was one other odd thing I just remembered," Hatch continued after another moment. "One of the men at that table was buying drinks for both his table of three *and* the table where Watts and Rhoads were sitting. He was very specific. He said that if any of the glasses became two-thirds empty, we were to refill them right away, and give him the bill at the end of the night."

"I see," Holmes said thoughtfully. Then with a quick glance at me he said, "Well, thank you, Mr. Hatch, for the information." Reaching into his pocket, Holmes extracted several large coins and placed them on the table.

"I trust this will cover the drinks and your time."

"Aye. That will do nicely," Hatch said as he put the coins into his pocket. "It's been a pleasure."

We rose from our seats and made our way outside. As we had dismissed our cab when we arrived, we had to hail another. It took some minutes but we were finally on our way back to Baker Street. As we rode, Holmes turned his excited eyes to me.

"Watson, I think we are getting closer to the perpetrators of this terrible act. By their own admission, both Colin Dunn and Basil Hart were in the pub the night Watts and Rhoads fought, and they broke up the altercation. We now have the publican saying that one of the men who broke

156

up the fight was buying drinks for Watts and Rhoads. No doubt to get Rhoads drunk and violent.

"We also have the publican recalling the shorter man who was sitting with Dunn and Hart. No doubt he was the murder victim wearing the clothes that were too large for him."

Holmes paused a moment, his eyes looking out the cab window. Then he struck his hand with his fist.

"But we do not have any direct evidence they orchestrated this affair. We can place them at or near the events, but we are hard-pressed to prove they were behind the scheme."

Holmes sat back and quietly looked out as the buildings and pedestrians passed by.

I had to agree with my friend. While it was becoming evident that Dunn and Hart were the culprits who planned and carried out the plot, we had precious little proof to present to the authorities. Also concerning was whether the authorities would even take action, in public, once proof was presented.

Chapter XVII: The Man Is Found!

As we entered the downstairs door to 221B Baker Street, we found Inspector Gregson sitting and talking with Mrs. Hudson in the parlour. Without stopping, Holmes bounded up the stairs to our rooms, calling loudly over his shoulder.

"Come, Inspector! *Il fait du soleil.* 'The sun shines' and we have much to discuss! Mrs. Hudson! Some tea, if you please!"

Inspector Gregson seemed a bit agitated, but he didn't say what was bothering him. I saw that Mrs. Hudson had already prepared tea so I motioned him up the stairs.

"Go ahead, Inspector. I'll bring up the tea."

The inspector led the way as I ferried the tray up the stairs and into our rooms, placing the tray onto the table. After removing our coats and hats, we sat and poured the tea.

"No Sergeant Cummings today, Inspector?" Holmes queried.

"I've not seen him all day," the inspector replied. "We were set to meet at Simon Rhoads' solicitor's office this morning at ten, but he never came. When our appointment time arrived, I met with the man. He was very helpful."

The inspector took another sip of his tea.

"After concluding my interview, I went to Scotland Yard to see if he was there or had left a message, but there was no message and no one had seen him. I left word with Sergeant Collins that if Sergeant Cummings came in to have him meet me here at this address. This behaviour is very unusual for the lad."

The inspector had a worried expression on his face. There had already been one close call. Perhaps, since we seemed to be getting closer to the heart of this affair, the danger was intensifying. But we had no proof or evidence that was the case.

"Well," Holmes said, "let's hope we see him before the day is out. Now, can you tell us what the solicitor said?"

"Aye," Gregson said as he took out his notebook and referenced his notations.

"It seems that Rhoads and Hart were not the best of friends. They barely tolerated each other near the end, according to the solicitor. Their wills stipulated that the other would receive seventy-five percent of the partner's share of the business should one of them die. The other twenty-five percent would go to a beneficiary they each designated."

"Who were these beneficiaries?" Holmes asked.

"Rhoads' twenty-five percent went to his wife, Mrs. Frances Rhoads, and would be paid until she remarried. Hart's twenty-five percent would go to a niece of his."

"So Mrs. Rhoads was entitled to twenty-five percent of the business until she remarried, at which time she ceased to benefit from the business?"

"That's right."

"So," I observed, "because she married Colin Dunn one year after her husband's death, she only benefited for a year. Hardly a motivation to be party to such an elaborate plan."

"Yes, that would seem to bring into question whether she had any motivation in seeing that her first husband was convicted of murder," Holmes agreed.

"Rhoads' finances," the inspector added, "were in good standing. There were no large outstanding debts to be paid. An account had been set up by the couple to benefit their housekeeper, Miss Haddie Shaw, in the event of the couple's demise."

"That must be the housekeeper we met this morning at the Dunn's residence," I suggested.

"Yes," the inspector continued, "Miss Shaw was Mrs. Dunn's nanny while she was growing up and became her housekeeper when she married. The Rhoads purchased a small house for her to live in, where she still resides.

"After Rhoads' death, Mrs. Rhoads remained in her house for a year until her marriage to Colin Dunn, at which time the house was sold and the proceeds were given to the new Mrs. Dunn. The business also held life insurance policies on both owners in case one of them died," the inspector added as he closed his notebook, "but the insurance would not pay off in Simon Rhoads' case because he was executed for a crime."

"All right, Inspector, that's helpful," Holmes said. "Adding the data you have brought us to what we learned this morning is painting a clearer picture of this affair."

Holmes then summarised what we had discovered from our conversations with Mr. and Mrs. Dunn as well as the publican at the Fox and Goose pub. I had the feeling that we were getting extremely close to our adversaries. I wondered if they were feeling the noose closing in on them.

As we were talking, we heard a ruckus from downstairs and then hurried footfalls coming up the steps. I rose and opened the door to find young Wiggins with another boy outside on the landing and Mrs. Hudson making her way up after them.

"'ello, Dr. Watson," he said with a slight bow. Then, looking past me, his eyes found Holmes.

"'ello, Mr. 'olmes. I was tellin' that lady downstairs that I think we've found the man you're looking for. Or rather, Pauley 'ere found 'im." Wiggins motioned to the boy standing beside him.

The lad was no more than twelve-to-thirteen years of age with a healthy head of dark hair, and freckles. He wore tattered black trousers that had been pinned up at the calves so they wouldn't drag the ground. A brown vest covered his grey shirt and he kneaded a grey flat cap in both hands. I noted that the last two fingers were missing from his left hand. His boots were covered with scuff marks from years of wear and I suspected bore holes in the soles.

"Come in! Come in!" Holmes said to the boys. Then to Mrs. Hudson, "It's all right, Mrs. Hudson. I promise they will only be here a few minutes."

"Very well, Mr. Holmes," she said with an exasperated sigh, "but I'm going to be watching me silver all the same." And she turned to go back down the stairs.

When the boys saw the Scotland Yard inspector sitting there, they became reticent to enter. But Holmes introduced the boys and let it be known that he was only working on the same case as they were.

Once they were seated at the table, Holmes said, "All right, tell me where you found our man."

The boys were quiet for a few moments, then Wiggins poked an elbow into the other boy's ribs and said, "Tell 'im, Pauley. Tell 'im what you told me."

The boy hesitated, not being accustomed to speaking with adults or Scotland Yard inspectors, I suspected. He finally cleared his throat and began.

"Well, sir, I was watchin' over by the fishin' docks, near Cubitt Town. Over there's beer 'alls, brothels, salvation 'ouses, and the like. Well, this mornin', a fishin' boat comes into the dock and off jumps this fella who's right 'and was a real light colour, like 'is skin was peeled away. I was standing on an old wooden box pretending to look through a waste bin so 'e didn't notice me. As he walked 'e kept pulling 'is coat collar up under his beard, but as 'e passed by, I looked over and I could see the same colour on the skin of 'is neck."

The lad seemed to be enjoying telling his tale and his initial reticence had disappeared.

"So," he continued, "I started to follow 'im. 'e went round the corner and stopped at a grocer's. 'e gave the grocer 'is list and after he paid for 'is food, 'e started to walk down Stebondale Street with 'is bags. 'e stayed on Stebondale Street until 'e turned on to Church Street. He kept looking behind 'im as 'e walked, like 'e was afraid someone was followin' 'im. But I was careful, so 'e didn't notice me.

"Finally, 'e reached into 'is pocket and pulled out a set of keys. Then quick as anythin', 'e turns and goes down some steps to a lower room, unlocks the door, and slams it shut so fast it was almost closed before 'e got in."

"Which room on Church Street?" asked Holmes.

"It was Number 100, just under the steps."

Holmes was quiet for a few moments.

"Well, that sounds like our man," he said as he reached into his pocket and extracted a shilling for Wiggins and a guinea for the young lad, Pauley. I'm sure I have never seen young eyes any larger.

"All right, boys, off you go." Holmes handed the boys their coins and opened the door.

"Thank you, sir!" they both said excitedly as they ran down the stairs and out the door to the street.

After Holmes had closed the door, he turned towards us and clapped his hands together.

"Finally! If they have located the elusive Asa Bloom we may get to the bottom of this affair and who has orchestrated it."

"We need to go speak to him right away," Gregson said, rising from his seat.

Holmes put up his hand.

"Inspector, I think he might be more willing to talk to Dr. Watson and myself rather than to an official from Scotland Yard."

Inspector Gregson thought about what Holmes had said and finally nodded his head.

"Aye, you are most likely correct, Mr. Holmes. As much as I'd like to meet the man, I want to find out what he knows about the people who put him up to making that false identification. That was the start of this whole nefarious affair."

The inspector paused a moment, then said, "Perhaps I can—"

He was interrupted by another loud commotion downstairs. At first, I thought something had happened with Wiggins and the other boy. But we heard heavy footsteps fast ascending the staircase to our door.

After a quick knock, I opened the door to find a police constable standing on the landing, breathing heavily from his exertions. He quickly scanned our faces until he found Inspector Gregson.

"Constable Franks?" the inspector asked, recognizing the man.

"Inspector!" he gasped, "I've been sent by Sergeant Collins. I'm to bring you right away. Something terrible has happened!"

"What is it?" the inspector asked as he grabbed his coat.

"It's Sergeant Cummings, sir! There's been an awful accident."

At the mention of Sergeant Cummings, we all looked at one another and quickly gathered our coats and hats and made our way down to the street. There, the police carriage the constable had arrived in was waiting by the curb. We all climbed in and were hastily off.

I thought as we drove through the traffic that it appeared to be just as we were finally making progress on this case, Fate had interceded to slow our advance. My first concern, as was everyone else's, was that whatever accident Sergeant Cummings had suffered was not too detrimental. My fear, however, was that, as with everything else in this case, we were about to be faced with yet another calamitous event.

Chapter XVIII: Tragedy Befalls the Investigation

As we rode to the scene, Inspector Gregson asked the young constable what had happened. Holmes and I listened intently as the man related the events that had brought this worrisome news to our door.

"Well, soon after you left Scotland Yard, Sergeant Collins was called out to an accident involving a pedestrian that had been run over by a horse and wagon." The constable's eyes were wide and his whole demeanour was one of anxiety and concern.

"I accompanied Sergeant Collins to the scene and when we got there, we saw that it was Sergeant Cummings who had been run over. Sergeant Collins immediately sent me to fetch you, sir."

"Do you know how it happened?" asked the inspector.

"No, sir. As soon as we got there and Sergeant Collins saw who the pedestrian was, he sent me to get you. I believe Sergeant Collins is still there with the driver now."

"Very well," the inspector said, and we rode the rest of the way in silence. The minutes seemed interminable. We had only known Sergeant Cummings a short time but he had become a vital part of our investigation, as well as a friend.

When we finally arrived, we exited the carriage and saw approximately twenty yards further down the road a sheet covering a form in the street. From our angle it did not appear to be a body, and I clung to the hope that perhaps something had fallen off the wagon during the accident, landing in the street. But I have to confess I had a sick feeling in my stomach. Another fifteen yards or so further stood a lorry laden with wooden boxes drawn by two horses. Two men and another uniformed constable were standing by the horses.

We first approached the sheet-covered form in the street. Inspector Gregson bent down and pulled back the sheet to reveal that it was indeed Sergeant Cummings lying dead. His body appeared to be broken, his face and hands bloodied. His clothes were torn from falling under the horse's hooves and lorry wheels. The strong smell of alcohol emanated from his clothes. My only hope was that his was a quick death with very little suffering.

Holmes bent to look closely, feeling the sergeant's hands, noting his position on the ground, and even going so far as to gently lift Sergeant Cummings' body slightly to look under it.

"This is not right, Watson," he said almost to himself. "This is not right at all."

In a few moments, Holmes completed his initial examination, and we walked over to the men standing by the lorry and horses. The driver was obvious because he had an extremely worried look on his face and was clutching his hat in both hands. He appeared to be of middle age, with a balding head and long side whiskers. His grey coat and trousers showed a considerable amount of wear, as did his shoes. He appeared to be a simple workman who had become involved in a terrible accident.

The other man standing with the driver greeted Inspector Gregson. He appeared to be about six feet one inch tall and approximately two and thirty years. He had brown eyes and hair that looked to have been recently trimmed. He was dressed in plain clothes consisting of a dark jacket, white shirt, and brown trousers. His black shoes were polished to a bright shine, suggesting he was meticulous in his appearance. He held in his hands a notebook in which I noticed he had been writing as we arrived. As I looked at him, I couldn't help but think that he and Sergeant Cummings were close in age.

"Inspector, the call came in not ten minutes after you and I spoke this afternoon at Scotland Yard. Once I saw that it involved Sergeant Cummings, I sent Constable Franks to get you."

"Thank you, Sergeant Collins," the inspector said as he turned towards us. "This is Sherlock Holmes and Dr. Watson. They've been working with us for the past couple of days." We all shook hands. Then Gregson turned towards the lorry driver.

"What's your name?"

"The name's Gibson. Fineas Gibson. I drive my lorry through 'ere every day and I ain't never 'ad an accident. Not a one." As he stated this, he tried to present an air of confidence, but his eyes betrayed his worry and concern.

"All right," the inspector said, "just tell us what happened."

"Well, it's like I was telling this sergeant 'ere, I was drivin' my team down the street. I wasn't going fast because the load I'm carryin' 'as some instruments for the museum and some 'eavy cartons of metal. I didn't want the load to shift.

"Well, like I said, I was driving my team down the street, when all of a sudden there's a loud explosion, like a firecracker or a gun being fired. It came from the pavement right beside the 'orses. Before I could look over to see what it was, the 'orses reared up and bolted down the street. I was almost thrown off the lorry."

While he spoke, the driver looked first at Inspector Gregson, then at the body in the street, then back to Inspector Gregson. It wasn't lost on the man that he had run over a Scotland Yard sergeant.

"Well," he continued, "just as the horses were boltin' down the road, this bloke comes stumblin' out of that alley up there." He pointed to an alley directly across from where Sergeant Cummings' body lay.

"'e was stumblin' like 'e was trying to get his balance, his arms wavin' all about. It was almost like 'e was drunk. I noticed blood on 'is forehead and thought 'e might 'ave stumbled and 'it his head on the alley wall before comin' out. 'e kept comin' towards the street, and as I watched 'im, I kept thinkin' to myself 'Surely 'e's going to catch 'imself.' But he never did, and just as my lorry got even with the alley, 'e fell under my horses and the wagon wheels."

He paused a few moments to look at the covered body in the street.

"It took me until 'ere to get the 'orses back under control. I ran back to see if I could 'elp 'im, but 'e was already dead."

We were all quiet as we contemplated what we had heard. Then Inspector Gregson turned back to Sergeant Collins. "Were there any other witnesses?"

"Aye," the sergeant responded, pointing. "The proprietor of the bakery shop across the street confirms his story. He looked out when he heard the shot, or explosion, and saw Sergeant Cummings stumbling out of the alley and into the street.

"There was also a husband and wife who are visiting from Exeter. They were walking along the pavement, heard the noise and saw Sergeant Cummings fall under the wagon. They are in the bakery now. The wife was quite hysterical right after it happened. She has probably calmed down by now."

Holmes, after listening to all of this quietly, turned to Gregson.

"May I ask a couple of questions, Inspector?"

"Aye, certainly."

Holmes turned to the driver. "Did you notice anyone on the pavement just before you heard the shot?"

"No sir, but then again, I wasn't really lookin' at the pavement. My attention was focused on the 'orses."

"Of course. Did you notice anyone else in the alley as Sergeant Cummings was coming out?"

"No, sir. By that time the 'orses were boltin' and I was tryin' to get them under control. If there was anyone in the alley, I didn't see them."

Holmes turned to Gregson.

"Inspector, I suggest that your sergeant here ask those same questions to the other witnesses, but I suspect he will get the same responses. Meanwhile, I'd like to look again at Sergeant Cummings' body and then at the alley."

169

Inspector Gregson agreed. He directed Sergeant Collins to go speak with the other witnesses. Then he had Constable Franks remain with the driver as we made our way back to the sheet-covered form in the street.

Once we were there, Holmes again pulled back the sheet and gazed at the corpse. Then he took out his lens for a closer look.

"Look here, Watson," he said after a few moments. "Look at these scrapes on his arms, head and hands. There are injuries around his mouth as well. These could indeed be injuries from the lorry, but they might just as well be the result of an altercation."

Holmes looked up at both of us.

"The description that the driver gave regarding how Sergeant Cummings came out of the alley 'stumbling' sounds to me like he was beaten in the alley and then pushed in front of the lorry as it was approaching."

Holmes replaced the sheet, rose, and led us to the alley. There rubbish, bottles, and bits of paper littered the alley throughout. The smell of sour milk wafted through the air, and bins overflowing with trash stood by the rear doors of the buildings at the back of the alley.

Holmes looked around on the ground for a moment until he exclaimed, "Ha! Look here, Inspector." He bent down and carefully picked something up from the ground with his handkerchief. "Here is an empty whisky bottle. Look at the label. It isn't scarred or weathered in the least."

He brought the empty bottle up to his nose, then continued. "The odour of fresh whisky is still strong. And look here, smears of blood on the mouth of the bottle. Recall the injuries we noted around Sergeant Cummings' mouth? I suggest that this is a brand-new bottle and some of the whisky it contained was forced upon Sergeant Cummings, with the rest being poured all over his clothes to make it appear that he was drunk."

Holmes then took out his lens again and began to inspect the walls on both sides of the alley. After a few moments he made another discovery.

"And look here, Inspector, bits of fresh blood on both the alley walls. This also indicates that Sergeant Cummings was subjected to some kind of beating."

After another few minutes, Holmes put his lens away and we began to walk out of the alley and back to where the lorry driver and horses were waiting.

"I believe I know what happened here," Holmes said in all earnestness, "and it is indeed a reprehensible occurrence. I believe the shot that startled the horses was intentional. I think that Sergeant Cummings was beaten in the alley and forced to drink from the whisky bottle. When the horses were stampeded, he was pushed out into the path of the out-of-control wagon.

"Recall the shot that missed us that first night when we were outside the Seaway Hotel after speaking with Chris Ross? I believe that shot was actually intended for Sergeant Cummings."

"Why would someone target Sergeant Cummings?" enquired I.

"Sergeant Cummings was the only person left from the original Rhoads investigation. I believe someone wanted to get rid of him because they believed he had discovered something, or perhaps knew something from the original investigation."

We turned at the sound of the coroner's wagon arriving to take Sergeant Cummings' body to the morgue. Sergeant Collins came out of the bakery and walked over to the two attendants. After some brief discussion, Sergeant Collins came towards us as the two attendants began to load Sergeant Cummings' body onto the wagon.

"I spoke to the other witnesses," Sergeant Collins said, "and they confirm what the driver said. After they heard a loud report, they saw the horses bolt and Sergeant Cummings come stumbling out of the alley and fall under the wagon's wheels. But no one saw who fired the shot, or anyone else in the alley, mainly because they were focused on Sergeant Cummings as he stumbled to his death."

Inspector Gregson was quiet for several seconds as he watched the attendants finish their work and drive off with the body of Sergeant Cummings. Then he turned to Sergeant Collins.

"All right, Sergeant. Collect everyone's names and addresses, then go back to the Yard and file the report. Let's see if the medical examiner can determine whether Sergeant Cummings' death was an accident or not. Did he have any family?"

It was a shame that I had worked so closely with the man, even for only a couple of days, yet I discovered just how little I knew about him.

"Aye," Sergeant Collins said. "His parents live in Norfolk. I've sent someone to notify them."

With a heavy sigh, Inspector Gregson said, "Very well, Sergeant Collins. I'll leave this with you. Thank you for letting me know about this."

Sergeant Collins nodded to us all and then turned to the driver to get his information. Holmes, Inspector Gregson and I went back to the police carriage that had brought us to the scene and Inspector Gregson had it take us back to Baker Street.

We were all silent as we travelled. This was indeed a situation that I don't believe any of us ever suspected could have occurred. Murder, in and of itself, was an extremely desperate act. But the murder of a Scotland Yard sergeant was a development I had not even imagined.

When we finally arrived at our Baker Street address, Holmes turned to face Inspector Gregson.

"Inspector, I'd like to suggest that you personally stay with Chris Ross until he boards his ship later tonight. With this latest turn of events, I think we have to consider him to be in very real danger."

"Aye," the inspector agreed, "but I first have to update Assistant Commissioner Sanders about Sergeant Cummings' death. I'm sure he will update the commissioner. I'll go stay with Chris Ross immediately after that."

"Good. Dr. Watson and I will provide tonight's update to Mycroft. I suspect that both the assistant commissioner and commissioner will also be there, but I'll explain why you're otherwise occupied."

I could tell the inspector was gutted and angry about Sergeant Cummings' death.

"He was a good man," Inspector Gregson seethed. "A fine young detective sergeant doing his job!" He struck his hand with his fist. Then looking at us he said, "This is another death associated with this affair. How many more deaths will there have to be?"

Neither Holmes nor I knew what to say. We were silent for another few moments until Holmes finally spoke.

"Dr. Watson and I will go see Asa Bloom tomorrow morning." He paused a moment, then added, "Be on your guard, Inspector. I do not believe any of us are safe while we are investigating this affair."

Chapter XIX: An Attack Too Close

We were not due to meet Mycroft and the others at the Diogenes Club for a couple of hours. And it was just as well because both of us were aggrieved by the death of Sergeant Cummings. Holmes picked up his violin but did not play. He only sat, staring into the fireplace. He had not said as much, but I suspected that he blamed himself for not anticipating a direct attack on one of our number.

As for me, when I wasn't gazing out the window, I was looking at the chair Sergeant Cummings tended to sit in while we were working. On this day, the investigation had taken a great step forward with the location of the elusive Asa Bloom, but had also suffered a tremendous blow with the death of the Scotland Yard sergeant. I wondered what the final cost in lives would be when we arrived at the conclusion of this case.

As the time of our meeting approached, I thought back over our progress since that fateful Monday afternoon in the Diogenes Club. While we had uncovered several important elements that pointed to a concerted effort to orchestrate a great deception, we still lacked any hard evidence pointing to the perpetrators.

A few minutes prior to our scheduled appointment, Holmes and I gathered our coats, hats, and walking sticks and left our Baker Street rooms for the Diogenes Club. The sounds of commerce and the boisterous voices of salesmen filled the air, but the cloudy late afternoon sky matched our dispositions as we made our way to our appointment.

We silently strolled down Baker Street to Oxford. Once we crossed, we continued towards Bond Street. Finally, Holmes spoke, keeping his gaze straight ahead.

"Watson," Holmes sighed, "the death of Sergeant Cummings is a very real blow to our investigation. I fully expect that he was murdered, and that the intent of his death was to greatly impede, if not also to discourage, our continued investigation."

"Then the perpetrators have badly misjudged us," I replied sternly.

"Indeed," Holmes stated firmly as we turned onto Bond Street. "I don't believe any of us will want to put this investigation aside. But Scotland Yard will not take the murder of a detective sergeant lightly."

"If they agree it *was* murder. At this point we only have our suspicions."

The clamour of the London thoroughfare continued to fill our ears as we continued our progress. I saw Piccadilly down the thoroughfare with Pall Mall soon to follow. It seemed we would arrive at the appointed hour.

Suddenly a series of shouts finally broke through our thoughts and conversation. They seemed to be coming from behind us. I also noticed for the first time a loud clanking and the sound of horse hooves pounding the street.

We turned at the reverberations and saw a carriage drawn by two horses bolting down the street. As we watched in stunned surprise, the entire contraption jumped the curb onto the pavement directly behind us and came straight for us.

There was barely time to react before the horses and carriage were upon us. Holmes quickly pushed me off the pavement and into the street. I went tumbling, landing about three feet into the thoroughfare. Holmes threw himself up against the building facing the street. The horses and carriage passed between us, just missing us by inches.

After it had passed, the driver steered back onto the street, the sound of wood bolted to metal being harshly jolted could be heard as the carriage went off the curb and onto the thoroughfare. Then the carriage continued its rapid course down to Piccadilly, where it turned and disappeared.

I quickly stood and saw Holmes leaning against the building.

"Holmes! Are you all right?" I cried, rushing to his side.

"Yes, Watson. I'm fine," he said, brushing dust off his coat. "But that was too close. It seems another 'accident' was about to befall us, and we are fortunate to have escaped with our lives."

"That carriage was trying to run us down deliberately!"

"Yes, I believe it was. But we can't prove it. This is just one more in a series of events that could be construed as simply an accident, or an intentional effort to bring us to harm. But there is no way to prove whether any of these incidents were deliberate or accidental. Just like Sergeant Cummings' death this afternoon. This whole affair is diabolical."

Holmes assisted me in brushing off the road dirt that had scuffed my trousers and coat. Once we felt we were as presentable as we could be, we continued our journey to the

Diogenes Club. Crossing Piccadilly, we searched but saw no sign of the carriage. Shortly we turned onto Pall Mall and arrived at the door of the Diogenes Club. In moments we were seated in the Stranger's Room, out of the night air, and for the moment, out of danger.

# # #

As we were the first to arrive, Holmes turned to me.

"Watson, I think we should inform everyone about our progress and suspicions, with the exception of the fact that we believe we have now found Asa Bloom. I think he is the ultimate key to this affair and the fewer people who know about him the better."

"Surely you don't suspect any of these people."

"No, but with the death of Sergeant Cummings, Scotland Yard may wish to become aggressive in trying to exact justice, or possibly revenge, upon the principals in this affair. They may not want to wait until we have all the facts. If they know where Asa Bloom is they may simply go get him, and possibly place him in the very danger he has, so far, been able to avoid. I'd like to keep his location quiet for another couple of days."

I nodded in agreement. It occurred to me that the death of Sergeant Cummings might put an entirely different perspective on this case for Scotland Yard. I knew they wouldn't take his death lightly. Would they simply collect whatever information we had so far, and take the case back over? Or perhaps they would decide to quietly exact their revenge on the principals involved at a time of their own choosing.

My thoughts were interrupted when the door opened and Mycroft, along with Assistant Commissioner Sanders and Commissioner Haliford, entered the room. All three wore grim faces. There were solemn greetings all around and then everyone sat.

Mycroft looked at Holmes and asked, "Is Inspector Gregson not attending?"

"Inspector Gregson is with Chris Ross, the business partner who accompanied Paul Watts here from America. From everything that has happened so far, we thought it best to make sure he gets safely on the ship back to America tonight."

Turning to Assistant Commissioner Sanders, Sherlock said, "I believe Inspector Gregson provided you a brief update this afternoon?"

"Yes, he did," the assistant commissioner replied, "but I would like to hear your summary as well."

"Very well," Mycroft said. "Perhaps, Sherlock, you can provide your update."

Sherlock gave a succinct summary of our findings so far. He included the differences between the two autopsy reports; the shredded clothes; where the body identification had gone awry eighteen months ago; our interviews with Basil Hart, Colin Dunn, and his wife, along with what we had learned from the Fox and Goose publican. He finally spoke about the death of Sergeant Cummings this afternoon, as well as the close call we had had on our journey to the Diogenes Club.

"I'd like to ask you, Mr. Holmes," the assistant commissioner queried when my friend had finished, "do you believe the death of Sergeant Cummings and the narrow escape you both had tonight were deliberate or accidental?" He glanced at the commissioner, then continued. "For me, once might seem accidental, but twice seems deliberate. The medical examiner could find no direct evidence of foul play regarding Sergeant Cummings' death, but I have my doubts."

"Well, sir, that's difficult to say. The lorry driver involved in Sergeant Cummings' death has worked for his company for several years without any issues. This was his first accident. Yet, something startled those horses and, according to witnesses, Sergeant Cummings came stumbling out of the alley into their path. I suspect he had been beaten, probably to find out what information we knew, and then thrust out into the roadway as the lorry passed by. But like everything else in this case, we cannot prove that his death, or our close call, was deliberate."

"But you know enough that we could bring these two, Dunn and Hart, in to Scotland Yard and see what we could get out of them," Assistant Commissioner Sanders said angrily. This was exactly the concern my friend had expressed to me earlier.

"Gentlemen," Mycroft interjected attempting to calm the atmosphere, "the tragedy of Sergeant Cummings' death this afternoon has taken a heavy toll on us all."

Turning to his brother, he asked, "What else do you need to uncover?"

"We are still in search of the man who identified the body in Battersea Park. I think we are close to locating him and when we do, I believe that he will provide the critical piece of information we are seeking to solve this case once and for all. There are also one or two additional points I want to investigate, but you now have the major elements before you."

As Mycroft made a few notes, I could tell that the assistant commissioner was none too happy with the situation. Commissioner Haliford had been silent during our conversation, but after a moment, he turned to Assistant Commissioner Sanders.

"I think we should contemplate what our next steps will be if Mr. Holmes here brings us the evidence necessary to bring those gentlemen, or whoever it is, to trial."

"Sir, I don't think a trial is possible," Assistant Commissioner Sanders said emphatically. "If we charge them publicly, they will not only claim innocence, but ask why Scotland Yard executed an innocent man."

The assistant commissioner shook his head and continued. "No sir, I say that when we have enough evidence to prove these people were involved, no option is off the table regarding how we deal with them; either publicly or privately."

"You should tread carefully, Assistant Commissioner Sanders," Sherlock advised. "I believe Scotland Yard was just as positive about Simon Rhoads' guilt before he was hanged. Surely you don't want to make the same mistake twice."

"The impertinence!" Assistant Commissioner Sanders exploded, his fury showing in his red face as he stood.

"Gentlemen! Gentlemen! Please!" Mycroft interjected in an attempt to regain control of the conversation. "We are getting ahead of ourselves. The investigation isn't over yet."

The commissioner bade the assistant commissioner to sit, which he reluctantly did.

Turning to his brother, Mycroft asked, "How much longer do you expect the investigation to take?"

"Oh, I think another two or three days should bring everything to a close."

"Very well," Mycroft said as he rose to end the meeting. "Let's plan to meet back here on Saturday at six o'clock. Agreed?"

Everyone agreed. We all stood and there were brief, if reluctant, handshakes all around before the assistant commissioner and commissioner left. As Holmes and I were preparing to leave Mycroft turned to us.

"You needn't provoke the man, Sherlock. He is only looking out for Scotland Yard and the death of one of his sergeants. He also recognises the poor position the police are in if they want to bring these people to justice."

My friend sighed. "Yes, I know, and I don't really blame him. Let's see what the next couple of days bring."

"Very well," Mycroft said as we shook hands. "I'll provide an update to the Home Secretary this evening." Then after a moment, he added, "Gentlemen, be on your guard."

Part V:

Day 4 – Thursday

Chapter XX: An Unexpected Visitor

It was mid-morning the next day when we finished our breakfast while anticipating our upcoming visit with the mysterious Asa Bloom. I could tell something was bothering Holmes as he had seemed distracted all morning. It was my experience that simply waiting for him to announce his inner thoughts might, or might not, provide insights into his thinking. But this time I was fortunate because he finally turned to me and voiced what he had been wrestling with.

"We want to be careful that we do not lead our adversaries to Mr. Bloom," Holmes said as he pushed his empty plate aside. "I suspect the deaths Inspector Lestrade brought to us Tuesday are related to the infamous Mr. Bloom."

"How so?" asked I.

"I need more data to confirm my suspicions, but once we have spoken with Mr. Bloom I believe we'll know for sure."

Just then there was a knock on our door. Holmes went over and opened the door to find a police constable standing on our landing.

"A message for you, Mr. Holmes, from Inspector Gregson," the constable said as he handed Holmes a folded piece of paper.

Holmes took the paper and read the note, then turned back to the constable.

"Thank you," he said, and closed the door.

"What's happened, Holmes?" I asked. Given recent events I was concerned about all members of our investigating team.

"It is indeed a note from Gregson," Holmes stated as he handed the note to me. It read as follows:

Mr. Holmes,

I have been called away to attend an urgent matter related to our investigation.

I should return to Baker Street sometime this afternoon.

Tobias Gregson

"Perhaps he has uncovered something regarding the death of Sergeant Cummings," I offered as I put the note down.

"Perhaps that is the case, but we will not know until we speak with him this afternoon. For now, we have an 'urgent matter' of our own in speaking with Asa Bloom. We should be on our way."

We began to gather our coats, hats, and walking sticks for our journey to Cubitt Town when there was a second softer, and seemingly apologetic, knock at our door. Holmes and I looked at each other.

"Perhaps the constable was supposed to get some kind of reply," I suggested as Holmes stepped to the door and opened it.

There on the landing, to our utter astonishment, stood Mrs. Frances Dunn, clutching a small purse in her gloved hands. She had her hair up under a stylish small-brimmed hat. Elegant diamond earrings were also in evidence. Her light-blue dress flowed down to the floor, just covering her small-heeled boots. Her fur jacket, while providing protection from the blustery weather, accentuated her figure and featured pearl buttons down the front. Her skin still possessed that youthful radiance I had noticed yesterday and provided an elegant contrast to a small gold locket that hung around her neck from a simple chain. I noticed that her green eyes seemed to reflect an uneasiness, as if haunted by a sense of dread and foreboding. Silently, she surveyed the room before she brought her full attention to Holmes.

"Please excuse this intrusion, Mr. Holmes, but I feel I must speak with you."

"Ah! Mrs. Dunn, please come in," Holmes said soothingly, stepping aside so she could enter. After closing the door, he assisted her with the removal of her fur jacket, then he took her by the elbow and guided her to a chair.

"Pray, take a seat and tell me how I may be of service."

When she was seated, I could observe that her blouse fit smartly and featured a pattern of small sequins on the pockets with gold piping along the sleeves. As she sat, she

185

continued clutching her purse, first holding her hands near her chest, then occasionally resting them in her lap. It was evident to me that something was troubling the woman and she seemed to be at her wits' end. After Holmes and I were seated, Holmes indicated he was ready to hear what was troubling her.

"Your visit yesterday was one more occurrence that has seemed to plague Colin over the past several months. I have noticed changes in Colin's behaviour that I believe portend some kind of disaster; although what it could be I do not know."

Holmes was silent while she spoke. After leaning back and closing his eyes, he waved for her to continue.

"When a man is continuously distracted, seemingly focused on minor business details, and evasive in his answers to the simplest questions, it is apparent that there is trouble looming nearby." She sighed quietly, then continued. "Mr. Holmes, a wife knows. And I know something disastrous is brewing, and my husband is either keeping it from me or trying to protect me from it."

After a moment, Holmes opened his eyes, looked into hers, and said, "Perhaps you can be more specific, Mrs. Dunn."

"Very well," she said. "Over the past three years, Colin's friendship with Basil Hart has grown immensely. At first, they were simply two business associates. But as time went on, they became closer and closer. I noticed their friendship, as I would occasionally work at Holtz Manufacturing. Basil seemed to hold Colin's opinion in higher regard than he did Simon's in matters of commerce. Near the end, Basil and Simon were hardly speaking with each other, so intense had their disagreements become. But

Colin seemed to always try to be the peacemaker between the two. When Simon's trial..."

She hesitated for several moments, reluctant to relive a horrendous period in her life. After gathering herself, she continued.

"When Simon's trial took place, we were all, Colin, Basil and I, often together in and out of the court. I found it extremely distressing. Colin made it a point to act as a shield between me and the press, and I must say I was grateful for his efforts.

"After Simon's death, I lived in our house and continued to work at the company, but not nearly as often as I had before. Colin took it upon himself to see that I kept myself busy and did not fall into a depression or hide from the world. He would often take me to the theatre or a concert so that I would get out and attempt to put my life back together. When he finally proposed marriage, he insisted that we wait a year after Simon's death, which we did. Ours was a happy marriage for the next several months."

"What happened to cast a shadow upon your happiness?" Holmes asked quietly.

"It seemed to begin one day four months ago. I recall that on that day, I brought the post into Colin's office and handed it to him. We were chatting as he would open the envelopes, toss them into the bin, and scan the letters. But when he came to one specific letter, he simply stopped speaking in mid-sentence, so focused was he on the letter he held in his hand. His eyes grew wide and the colour seemed to drain from his face.

"When I asked him what was wrong, he quickly recovered and said it was nothing. But he put the letter in his pocket, gathered his coat, and told me he had to see Basil regarding some business issue and that he would be late returning home that evening.

"He had tossed the envelope containing the letter into the bin beside his desk along with all the other envelopes. So, after he left, I retrieved the envelope to see if I could discern what had caused such a strange reaction in my husband."

Holmes opened his eyes and asked, "I don't suppose you still have the envelope?"

Looking at Holmes, Mrs. Dunn replied, "I have it here." And with that she opened her purse and withdrew an envelope which she handed to Holmes.

Holmes immediately sat upright and took the offered envelope. Reaching into his pocket he took out his lens and studied the outside of the envelope and the postmark. After several moments, he handed it to me.

The envelope itself was nothing special. It was of standard stock available from any print shop. However, the postmark was from America, and it was dated November 16, 1895. Given the speed with which mail traversed the Atlantic, the letter would have arrived near the end of November last.

I noticed that in the upper left-hand corner was printed *Cross Seas Export* with an address in New York City. This had to have contained one of the letters Paul Watts had sent to his friends announcing his intention to return to London. It seemed that another firm piece of evidence was finally falling into place.

"Do you have any idea what was in the letter your husband received?" Holmes asked.

"None at all."

After a moment's thought, Holmes asked, "May I keep this envelope, Mrs. Dunn?"

"Yes. Colin has forgotten all about it."

"Thank you. Now, what else has caused you concern over the previous months?"

She shook her head as if she were trying to place her finger upon the issue.

"Well, he would sometimes stay out late at night, often three or four nights in a row, only to later resume his regular hours at home. When I asked what had his attention during those late nights, he would say that he and Basil were working late to keep Holtz Manufacturing profitable. I know he invested a large sum of money into the business so he would naturally have an interest in protecting his investment. Yet I had the sense that there was something more sinister afoot involving both Colin and Basil."

"You said he seemed to stay out late 'three or four nights in a row' before resuming his regular home hours. Did you notice any kind of pattern? For instance, did he spend three or four nights in a row out late and then eight or ten nights keeping regular hours?"

She gave Holmes' question some consideration, but then shook her head.

"I just recall that there seemed to be perhaps three periods when he stayed out late several consecutive nights. In fact, as recently as last week he was out late for four nights, but then resumed his normal schedule a couple of nights ago. On the various occasions I spoke to Basil, I'd ask him about those evenings, and he confirmed that they were working to keep the business profitable. But I still feel a sense of evasion in both of their responses."

Holmes was quiet for a moment, then ventured, "Mrs. Dunn, please excuse the indelicacy, but could there perhaps be some other 'interests' that your husband is pursuing? Could it be a matter of *nostalgie de la boue*, a 'yearning for the mud,' so to speak? He would not be the first."

At this she gave a wry smile. "No, Mr. Holmes. As I said, a wife knows. Colin is somewhat fastidious and so would, I think, be loath to degrade himself with other women. And frankly, I believe that the trouble brewing is much more severe than another woman. Since your visit yesterday, Colin and Basil have been unusually secretive."

Holmes was silent for almost a full minute. Finally, he asked, "What would you like for me to do?"

"Tell me!" she implored. "If you know what these troubling circumstances are, please tell me. I have withstood the most terrible thing a wife can endure, and if I or Colin are about to be subjected to something just as horrible, I'd like to know before it befalls us. I don't believe I can survive another crisis like the one I have already endured."

As tears began to well in her eyes, she took a small handkerchief out of her purse.

"Tell me, Mr. Holmes, truthfully, why are you looking into the death of Paul Watts and investigating this awful time in our lives? We've only just been able to put that ordeal behind us and now you have brought it all up again."

"Well, Mrs. Dunn," Holmes said apologetically, "as I said yesterday, some distant relatives of Paul Watts have asked for some clarification on his life and passing."

"I'm not sure I completely believe your story, Mr. Holmes," she said as she rose from her seat. Both Holmes and I stood as well. "But whatever you are looking into, I can tell you that I do not believe any good will come of it."

Holmes assisted her with her fur coat and then opened the door. She stepped through the threshold, then turned and said, "I'm asking you, Mr. Holmes, to please stop."

With one more glance at both of us she said, "Good day, gentlemen."

"Good day," we both said. We silently watched her go down the stairs and exit the outside door. Then Holmes quietly closed the door.

Neither of us spoke for several minutes after she left. As I replayed the conversation in my mind, it became clear that this woman was yet another victim of this murderous plot. And as we pursued, and eventually achieved, our ultimate objective, I feared that we would lay waste to any hope she might hold of ever having a happy and normal life.

I believe Holmes read my mind because he turned to me and sighed. "I disliked lying to the lady, but I don't believe we can reveal our evidence just yet."

"But Holmes," I interjected, "she trusts you. She's begged you to forewarn her if trouble is about to befall her. Can you really carry on without providing her some kind of warning?"

"I don't know, Watson. I feel that our hands are tied at the moment."

After another few moments, Holmes said, "Let's see what Asa Bloom has to say, and later today, what Inspector Gregson's urgent matter is. Perhaps that additional information will provide us with some guidance as to how we can inform, and possibly protect, Mrs. Dunn."

I agreed that perhaps we might find some information that we could use to at least forewarn Mrs. Dunn if at all possible.

So, Holmes and I again gathered our coats, hats, and walking sticks, but as we were doing so, Holmes turned to me.

"I wonder, old fellow," he asked surreptitiously, "if I could impose upon you to empty your medical bag and bring it with you."

I gazed at my friend as if he had lost his mind, my mouth open in astonishment. This was indeed the strangest request he had ever made.

"You want me to do what? Why would I need my medical bag? And what purpose would it serve to have it *without* my medical instruments?"

"I assure you my reasons are sound. It will assist us in bringing this critical part of the case to a close."

I continued to gaze at my friend, searching his eyes for some sign of jest, but there was none. He was completely serious. I had to admit to myself that in all my experiences with Holmes, his occasionally strange requests, regardless how unusual, were always shown in the end to be reasonable. So, I acquiesced.

"Very well," I sighed. I picked up my medical bag and emptied its contents onto the table.

Once that task was completed, I retrieved my walking stick and we began to make our way downstairs. However, when we reached the bottom of the stairs, Holmes again turned to me.

"Watson, go ahead and secure a cab for us. I need to speak with Mrs. Hudson for a moment. I'll join you directly."

He turned to go find Mrs. Hudson in the kitchen as I opened the door and went outside. In just moments I had hailed a cab and climbed inside. Holmes joined me shortly and we were off.

"What did you need to speak with Mrs. Hudson about?" asked I.

"Oh, I was just making some preparations so that if the need arises, we are ready."

He would not explain any further so I resolved to sit back, my empty medical bag at my feet, and watch the city go by as we made our way to Cubitt Town and the mysterious Asa Bloom.

Chapter XXI: Mr. Asa Bloom

By late morning the blustery weather had not lessened its grip on the day. We had received almost two inches of snow overnight and it appeared that there would be more before the day was out.

As we were riding in our cab towards Cubitt Town, Holmes suddenly rapped his cane against the top of the cab and called out, "Cabman! Cabman!"

The cabman opened the small door in the roof of the cab and looked down.

"Please take us to the Esquire Arms on Gresham Street."

"Aye, sir," was the curt reply, and the door was promptly shut.

"Holmes!" I exclaimed. "Why are we going to a pub? This is hardly the time for a lager!"

"You're quite right, Watson. However, we aren't going there for a lager. You'll see shortly what I have planned."

He would not say any more and we rode the rest of the way in silence. As we rode, I could see the frost of our exhalations as the chill of the late-morning air began to penetrate my coat.

I again replayed our conversation with Mrs. Dunn over in my mind. I believed she was innocent in this horrible ordeal and was about to be overrun by events. It was clear that she felt an uneasiness, yet she did not know from where it might come. For me, I wanted to alert her that she should seek her answers closer to home, but we still lacked the evidence we needed to confirm our suspicions.

My thoughts were interrupted as the cab pulled over to the curb. I looked out and saw that we had arrived at the Esquire Arms. I gathered my medical bag and once we were out of the cab, Holmes paid the driver and we walked into the establishment.

The pub was similar to the Fox and Goose we had visited the previous day with a large bar and tables and chairs scattered throughout the room. There was a roaring fire in the fireplace and the room held the scent of burning wood and a welcoming warmth. It was too early for the lunch trade, and in fact there were only two people at the bar: one of them the publican. They both turned to face us as we entered.

"Gentlemen!" Holmes enthused as we approached the bar.

"What can I do for you?" the publican asked as he took up a white rag and began to polish the top of the bar.

"Direct us to the back door, if you please. And if anyone should ask, you haven't seen us," Holmes said as he extracted two coins from his pocket and placed them on the bar.

The publican saw the coins and a smile crossed his face as he pocketed the windfall. Then he hitched a thumb behind him and said, "Just down the hall, then turn left. You'll see the door."

"Thank you, my good man!" Holmes said. "Come along, Watson," and we were off down the indicated corridor. In moments we found ourselves outside standing at the back door of the pub. The street we were on was a secondary avenue but we had no trouble hailing another cab, and we were soon on our way.

"Are we actually going to Cubitt Town this time or do we have somewhere else we need to pass through?" I asked somewhat flummoxed.

Holmes saw my bemused expression.

"*Abundans cautela non nocet,* Watson. 'One can never be too careful.' You recall, of course, that I was concerned we might inadvertently lead our adversaries to Mr. Bloom? Well, if we were being followed, I believe we have just evaded our pursuers for the time being."

I had to smile to myself as we rode along the thoroughfares. If someone had been following us, I wondered just how long they would sit outside the Esquire Arms waiting for us to come out. Eventually they might venture inside, only to find that we were not present.

As we rode, the clip-clop of the horse's hoofs were muffled somewhat by the snow and slush on the thoroughfares. Finally, after some time, our cab turned onto Church Street. Holmes immediately had the cab stop and we exited in order to walk the rest of the way.

The neighbourhood was quiet and many of the houses and buildings were in need of repair. There were areas where the fencing had fallen over and other places where the fencing had been taken away completely. Snow covered the pavement so we were obliged to walk in the street where cab and lorry wheels had cleared the snow. I could tell we were near the Thames; the cold air carried the odour of fish, along with the distant sounds of ship horns and bells.

We saw the door to number 100 just under some steps that led to an upstairs apartment. To the right of the door was a large window with drawn curtains that faced out onto the street.

Holmes looked up and down the street. I did the same and it appeared there was no one watching us. We then made our way to the door of number 100 and knocked.

We waited but there was no answer. I watched the drawn curtain for any movement, but there was none. Holmes knocked again, then turned to me.

"No doubt this man is in fear of his life. I would be surprised if he opened this door to anyone."

We waited another few moments, stamping our feet every so often to keep our circulation going. Finally, Holmes decided to try something else.

In a voice loud enough for someone inside to hear, but not so loud that someone on the street could hear, Holmes said, "We are seeking a man who once called himself 'Asa Bloom.'"

No response. Then he continued.

"It is in your interest to speak with us."

Still there was no answer.

"I can assure you we mean you no harm. If we were here to injure you, would we remain standing outside knocking at your door? We only wish to speak with you and possibly help you."

We were silent again, listening intently for any sounds from inside. If the drawn curtain covering the window moved, it was imperceptible.

Finally, we heard the faintest sound as the doorknob slowly began to turn. In moments, the door slowly opened about five inches. I could just make out the left eye and part of the beard of the man inside as he looked us up and down.

"What do you want?" he asked.

"To help you, sir," Holmes said. "We believe you are in danger. We know what has happened, and we want to help you so you do not have to continue hiding. I can assure you we are unarmed and we are not with the police. May we come in?"

The man hesitated for a moment as he continued to eye us through the partially opened door. Then he stepped back and allowed us to enter. As soon as we were in, he quickly looked outside, then closed the door, locking the two deadbolts.

Upon entering the room, I was at once struck by the thick odours of cooked onions and boiled potatoes. Surveying the dark room, I saw it was a one-room flat measuring approximately twenty feet by thirty feet. An old dresser and mirror stood along one wall; a single bed was placed against the opposite wall from the door. Against the third wall stood a small table and two chairs, as well as a small coal stove, which was the only source for heat and cooking. Next to the door was the large window looking out onto the street. A heavy curtain had been drawn tightly across the window so that no light escaped. Two large carpet remnants covered the wooden floor. An oil lamp burned on the table, the only source of light in the room.

Holmes turned to the man and said, "Are you the man who presented himself in Battersea Park as 'Asa Bloom' eighteen months ago?"

The man hesitated before answering, looking from Holmes and then to me. There was genuine fear in his eyes. Finally, he nodded and said, "Yes, I am."

"Then it is urgent that we speak. May we sit down?"

"Aye, but just know that I may not answer all of your questions. There are people after me, and now that you have found me, I'll have to move."

"Hopefully, sir, we can help get you to a place of safety," Holmes said as we removed our coats and hats.

My head was spinning. We were finally getting to the crux of this matter. This one man held the key to the entire mystery and now, finally, we were moments away from finding out the truth.

# # #

I placed my empty medical bag on the table as Holmes and I sat in the two chairs. Our host sat on the bed. I took a few moments to look over the man we had been so desperate to locate. He stood about six feet tall, with an angular build. He had thick eyebrows, and his hair and beard were dark brown with flecks of grey throughout. He wore a white shirt, a dark vest, and a pair of dark trousers. His shoes bore small tears and scuffs from hard use. The discolouration on the top of his right hand was evident and he seemed to make no effort to conceal it. His beard, however, made it difficult to see the discolouration on his neck, but as he moved his head it would occasionally come into view.

When we were all settled, Holmes said, "My name is Sherlock Holmes, and this is my good friend and colleague Dr. Watson. May I ask what your real name is?"

Still hesitant, he finally said, "My name is Harvey Wise. I'm a carpenter and seaman when the jobs are available."

"Mr. Wise," Holmes began, "am I correct in assuming that you were paid to provide an identification in Battersea Park some months ago and that now you are in fear of your life from the people who hired you?"

Wise looked intently at Holmes, then said, "That's right. They offered to make two payments. One before I made the identification in the park, then the second one afterwards. But I didn't go back for the second payment. Not after what they done."

"I see," Holmes said thoughtfully. Then, "Would you please relate the entire story to me? I must tell you that I am in possession of most of the facts, I simply need a few minor points clarified. As I said, we are not affiliated with the police so you have nothing to fear from them. And at the end of your story, I believe we may be able to rid you of the fear you hold."

"All right," Wise said as he reached over to one of the dresser drawers and took out a pipe and a pouch of tobacco. After getting his pipe going, he began to tell his story.

"Me and several mates find work where we can. We try to look out for one another, so if one of us gets a job, they try to get the others taken on as well. Sometimes we can get everyone on the job; sometimes only a couple; sometimes we can't get anyone added. And sometimes, there's no work to be had. When we fall on hard days, we seek out the comfort and benevolence of the various charity houses.

"Well, one afternoon several months back, one of my mates, Kelwin Hooper, came to me and said he'd just gotten a simple job and the pay was overly generous. He said two 'dandy' gentlemen hired him and that it was easy money because they didn't know they were paying too much for the job. They wanted him to sign onto a fishing boat they said they owned that was leaving late the night of Thursday, the 12th of September. They told him he would be working the nets, but they were paying him to watch the captain. They said the captain was taking some of the catch and selling it for his own benefit. Kelwin was to report back to them when the fishing boat returned after a week."

"Did he say where he met these 'dandy' gentlemen?" Holmes asked.

"Aye. He met them at the Randall House.

"I see," Holmes said thoughtfully. "Pray, continue."

After drawing on his pipe, Harvey Wise resumed his narration.

"Well, the next day I was going round to all of the charity houses looking for work. It was late in the afternoon when I came to the Randall House. As we were gathering for the evening meal, one of the cooks announced that there were some gentlemen looking to hire someone for a special job.

"I hurried to the office where these gentlemen were and found two gentlemen dressed in fine clothes. I introduced myself and asked them what the job was.

"'Well,' they said, 'We need someone who can be in Battersea Park in the early morning hours this coming Friday, the 13th of September.'"

"Did they tell you what they wanted you to do?"

"Oh aye. They said 'We are going to have a body from one of the universities placed under the oak tree in

Battersea Park nearest the memorial. We need someone to provide a specific identification to the police.'"

Wise drew on his pipe again, then continued.

"They said it was some kind of elaborate joke they were playing on someone. I was offered ten pounds; five on the spot and five more after I made the identification. After they gave me a suit of clothes to wear, I was told I couldn't tell anyone or it would spoil the joke and I wouldn't get paid, so I kept quiet."

Harvey Wise slowly shook his head as he recalled the events that had led up to his current situation.

"When the morning came, it was still dark when I got to the park. I wanted to be early to be sure I was there when everything started to happen. I sat on one of the benches about fifty yards from the memorial so I could keep watch for when things began to happen around the oak tree. I could see what appeared to be two dark shapes lying at the base of the oak tree behind the memorial. From where I was sitting, the shapes appeared to be two rucksacks. But I suspected that one of them was the body the gentlemen said they were taking from the university.

"After a few minutes of waiting, I saw two constables come up to the oak tree and stop at the shapes. Then one of them ran off. Several minutes later more policemen arrived and a crowd began to gather as the morning light grew brighter. I eventually made my way up to the crowd and stood back, just watching.

"I looked around the crowd but didn't see either of the two gentlemen who hired me. But I decided they, or someone else hired by them, was probably there to see that I did what they hired me to do.

"Finally, two detectives who seemed to be in charge came up and started looking at the body and that's when I saw there were *two* bodies. I hadn't expected that and it was the first time I became nervous that I might have gotten myself into something unsavoury. But then I heard one of the policemen say the other bloke was drunk and they were taking him to jail to sleep it off.

"After he was taken away, they went back to look through the pockets of the dead man. That's when I said, 'Hey, that's Paul Watts' as I had been paid to do. The police called me forward and I got a closer look."

At this point, Harvey Wise paused to relight his pipe. Then he looked off into the distance without really seeing anything. I could imagine he was reliving that fateful morning, something he had no doubt relived time and again ever since he had become involved in this affair.

"As I got closer, I looked at the face and thought I recognised the man. But then I saw the tattoo on his left arm through the torn clothes and I knew it was Kelwin. Panic overcame me and my heart almost stopped.

"I was thinking fast. The gentlemen must not have realized that Kelwin was known to me or they would not have asked me to provide the false identification. Then I thought, *if they could do that to Kelwin, they could do it to me, too.* All of this was rushing through my mind when I saw that heart tattoo."

Harvey Wise finished his pipe and knocked it against his shoe, scattering the ashes onto the floor.

"I gave the police a made-up name and address and left as soon as I could. I never went back to collect the second payment. Ever since that day I have been laying low. I have not been back to the Randall House or any of the other charity houses. I don't want those two to find me. I was afraid that you both had been sent here by them."

It was clear that Harvey Wise was still shaken by the events he had just related. To see a friend who had been murdered and have to participate in giving the police a false identification would weigh on anyone's conscience.

"Had you seen the two gentlemen before?" asked Holmes.

"Aye. I had seen them a few times when they volunteered at the Randall House. But between you and me, I suspect they only came by when they were looking to hire someone to do something for them."

"Can you describe the two gentlemen?"

"Aye. One was shorter than the other; perhaps five feet eight or ten, and the other perhaps six feet tall. The shorter one seemed to be frailer than the taller one. And the taller one had black hair but no grey. The smaller one had dark hair but there was some grey in his hair and beard."

"Did the taller one have a beard?"

"No, not at the time I saw them."

Holmes was silent for almost two minutes as he thought through the events Harvey Wise had related. While he waited for Holmes to ask something else, Harvey Wise placed a kettle of water onto the coal stove to warm.

Finally, Holmes said, "Let me confirm something else that I suspect. These 'several mates' of yours, how many men are in this group?"

"There's five of us who try to look out for one another. Kelwin was one."

"Would another of your friends be Roy Hallis?"

Wise looked startled at Holmes.

"Aye, he would be."

"How about Liam Norwell?"

"Now look 'ere!" Wise shouted as he stood up, "Have you been spyin' on me?"

"No, no, Mr. Wise. Calm yourself. I assure you I have not," Holmes said in an effort to relax the man. "But I'm afraid I have to tell you that both Hallis and Norwell have been murdered, along with another man, over the past several months. I believe that they were killed by the people who are seeking you."

Wise's eyes were wide open in shock as he resumed his seat on the bed.

"Both of them killed? By the men who are looking for me?"

"I believe so. Do you also know a man with red hair who is missing his right thumb?"

Wise looked forlornly at Holmes.

"That would be Hal Estes. Has he been killed, too?"

"I'm afraid so. Whoever killed each of them believed that they knew where you were hiding."

"I avoided seeing anyone who knew me for that very reason," Harvey Wise said, shaking his head. "I didn't want to put anyone else in danger."

"Well, somehow your adversaries discovered who your friends were and over the past four months have been torturing and murdering them in an effort to find you."

The look on Harvey Wise's face showed a man who felt he'd lost every friend he ever had. Worse still, he began to understand that their deaths were directly related to the job he had taken, and his hiding out these past few months. I could tell from his troubled expression that those deaths would be a lifelong burden.

"I must warn you," Holmes said, "that if I could find you, they will eventually find you. It will only be a matter of time."

"Then what am I to do?" he asked desperately. "How can I throw off this curse that plagues me?"

"I believe we can help you, and in just a few days put an end to this terror you have been facing. But you need to place yourself completely in our hands. You must do exactly as I say."

Harvey Wise considered what Holmes had said for several moments, then nodded his head.

"All right, what should I do?"

"Excellent! First gather some of your clothes and possessions, but only what can fit into Dr. Watson's medical bag." Holmes pointed to my medical case resting on the table. Then he continued. "I have a safer place for you to hide out and I want to get you there as soon as possible."

I handed my medical bag over to Harvey Wise, who began to go through his dresser drawers selecting which articles he wanted to bring. While he went through his possessions, Holmes pulled me aside.

"Watson, I want you to take Mr. Wise to Baker Street."

"Baker Street? Why there, Holmes?"

"I have arranged with Mrs. Hudson that Mr. Wise can stay in her basement for a short period of time. There is a small bed and cabinet down there and the coal furnace provides enough heat that he should be comfortable."

As he said this last, he picked up his own coat and hat and placed them on the bed. A couple of minutes later, Harvey Wise had completed his packing.

"All right, Mr. Wise," Holmes said, "please put my coat and hat on. Dr. Watson will go out and hail a cab. Once he has one, you will go out and join him and take the cab to Baker Street. When you are out in the open, such as between this house and the cab, and from the cab into Baker Street, try to keep your beard tucked in. If there is anyone watching our rooms, I want them to believe it is Dr. Watson and myself whom they have observed. I will come into our Baker Street residence by the back way. May I have your coat and hat?"

Harvey Wise handed his coat and hat to Holmes, who put them on.

"Is there a back way out of this building?" Holmes enquired.

"No, I'm afraid the only way out is through the front door."

"Well, no matter. Watson, please be so kind as to take your medical bag and secure a cab. I have another stop I want to make, but I should not be too delayed and will join you at Baker Street shortly."

I did not like the idea of Holmes being out by himself, but he seemed to have a plan already prepared, and now I was going to be responsible for getting Mr. Wise safely to Baker Street.

After retrieving my coat, hat, walking stick, and now-full medical bag, I left the room and went out to the street. It took some minutes but I was finally able to hail a cab. When it arrived, I got in and as I did, I saw a tall figure exit the apartment and walk towards the cab. The man's gait told me it wasn't Holmes, but someone observing from further away would have difficulty ascertaining the difference. Mr. Wise, wearing Holmes' coat and hat, tried to walk calmly but I could tell from his stride he was feeling exposed. Carrying Holmes' cane waist high, it was obvious he was unaccustomed to using a walking stick.

Once Harvey Wise was in the cab, we pulled away from the curb and were on our way to Baker Street. All during our journey it was evident that Harvey Wise was extremely nervous from the way he continuously glanced out the back window. He was with unfamiliar people and going to an unfamiliar place. After living his life so carefully, I could understand his unease.

When we finally arrived at Baker Street, we exited the cab and went straight inside. Once the door was closed, we met Mrs. Hudson in the parlour. She was as gracious as ever and we all went downstairs to the basement where Harvey Wise would spend the next few days.

I assisted with his unpacking and saw that he was situated comfortably. A few minutes later, Mrs. Hudson came down with a sandwich and tea for our temporary guest, who was most grateful. I took my leave and, carrying Holmes' coat, hat, and walking stick, along with my now-empty medical bag, went up to our rooms to await Holmes' return.

It seemed to me that we now had all the parts of the puzzle. Harvey Wise would be able to identify the 'dandy' gentlemen who had hired him and testify that it was Kelwin Hooper's body he saw in Battersea Park. Given all the other evidence we had obtained, it seemed to me that we could move forward with handing the matter over to the police.

Perhaps we were finally seeing an end to this horrible affair.

Chapter XXII: Another Tragedy

It was early afternoon when Holmes returned to Baker Street. I had just completed replacing the contents of my medical bag when I heard him talking with Mrs. Hudson downstairs. In moments he had joined me in our rooms.

"Ah, Watson, thank you for getting Mr. Wise here and settled in his new room. I believe he is much safer, for the moment."

"Well, I agree he is much safer here with us, but tell me, where did you go after we left you in Cubitt Town? I'm not sure that it is wise for any of us to travel alone."

"Yes, well, I had another line of enquiry I wanted to follow up. I believe we are at the point where we can fit the pieces of the puzzle together and get the full picture of this incredible affair."

Just then, we heard the sound of the downstairs door opening and closing, followed by footsteps ascending to our rooms. After a brief knock, Holmes answered the door to find Inspector Gregson standing on our landing, hat in hand.

"Inspector," Holmes said as the inspector entered. "We have some news for you, but you indicated that you had to attend to an urgent matter this morning. Pray, what was the issue?"

"This confounded case may be the death of us all before it is finished," Inspector Gregson growled as he set his hat and coat down and took a seat at the table.

"What has happened?"

"I've been in Essex all day. There is no easy way to say this. Inspector Jack Hall killed himself early this morning. He was found in his garden by his wife at about five thirty. He had gone out there and shot himself in the head."

We were all shocked! Inspector Hall, a competent and proud former member of Scotland Yard, taking his own life. It was something none of us had even imagined. This was indeed a devastating event.

Inspector Gregson continued after a few moments.

"When the call came in, I was sent by Assistant Commissioner Sanders to investigate whether it was actually suicide or possibly another murder. When I got there, I inspected Jack's body. It was out in the back garden. He had been sitting on a small planter wall where some evergreen plants had been covered by the snow last night. He had placed the gun in his mouth and fired, causing his body to fall backwards into the plants. His revolver was at his feet; one shot had been fired."

Inspector Gregson was having trouble keeping his emotions in check. It was evident that he and Jack Hall had been good friends.

"He had always been extremely proud of his garden. Even when he was still at Scotland Yard, it was all he would talk about."

After another few moments, Holmes asked, "Inspector, I hesitate to ask, but how certain are you that he died by his own hand?"

Gregson seemed to be startled by the question. He quickly looked at Holmes, then sighed.

"I'm certain. I spoke with his wife. She said that ever since he returned from his trip to London last Tuesday, he had seemed distracted and despondent. She would often find him out in his garden just staring at the clouds. She asked him what the trouble was but he wouldn't say. He started drinking Tuesday night and drank until he fell into bed. Later, she heard him wake up in the early-morning hours and go wandering around in his garden.

"On Wednesday, his wife said he continued drinking all day, lamenting some 'failure,' but he would not say what. He maintained his despondency until he went to bed that night. She never heard him get back up, but awoke abruptly when she heard the sound of a gunshot. She immediately went looking for him and found him out in the garden."

Inspector Gregson turned to Holmes.

"She asked me what had happened on Tuesday. 'Tobias,' she said, 'you were one of his best friends. What happened to make him do this terrible thing?'

"I knew I couldn't give her the real reason. I just tried to comfort her as best I could and to get the investigation away from the house as quickly as possible.

"I reported back to Assistant Commissioner Sanders just before coming here. The medical examiner will perform an autopsy, but there is little doubt he took his own life."

We were all silent as we contemplated the growing number of lives that had ended prematurely because of this scheme. As we sat, I noticed the expression on Holmes' face. His cheeks were flushed and his eyes narrowed with a stern look. He was not one who would normally reveal emotions, but it was evident he was angry.

Holmes finally rose from his seat and struck his fist on the table.

"Damn!" he exclaimed. "This is another death associated with this dastardly affair. There have been eight, possibly nine, innocent people who have lost their lives during the course of this case."

Then he looked resolutely at us both and said, "However, I believe we now have the means to bring this case to a close, and I think we will soon be in a position to do so."

Chapter XXIII: Mr. Holmes Has Some Thoughts

"How can we do that?" Inspector Gregson asked, adding his own anger. "I am ready to confront these people."

Holmes then summarised our conversation with Harvey Wise: how he was recruited to give a false identification by two gentlemen; why Mr. Wise felt he had to go into hiding; and the fact that Mr. Wise now resided in the basement of 221B Baker Street.

We spent some time going over the information Wise had provided. We even went so far as to go down to the basement and introduce Inspector Gregson to Harvey Wise. We watched as the two of them spoke about the actions and dangers Mr. Wise had experienced over the past eighteen months.

As we were leaving to go back upstairs, Mrs. Hudson handed us a tray of food for our evening meal: tea, pot roast, greens and potatoes with gravy were a welcomed change from the sandwiches we had been living on over the past few days. We thanked her and took the food up to our rooms.

As we ate, Inspector Gregson summarised the crucial element of this entire case.

"So," Gregson stated, "we now have someone who can provide eyewitness testimony regarding who hired him to be in the park that morning and set the police on the wrong course. *And* who the body found in the park actually was."

"That's correct, Inspector," Holmes replied. "I have felt all along that this single piece of information was critical to the case. But now we must seriously consider the political aspects of this affair. We have all known that it could very well be that because this case involved the execution of a demonstrably innocent man, a court trial would almost be completely out of the question."

"Perhaps," the inspector agreed. "However, we should present all of the evidence we have and let those in charge make the decisions."

"I agree with you, Inspector. I would like for us to review the entire case, now that we seem to have almost everything related to this matter."

Inspector Gregson had a puzzled look on his face as he considered Holmes' words. "You said we have 'almost everything' related to the matter. What are we missing?" he asked.

"I do not believe that we are completely clear as to the motivations behind this deception. Oh, Basil Hart's motivation seems clear enough: to gain sole control over Holtz Manufacturing. But Colin Dunn's motivation is unclear to me. If he wanted to own some or all of Holtz Manufacturing, all he had to do was wait until the business went bankrupt and he could purchase it. But that is not what he did. So exactly what was his motivation? Before we present our findings to Mycroft and the others, I believe we need to have that information."

"How can we ascertain his motivation?" asked I.

Holmes paused for a few moments as he pondered the question. Then in frustration he sighed.

"Perhaps, if we review all of the evidence, all of the information, and see what we can infer from the data, we will be able to work out his motivations. Maybe we've missed something. Something obvious."

Inspector Gregson and I looked at one another. We'd all been over and over the evidence that had been collected these past several days. But I had to admit that only recently had we acquired the critical information from Harvey Wise. It seemed a reasonable course of action to now reconsider everything we knew in light of this new information.

Gregson and I turned to Holmes and nodded our agreement.

"Very well," Holmes began. "Let me present some thoughts and observations. All of this is based on information we have gathered so far. I'd like to see if we can put this entire plot together. If either of you find that I have missed something of importance, please point it out."

After a moment's pause to gather his thoughts, he began.

"First, let's go back eighteen months, to the 13th of September, 1894. It seems to me that someone went to great lengths to get Simon Rhoads convicted of murdering a man whom they knew would be out of the country. We know that a body, which we now know belonged to Kelwin Hooper, was found with Simon Rhoads in Battersea Park. We know someone, whom we now know to be Harvey Wise, identified the body as Paul Watts. We know the body was dressed in clothing that had once belonged to Watts and the weapon was a possession of Simon Rhoads, who himself was found near the body. We also know that Watts departed for America from the London port the morning Rhoads was arrested for Watts' murder.

"I believe one or more people conspired to create evidence in an effort to deliberately guide the Scotland Yard investigation to convict Rhoads for the murder of Paul Watts and have the English government execute him. These were calculated murders; both the murder of the man in Battersea Park, and the eventual execution of an innocent Simon Rhoads."

Holmes paused a moment as he took a sip of tea, then pressed on.

"Now, let's consider how this case began to take a different track approximately four months ago. Paul Watts, still in America and completely unaware that anyone had been executed for his supposed murder, wrote to some friends that he would be returning to England in the hopes of expanding his American business. Now, for the people who had orchestrated this charade this was the worst possible news. So far, their crime had gone undetected and would have remained so, as long as Paul Watts stayed in America. But when they learned Watts was returning, they had to take drastic action.

"They knew that there was only one man, Harvey Wise, who could identify them as the men who had paid to have a false identification given to the police. So far, they had not been able to locate him, but as long as Paul Watts was in America, they believed their secret was safe. However, when they learned that Watts was returning to London, they desperately had to find Harvey Wise and eliminate him. They located his friends – Hal Estes, Liam Norwell, and Roy Hallis – and over the next four months they tortured and killed each one in an effort to find out where Harvey Wise was hiding. Inspector Lestrade investigating those murders now, but is unaware of their connection to our case."

Holmes shook his head slowly.

"Those unfortunate men had no idea where Harvey Wise was and died because of it. When Paul Watts wrote to his 'friends' announcing his intentions to return to London, he inadvertently sealed the fates of those three men as well as his own."

"But this is fantastic, Holmes," said I. "The cold-bloodedness needed to contemplate, much less carry out, such a scheme seems too great."

"No, Watson. These people are playing for stakes that we do not yet understand. And these stakes must be very high indeed, because the people behind this are still carrying out their deadly scheme."

After another brief pause to drink his tea, Holmes continued.

"When it became necessary, and I believe it did become necessary because of his return from America, the murder of Paul Watts had to be carried out last Monday morning. That, of course, is when Sergeant Cummings made his discovery of who the victim was and we became embroiled in this affair. All of these murders were planned with precision and in such a way that it seems there is scant evidence to reveal that any overall plot ever existed."

We were all silent for several moments as we considered what we had heard. I believe that we were only now beginning to understand what we were really up against.

But Holmes wasn't finished. He cleared his throat and continued.

"From what I have observed, I believe I can give you some specific characteristics of the killers who committed these murders. I believe there were at least two people involved. One man approached each victim from the front and gripped him by the upper arms.

"Let's confine ourselves to this individual first. This man was someone both victims knew and trusted. They were not afraid of him. He is approximately five feet ten inches tall and fairly strong."

"How do you derive his height?" asked I.

"You remember the bruising on the upper arms of both victims from the autopsy reports? If you recall, the bruising is located high on the upper arms near the shoulders of the victim found in Battersea Park eighteen months ago. This man was smaller in stature and thus the assailant's grip would naturally be higher up on the shorter victim's arms. However, the bruising on the upper arms of the real Paul Watts found last Monday was lower down, closer to his elbows, because he was a taller man in relation to his attacker."

We considered this new insight and could find no flaw. Holmes continued.

"Now the second attacker approached from the rear. I would estimate his height to be at least six feet tall; tall enough to wrap his arm around each victim's throat from behind. You'll recall the slight irritation present around the neck area of both stabbing victims that was noted in the autopsy reports.

"Based on the location of both wounds, I suggest that the man is left-handed. Watson, that will eliminate Basil Hart as our knife wielder. You'll recall that as we watched him writing in the warehouse, he was writing with his right hand. He could still be involved, but he wasn't the one who delivered the fatal wound.

"Now, Colin Dunn is left-handed. Watson and I observed that fact yesterday. So far, he is the only person we have encountered in this affair who is left-handed. Our murderer also has some knowledge of the human body; perhaps he was formerly an army medic or served in some other medical capacity. One thing is for sure, our murderer knew exactly where to place the stab wound for best effect. We do not yet know whether Colin Dunn possesses any such knowledge.

"Once the killing took place, both men gripped the victim by the upper arms and carefully laid him back on the ground placing the victim's hands by his side. Hence, what Sergeant Cummings noticed as the lack of 'crumpling' of both victims after they were stabbed."

"Why did they do that?" Gregson asked.

Holmes replied, "I believe they knew their victims and so took some care as they placed them on the ground. Perhaps they also have a driven need to keep things tidy, neat, orderly, well-balanced."

"By Jove! Holmes," I ejaculated. "Did you notice Basil Hart's mannerisms? When we spoke with him in his office, as he sat at his desk, he made quite a production of straightening and aligning everything on his desk. It all had to be just so."

"Yes," Holmes agreed, "I noticed that as well."

Holmes paused a moment, then added, "This is a diabolical business in the extreme."

No one could find a flaw in Holmes' reasoning up to this point. All of the conclusions he had voiced were supported by the facts.

After some moments, Holmes resumed. "Now, as to who is involved in this affair, I believe we have to seriously look at Basil Hart, Colin Dunn, and Mrs. Frances Dunn.

"Both Mr. Hart and Mr. Dunn knew Paul Watts and Simon Rhoads, and both knew them reasonably well. They all were aware that Paul Watts was destined to depart for America. Hart and Dunn were both in the Fox and Goose pub the night Watts and Rhoads were drinking. In fact, one of them was paying for the drinks at their table.

"We also know, from information provided by Mrs. Dunn, that some time ago Colin Dunn received a letter that caused him great concern, if we are to believe her. While she could not provide the actual letter, she provided the envelope. Inspector, we have it here."

Holmes rose from his seat and looked through some papers on his desk until he found what he was looking for. He returned to the table and handed the envelope to Inspector Gregson, pointing to the address in the upper left-hand corner.

"Note the address, *Cross Seas Export* in New York City. That is the name of Paul Watts' company in America. The postmark confirms it was mailed from America. Mrs. Dunn said the letter arrived about four months ago, which is about the time the other murders began. All of this seems to point to Colin Dunn as the other perpetrator in these murders."

"What about that Cahn fellow?" I asked. "He could certainly have been the one who crushed those other men."

"Yes, you're right, Watson. And I believe he was also the person who sent Sergeant Cummings into the path of that lorry yesterday.

"But we have no proof of his participation in any of these murders, just like we do not have any proof of Hart's or Dunn's involvement."

"But Harvey Wise could identify them," Gregson offered.

"Yes, he could," Holmes agreed. "But it would be his word against two gentlemen. Tell me, Inspector, in any other Scotland Yard case, if you had to choose between the word of two gentlemen or a man with no steady job who depended on charity houses, which would you believe? No, I'm certain their word would not be doubted unless we could find some additional evidence or someone else to support Harvey Wise's identification."

It seemed to me that any way we tried to pursue this case, we came to a dead end. None of the evidence we had just reviewed would be sufficient to bring the people involved into a court of law. Every death related to this affair could be explained as an unfortunate accident or completely unrelated to the case. In frustration I struck the table.

"Then what are we to do, Holmes?"

Holmes was silent for several moments

"It occurs to me that the Randall House seems to have played a central role in this scheme. The three murdered men, as well as Kelwin Hooper and Harvey Wise, were all frequent visitors of the charity house. I think that is where all of these men came into contact with the perpetrators and became an unfortunate part of this scheme."

"Well, what is our next step?" Inspector Gregson enquired.

"I suggest that we sleep on what we have tonight and begin fresh tomorrow," Holmes suggested. "Watson and I must attend to some other business later in the day, so I suggest that we meet back here tomorrow evening at six o'clock."

"Agreed," Inspector Gregson said as we all rose and he retrieved his coat and hat. "I will need to spend most of the day tomorrow at Scotland Yard closing the case of Inspector Hall's suicide. I'll return sometime after six o'clock. Good evening, gentlemen."

"Good evening, Inspector," we both said as I opened the door and watched the inspector descend the stairs.

Closing the door, I turned to Holmes.

"What 'other business' do we have tomorrow, Holmes?"

Holmes smiled as he lit his pipe, a thick stream of blue smoke billowing into the air.

"I stopped by the Randall House this afternoon when I was returning from Harvey Wise's room. I requested a list of the people who volunteer there. I led them to believe that I, or rather, that you, were writing an article to highlight their charity and good work. Watson, when this is over, might I impose upon you to write a small article on the organisation?

"Anyway, after looking at the roster of volunteers, I found two names of people that I believe know more than they have revealed to us: both Mr. Basil Hart and Mr. Colin Dunn. I believe they are the two men who convinced the ill-fated Kelwin Hooper and Harvey Wise to participate in their evil game."

"So, what are we to do?" asked I.

"I want us to speak with both Basil Hart and Colin Dunn tomorrow afternoon at the Dunn residence. I'll send a telegram shortly, stating that it is vitally important that we meet with them, together, tomorrow afternoon."

"But what do you hope to accomplish with such a meeting?"

"When we confront these men with what we know, I expect that we will find them confident, arrogant, but too clever by half. Their own arrogance may lull them into a sense of invulnerability and that, my dear Watson, may lead them to overplay their hand and make some incriminating statements. If that happens, we will be there to witness their braggadocious admissions."

"Perhaps. But shouldn't Inspector Gregson accompany us as a representative of Scotland Yard?"

"Don't you see, Watson? If Hart and Dunn were to admit to their crimes and Inspector Gregson were present, then he would have no choice as a representative of Scotland Yard but to arrest them and take them into custody. That would initiate the very proceedings everyone has been trying to avoid ever since this investigation began. No, I think we have to see what you and I can elicit from these scoundrels ourselves. Then we can present our results to Mycroft and the others."

Holmes took a few more draws on his pipe, then gazing into the fireplace, he concluded. "This affair has gone on long enough, Watson. It is time we bring it to a close."

It appeared that Holmes was prepared to confront the two men on their activities. Whether they would admit their involvement or claim ignorance of the events remained to be seen. But we had Harvey Wise, and he could provide an eyewitness account, at least to Holmes and I, regarding whether these two men had hired him for this nefarious affair.

Chapter XXIV: Mr. Holmes Teaches a Lesson

It was just getting dark when Holmes left our Baker Street rooms to send telegrams to both Basil Hart and Colin Dunn. I asked to accompany him but he insisted that he go alone. He wanted to take in the air as he focused his thoughts on our case. After some discussion, he agreed to at least take my revolver with him for some protection, but I found after he left that he had conveniently forgotten to pocket it. So, I waited in anxious anticipation for his return.

As I considered the events of the day – the unexpected visit of Mrs. Dunn, the envelope she had given to Holmes, and the delivery of Harvey Wise to a place of safety – each incident was yet one more brick in a carefully constructed case that we were building to uncover the minds behind this scheme.

It was not lost on me that, in apparent desperation, these minds would stop at nothing to keep their actions from being revealed. But if anyone were up to the task, it would be Holmes.

So, I sat for the next hour, nervously waiting for my friend to return from his errand.

# # #

As the clock on the mantel chimed the hour of seven, I suddenly heard some kind of commotion downstairs, followed by the slamming of the front door and a strident cry from Mrs. Hudson.

"Oh! Dr. Watson! Dr. Watson!"

I rushed to the door and found at the bottom of the stairway Mrs. Hudson assisting Holmes towards the steps. His hat had been damaged, his clothes were dirty and dishevelled, and there appeared to be scuff marks on both his shoes and walking stick.

"Holmes!" I cried as I bounded down the stairs. His movements were stiff, as if he were fearful of breaking, and his eyes reflected a dull awareness which troubled me greatly.

As I reached him, he softly stated, "I just need to sit, and perhaps you can provide some ministrations to me, if you would be so kind."

I placed his arm over my shoulder and took him towards the stairs, calling back to Mrs. Hudson as we went.

"Mrs. Hudson, please bring some clean towels and a bowl of water." As she left to gather the items I'd requested, I guided Holmes up the steps to our rooms.

It was slow progress getting Holmes up the stairs, so that by the time we entered our rooms, Mrs. Hudson was behind us with the towels and water I had requested, wearing a worried look on her face. I had Mrs. Hudson place the water bowl and towels on the table.

"Thank you, Mrs. Hudson. I must give Holmes a full examination so if I need any additional items, I will call you."

"Oh, Doctor," fretted Mrs. Hudson, "I don't believe I've ever seen him in this state. It's terrible." Then an idea came to her. "I can put some soup on and have it ready when you have finished," she offered.

"That's an excellent idea, Mrs. Hudson. When we are finished here, I'll come down and get the soup. Thank you."

That seemed to satisfy her, but there was still a look of distress on her face when she closed the door behind her.

I turned my attention to Holmes. There was a large scrape on his forehead and due to the look in his eyes I feared a possible concussion. I could tell that the rest of his body seemed to be in considerable pain as well. Moving slowly, I gently helped him remove his coat. As I did so, I noticed tears along the elbows as well as what appeared to be two oblong marks on the left side of his jacket.

Then I began to slowly remove his shirt. He winced with each movement and his breathing was ragged. I was astounded to see the injuries he had sustained. His ribs, which at first appeared to present a light purplish colour, were beginning to turn a bluish black along both sides. I again noticed the presence of two oblong bruises near his left kidney.

After helping Holmes to sit, I opened my medical bag on the table and said, "All right, Holmes. Tell me what happened."

Holmes had closed his eyes, wincing as I started to clean the laceration on his forehead and emitting an occasional groan. After another moment, he began.

"I was foolish for not taking your revolver with me. But even if I had, I suspect it would have been of little use. The attack was quite sudden."

All manner of dirt and grit were in the wound on Holmes' forehead. It was evident that he had suffered a number of severe blows not just to his head but to his entire body. His breathing had finally improved but was still uneven. After another wince due to my attentions, Holmes continued.

"I enjoyed a pleasant walk down to Oxford Street and then over to Regent Street. The telegram office at Piccadilly Circus was still open so it was from there I sent telegrams to the two gentlemen involved. In the messages, I stated that there would be a meeting at Colin Dunn's residence tomorrow afternoon at four o'clock and they were both expected to attend. I also indicated that it would be to their great advantage to keep the appointment."

He pulled back a moment to look directly at me. Even with the pain he was experiencing, he still managed to chuckle as he said, "I signed both telegrams 'Harvey Wise.' That should ensure they keep the appointment."

Indeed, thought I. That should get the attention of both men. The one person they had been desperately seeking was now contacting them.

I brought Holmes' head closer so I could complete my treatments to his wound. Holmes continued his narration.

"I also received a reply to an enquiry I sent to the Spanish police regarding an incident that I'm not sure has any bearing on our case. Anyway, as I was returning, I was about to leave Regent Street for Oxford, just passing the tobacconist shop I frequent, when I felt an enormous shove from behind. I had not heard any sound approaching so I was caught completely unawares. I fell to the pavement, my hat falling off my head as I dropped my walking stick. Turning to get up, I saw someone, a man about five feet eight or nine, wearing a handkerchief over the lower half of his face approach me and deliver a brutal kick to my ribs. The blow knocked the wind out of me, and before I could turn over the assailant delivered another kick very near the first one. I can tell you, old fellow, I have never experienced that level of pain before and hope to never experience it again.

"In just moments, the assailant who had kicked me stepped back and I was suddenly lifted off the pavement by a second assailant. I might have been a sack of feathers, so easily did this brute handle me. He turned me around and with his arms encircling my body he began to squeeze. The pressure was so great that in moments breathing was almost impossible and I could feel my ribs and spine begin to crack. I pounded on the arms that encircled me but to no effect.

"It was then that I looked at the face of the man who had a death grip on me. A small, flat cap sat on his long, dark hair and the smell of sawdust emanated from his clothes. He wore a handkerchief covering his nose and the lower half of his face, but the bridge of his nose and his eyes were visible. I saw a small brown mole on the bridge of his nose by his right eye."

"Cahn!" I exclaimed.

"Yes, indeed. And I'm sure he knew I was aware of who he was. I'm convinced I heard a soft chuckle emanate from the scoundrel and as I struggled, I could imagine a smile beneath the mask. I believe that he fully intended that I not survive the encounter."

Having finished attending to the gash on Holmes' forehead, I began to look at the bruising on his ribs. It was evident that Holmes had suffered at least one cracked rib, possibly two. Fortunately, his spine seemed to have survived the attack without injury; at least there were no protruding disks, and he didn't seem to react as I pressed various places up and down his back.

As I poked, prodded, and began to wrap Holmes' ribs with bandages, he resumed his narrative.

"Seeing that my attempts to break free were fruitless, I decided that I had no other choice but to strike at the most vulnerable spot available to me. With a rigid hand I struck out at his neck, striking his Adam's apple. That had the desired effect.

"He immediately dropped me to the pavement and staggered backward, clutching his throat with both hands. I landed on my back and I immediately saw the first assailant approaching, no doubt preparing to deliver another series of kicks. Fortunately, I found that I had landed beside my walking stick, which I had dropped when I was first knocked to the ground.

"I barely had time to pick it up when the smaller assailant was upon me. I did the only thing I could: I thrust my cane upwards into the man's midsection, just below the breastbone. He too, staggered back, although I believe more in surprise than injury. But that gave me the time I needed. I rose to one knee and as he approached me again, I swung the cane around smartly and brought it down upon his left knee. He emitted a pained howl.

"I was about to deliver another blow when I was suddenly pushed away harshly towards the tobacconist shop, causing my head to strike the wall as I fell onto the pavement. I rolled back over, prepared for another attack, when I saw the bigger fellow helping the smaller one limp off towards an alley. They weren't running, but they were going as fast as the smaller fellow could move. They turned down an alley and disappeared into the night."

"Great Scott, Holmes!" I exclaimed as I finished wrapping Holmes' ribs. "You could have easily been killed. Did you get a look at the smaller attacker?"

"No, as I said he also had a handkerchief covering the lower part of his face and he never came close enough for me to see his eyes. The attack was well planned. It took place at a location where the lampposts did not provide a sufficient amount of light, so it was quite dark. Had we not seen Mr. Cahn that day at Holtz Manufacturing, I would not have known who he was."

I began to replace my supplies into my medical bag. I realized that I should not have been surprised by the level of brutality we had witnessed during this case. If we had discovered anything over these past few days, it was that the people behind this affair were ruthless and would stop at nothing to protect the secret they had guarded these past eighteen months.

I helped Holmes over to his chair and saw to his comfort. Then I went downstairs to retrieve the soup Mrs. Hudson had prepared. After reassuring her that Holmes would indeed survive, I brought the soup up to our rooms.

After the soup, Holmes accepted my offer of a sleeping draught and soon went to bed. Once I had returned the soup dishes to Mrs. Hudson, I, too, turned in for the evening.

As I thought about the day's events, I recalled that Holmes had told Harvey Wise this morning that he expected to bring this case to a close within the next couple of days. For me, this case couldn't end soon enough.

There had already been too many deceptions; too many deaths. In my mind, it seemed that there now needed to be a harsh reckoning. Whether in public, or privately, as the assistant commissioner seemed inclined to pursue.

However it would eventually be resolved, I did not believe that these atrocities would go unpunished.

Part VI
Day 5 - Friday

Chapter XXV: The Final Piece

Holmes awoke sore and stiff as a result of his encounter the previous evening. As we ate our breakfast, he thanked me for the sleeping draught I had concocted for him and indicated it had indeed helped him experience a restful night. Soon after we finished our breakfast, and as I was beginning to read the morning paper, he turned to me.

"Watson, I wonder if you'd be so kind as to accompany me on an errand I want to complete before this afternoon's meeting with Colin Dunn and Basil Hart."

"Certainly," I replied. "Where do you want to go?"

"You'll recall that when we spoke to Basil Hart at his business, he mentioned that he and Colin Dunn had been featured as one of several business partners in the London area with growing enterprises. I'd like to take a look at that article. As I remember, he said the article came out one or two months after Simon Rhoads' death and had been published in *The Strand Magazine*. I would like to look through the archives of that publication, and since you already have a relationship with the editor, I thought you might be of assistance in gaining access to the past publications."

I had to admit his reasoning was sound. I had developed a good relationship with the editor over the past few years as my accounts of Holmes' adventures had been published.

"Then we should leave soon," I said as I rose from my seat. "It may take us sometime to locate the specific issue we are seeking."

Holmes agreed and rose slowly from his seat. We gathered our coats, hats, and walking sticks and made our way down to the street where we hailed a cab and were soon on our way.

The brisk morning air permeated the hansom cab, our breath visible as we rode in silence. The sounds of the London business district were prominent as wagons of freight drawn by teams of horses moved up and down the thoroughfare.

When we finally arrived at our destination, 12 Burleigh Street, we exited the hansom cab and entered the grey, stone building that housed the publishing offices and printing facilities for several publications, including *The Strand Magazine*. The printing and shipping of the magazine took place on the ground floor. We made our way up to the first floor where the offices for *The Strand Magazine* were located.

At the top of the stairs, we encountered a large room with desks and filing cabinets scattered throughout. Some people were standing about talking, some were walking back and forth to filing cabinets, while others were seated at desks typing. It was so loud I found it hard to believe that anyone could think in such an environment, much less write a coherent article.

I led my companion past the desks to the line of offices located at the back of the space. No one seemed to pay us any mind as we made our way to the centre office and knocked on the open door.

My friend, Gavin Pope, had been one of the editors of *The Strand Magazine* over the past five years. He was a tall man, thirty-one years of age, whose lean figure belied an athletic prowess. He was an energetic man with a booming voice who would be easy to locate in a crowd. His thick moustache and fingers were stained due to chain smoking. We had come to know one another after I had submitted my first account of one of Holmes' cases. We had remained on friendly terms ever since, although he would often press me for a new story each time we were together.

"Dr. John Watson!" he exclaimed as we entered his smoke-filled office. He wore a broad smile as he came around his desk to shake my hand. "It's good to see you. You really should come by more often."

"Well," I replied, "my growing medical practice keeps me quite busy these days."

I turned to my friend and said, "Gavin Pope, I'd like to introduce you to Sherlock Holmes."

"Ah," he said as his smile became even wider, "the great Sherlock Holmes! I have to say I have greatly enjoyed reading of your cases through Dr. Watson's accounts." Leaning in closer, he asked in a conspiratorial tone, "Tell me, do you *really* solve those cases the way he says in his stories?"

"Well," Holmes said as he shook Pope's hand, "Dr. Watson does tend to romanticize the cases a bit. But I can assure you he is quite accurate in his account of my methods." I might have seen just a hint of annoyance on Holmes' face, but I wasn't sure.

In an effort to move things along, I said, "Gavin, we have a favour to ask of you."

"Yes! What can I do for you?" he asked waving us to sit in two chairs as he sat behind his desk.

"We are looking for an article that we believe was published in *The Strand Magazine* sometime after October, 1894. We are not sure which monthly edition, so we may need to search through several months until we can locate the right issue."

Gavin nodded his head as he heard our request. Then he said, "As you know, we publish several periodicals here. But we keep archived copies of all the periodicals downstairs in the basement. We also have negatives for all of the photographs in the magazines as well."

Pope paused a moment, then, as if an idea had just struck him said, "I can send young Tolson down with you to help you find what you're looking for. He is learning all aspects of the publishing business and knows where everything is. TOLSON!"

Both Holmes and I jumped at the sudden outburst. Almost immediately, a young boy, perhaps sixteen or seventeen years of age, appeared in the doorway of the office.

"Yes, sir, Mr. Pope," he said as he looked us over. He stood about five feet eight inches tall with sandy blond hair and freckles under his eyes. His dark trousers and white shirt were a bit dingy and his hands seemed to be stained with ink.

"Tolson," Pope began, "take these gentlemen down to the basement and show them where the archives are located. They're looking for archived versions of *The Strand Magazine*. Please give them any assistance they need."

"Yes, sir," Tolson said smartly.

Pope turned back to us. "Gentlemen, Tolson here can show you anything you want to see. Let me know if you need anything further."

"We will," Holmes said to Pope as we rose from our seats and started for the office door.

Then to Tolson, Holmes said, "Lead the way" and we were off to roam through the archives of *The Strand Magazine*.

# # #

We followed the boy Tolson down two flights of stairs to the basement of the building. Once we were at the bottom of the stairs we were taken through a set of large double doors into a vast open area where there were tall, metal shelves arranged along the walls and throughout the basement in rows. A light, musty smell was evident in the entire room. Narrow, horizontal windows were set high in the concrete walls to let in light from outside. The brightness from the windows fluctuated as the legs of passersby on the street above interrupted the streaming daylight. At the start of each row of shelves were placards that had months and years written upon them indicating the issues that were located in each specific row.

"What month and year are you looking for?" Tolson asked.

"We're not quite sure," Holmes replied. "We know it will be a few months after October, 1894. Perhaps we should begin with November, 1894, and gradually work our way forward until we locate the issue we need."

"Well," Tolson said, "these first two rows contain archived copies of some of our other publications."

Then he pointed down to the third row, "Archived copies of *The Strand Magazine* start in the third row. The 1894 issues will be midway down the row. You'll find November near the end of the shelf. Further down that row will be another set of shelves that will have the 1895 issues beginning with January. You'll see each month in order."

"Very well, Tolson. Thank you. We'll take it from here."

"I'll just wait up here in case you need anything," Tolson said as he sat in a chair and took out a small book.

Holmes and I walked down the indicated aisle until we came upon the 1894 issues. Four copies of each month's magazine had been placed into a small wooden box that was labelled with the month and year of the issue it contained. The box had been constructed so as to protect the stored magazines from dampness, and to hopefully preserve the paper.

Holmes took out one of the November, 1894, issues and I took one of the December, 1894, issues. We looked through the table of contents of both magazines to see if an article relevant to the subject we were seeking was listed. There was not. So, we placed the magazines back into their boxes, replaced the boxes on the shelves, and moved down the row to the next month's issues.

Holmes reviewed the January, 1895, issue while I searched the February, 1895, issue. As I scanned the table of contents one entry brought my perusal to a halt. An entry entitled "Growing Businesses in London" was listed as beginning on page 42.

"Holmes," said I, "I may have found it here."

He came over as I turned the magazine to page 42. The author of the article began by stating he was reporting on small to mid-sized businesses located in London that were expected to grow over the next several years.

The first company he wrote about was Harland and Sons who were just coming out with an innovative bridle that would make it much easier for carriage riders to control their horses. They were so sure this new bridle would take the world by storm and replace every bridle used by carriage horse owners, they were offering a free buggy whip with every purchase. The article was accompanied by a picture of an older and younger man, presumably Mr. Harland and his son, holding what looked like a bridle, standing by a horse next to a wooden fence.

The second company featured was Holtz Manufacturing. The article briefly mentioned the execution of Simon Rhoads and his affiliation with the company. But it quickly moved on to say that Colin Dunn had now partnered with Basil Hart and the two expected great things to happen over the next several years.

"Ah! Look here, Watson," Holmes said as he turned the page. There on the page was a photograph of Dunn and Hart, standing by one of their warehouse bay doors.

"Tolson?" Holmes called out. Tolson was by our side immediately. Holmes showed him the picture.

"Can we get a copy of this photograph?"

"Aye, sir," Tolson said pointing to the back wall of the basement. "We keep the negatives of all the photographs over there."

"Can we see the negative?"

"Sure," and Tolson led us over to another set of shelves that contained metal boxes. He opened one of the metal boxes labelled "Jan – Jun 1895" and began to search through the negatives. Each negative had a label that identified the month of the issue it appeared in, but not the specific article, so it took some minutes to locate the exact picture we wanted. However, he eventually found the negative and handed it to Holmes.

Holmes held it up to the light. We could see a reverse image of the one that had appeared in the magazine.

Satisfied, Holmes asked, "How long would it take to produce a picture from this negative?"

"Probably about two hours. It depends on how long it takes for the chemicals to dry. But it shouldn't be much longer than that."

"Do you know how to produce a picture from a negative?"

"I sure do," Tolson said proudly.

"Excellent!" he said as he handed the negative back to Tolson. "Please make a picture from this negative and as soon as it is ready take it up to Mr. Pope's office." As Holmes said this, he handed Tolson four shillings.

"I'll get started straight away!" the boy said excitedly and left with the negative to begin his task.

Holmes and I made our way back up to the first floor and to Gavin Pope's office. While we were slow in our strides due to Holmes' injuries, I have to say that I believe we were both excited by our find.

"Well, did you locate what you needed?" Pope asked after we entered his office and sat.

"Yes, I believe we may have found something that can be of assistance," Holmes replied nonchalantly. He did not want to raise the interest of Gavin Pope too much. After all, Pope was still a newspaper man, and would want details that we were not yet ready to reveal. We had been very fortunate to locate this key piece of information and I believed it would be invaluable to our case.

"I've asked young Tolson," Holmes continued, "to make a photograph from a negative that we found, and to bring it to your office when it is ready. Would you please send it by courier to 221B Baker Street as soon as he has it ready?"

"I'll be glad to help in any way I can," Pope replied as he wrote the address.

Turning to me, Pope said, "Hopefully, I'll be able to publish a story where *The Strand Magazine* figures prominently."

I wanted to gently put him off since I knew this was a case that would most likely not be seen by the public.

"Well," I said, "let me take some time to look through my notes and see what cases might be of interest to your readers."

That seemed to satisfy him. We shook hands and made our way down to the ground floor and outside where we hailed a cab.

# # #

We arrived back at Baker Street to await delivery of the photograph. While we had only been gone a couple of hours, Holmes was quite tired and a bit sore from his exertions. I prepared a cold compress for his ribs which he gladly accepted. After I relit the fire, Holmes sat quietly in his chair and in minutes he had fallen asleep. His breathing was steady but shallow due to his cracked ribs. His chin rested comfortably upon his chest.

After an hour quietly reading the morning paper, I went downstairs to ask Mrs. Hudson to prepare some soup which she did, asking all the while how Holmes was faring. I reassured her as best I could. Harvey Wise was also in the kitchen making repairs to some cabinets, but I could tell he was also concerned about Holmes' well-being. He had put his faith in Holmes to alleviate the fear he had been living with for eighteen months.

I took the soup back upstairs and found Holmes awake, still in his chair, and staring into the fireplace. While he was still sore, I could tell he was refreshed from his nap.

I set the soup on the table and helped him over to a chair. The soup also seemed to have a restorative effect on my friend.

It was about noon when we heard a knock on the downstairs door. Mrs. Hudson had a brief discussion before closing the door and calling up to us.

"That should be the photograph we have been waiting for," Holmes said to me as he rose from his seat. I accompanied him downstairs.

"Oh, Mr. Holmes," Mrs. Hudson said, standing by the door holding a brown envelope, "a courier has just left this for you." She handed the envelope to Holmes before returning to the kitchen.

"Thank you, Mrs. Hudson," Holmes said as he took the package. Printed on the front in black ink were the words *'Mr. Holmes, Dr. Watson, 221B Baker Street'*. When he opened it, he found a folded piece of paper inside which he handed to me, then he took out the photograph and looked closely at it. The note was from Gavin Pope saying that he was looking forward to publishing our next story. After another moment, Holmes handed the picture to me. I immediately recognized the two men. Basil Hart's thin frame and moderate stature and Colin Dunn's slightly broader build and his dark beard. I took a closer look and saw the same dark eyes I had noticed upon my first meeting with Colin Dunn. I looked for anything in their appearance that would indicate the evil that we knew these men had perpetrated, but I found nothing.

After a few moments, Holmes and I took the photograph into the kitchen where Harvey Wise was still working. He had just finished attaching one of the cabinet doors. As we entered, he stood up

"Ah, Mr. Wise," Holmes said. "I wonder if you would please take a few moments to look at a photograph for me."

"Aye," he said. He sat at the kitchen table, accepting a glass of water from Mrs. Hudson. I stood on the other side of the table so that I could watch Harvey Wise's reaction when he saw the photograph.

Holmes placed the picture in front of Harvey Wise.

"Do you recognize anyone in this photograph?"

Harvey Wise stared at the picture for several seconds, even turning it slightly to either side to get a different perspective. After some moments, he looked up at Holmes.

"I'm not sure. I may have seen these men before, but I can't say for certain."

Holmes was quiet for a moment, then moved closer to the table.

"How about now?" he asked as he placed his fingers over the lower part of the image of Colin Dunn's face. This made his beard disappear.

In moments, Harvey Wise's eyes grew large and he abruptly stood up from the table.

"That's them!" he exclaimed. "That's them! They're the ones what paid me to identify that body."

"Are you sure?" Holmes asked.

"Sure as I'm standin' 'ere! That's them!"

I felt my heart flutter at this outburst. Here was the first tangible bit of direct evidence that pointed to these men as the culprits in this affair. And I have to say I believe I saw just the smallest of smiles cross my friend's face as he heard Mr. Wise's adamant statement.

"Very well, Mr. Wise," Holmes said as he gathered up the photograph. "That will do for now. I can tell you we are making good progress and I believe your ordeal will soon be over."

"Thank you, sir. Thank you," Wise gratefully said as Mrs. Hudson gave him a consoling pat on the back.

As Holmes and I left the kitchen with the photograph, he turned to me.

"Watson, would you please go upstairs and get our coats, hats, and walking sticks? I want to show this picture to the publican at the Fox and Goose pub. You can manage the stairs better than I at the moment. I will go out and hail a cab."

"Right away," I said as I turned and quickly ascended the stairs. I gathered our things and was back downstairs and out the door in moments. Holmes had a cab waiting and in short order we were on our way to the Fox and Goose pub.

# # #

We arrived at our destination in the early afternoon soon after the lunch trade had ended. After asking the cabman to wait, we walked into the pub. The place was almost empty. There were only two tables with customers finishing up their midday meal. The waitresses were picking up dishes and wiping down the empty tables. The smell of tobacco smoke and burning wood from the fireplace filled the room.

The publican, Clint Hatch, was behind the bar wiping a glass. When he saw us enter, it was clear he remembered us because he put down the glass and came around the bar to meet us.

"Gentlemen, have you come to dine? We've just finished lunch, but I think we still have some bread and cheese."

"Thank you, sir, but no," Holmes said. "I'm afraid we are pressed for time. I would like to ask you to look at a photograph and tell me if you recognize anyone."

Pointing to an empty table nearby Hatch said, "Here, let's sit down."

We sat and Holmes took out the photograph from his pocket and placed it in front of the publican.

"Do you recognize anyone in this picture?"

Moving the photograph so he could look at it, Hatch said, "If this is about that murder we spoke of the other day, I'm afraid that was a long time—"

Hatch stopped as he looked closely at the photograph. He even picked it up so that more light fell on the image.

After a few moments, he said, "This thin one was definitely here that night. I remember he seemed a bit wiry but showed he had some strength when he separated those two that were fighting."

He kept looking at the picture. Finally, he set it down on the table.

"And the other one, he was definitely here as well. I remember his eyes. Those were empty eyes that didn't seem to hold a soul. He didn't have a beard back then, but I remember him, too. He was with the wiry one."

After another moment, Hatch asked, "Do you have a picture of the third man who was with them?"

"No, I'm afraid we don't," Holmes said as he took the photograph and rose from his seat. "But this has been extremely helpful, Mr. Hatch. Thank you."

Holmes paused a moment, then said, "We may have need to call upon you again."

"You can find me here anytime," Hatch said as he waved and started back to the bar.

In the cab on our way back to Baker Street, Holmes turned to me.

"That's two people who can identify Dunn and Hart. We will not have to rely solely on the word of Harvey Wise. This should set our case on firmer footing. I feel more confident now that we may be able to bring justice to bear."

I had to agree. We finally had eyewitnesses who could confirm the involvement of Dunn and Hart. Finally, all of these seemingly unrelated incidents we had uncovered, that had taken place over these past eighteen months, might be brought together if we could only bring pressure on one or both of the culprits.

Upon our return to Baker Street, Holmes and I went back upstairs. After all the time spent on this case, we finally had some solid evidence. Holmes was calm and quiet on the outside, but I knew that like me, he was excited that we now could put names and faces to the evils that had been carried out.

Once we were back in our rooms, Holmes placed the photograph next to the evidence boxes. There was no doubt that it would soon become a critical part of this case.

Holmes and I settled back into our chairs. With our appointment not scheduled until four o'clock and Inspector Gregson occupied with closing the sad case of Inspector Jack Hall, there was not much to be done until the appointed hour.

Chapter XXVI: A "Theoretical" Discussion

As the afternoon progressed, the nervous energy we both were feeling began to present itself. Neither of us could sit for very long. At about two o'clock we left our Baker Street residence to take a short, but cautious, stroll into Regent's Park. Holmes' injuries still required that he proceed slowly at first, but after some minutes he seemed to become more comfortable in both his movements and breathing.

The air was brisk but clear. Our strides were measured and even though we only walked a short distance in the park, by the time we returned to Baker Street we had only one-half hour before we needed to depart for our appointment. Thankfully, Holmes used this time to recuperate from his exertions. I also made use of the time to redress his head wound and to check the wrappings around his ribs I had replaced earlier that morning.

When it was time to leave, we gathered our coats, hats, and walking sticks and made our way down to the street. We quickly hailed a cab and were on our way.

As we travelled, I could not help but consider Mrs. Dunn's unexpected visit the previous day and her plea to Holmes. We were about to confront the people we now knew were responsible for a most reprehensible crime. A crime that also involved Mrs. Dunn as an unknowing victim. Her world, the peaceful world she had built with Colin Dunn after the destruction of the peaceful world she had built with

Simon Rhoads, was about to be shaken, and most likely torn asunder.

# # #

Our cab ride to the Dunn residence was brief, and in minutes we were exiting the cab in front of the porch. After telling the cabman to wait, Holmes and I ascended the stone steps. The housekeeper opened the double wooden doors to our knock, and after a look of recognition, she offered a sombre greeting.

"Good afternoon, gentlemen," she said with a slight nod of her head.

"We are here to see Mr. Dunn and Mr. Hart, if you please," Holmes stated.

"Come in, gentlemen," she said, and stepped aside so we could enter.

We again placed our things on the large, circular table in the entryway. I noticed that the vase sitting in the middle of the table was empty and wondered how often the flowers were replaced. The housekeeper then led us towards the open double doors to the dining room.

The dining room itself was similar in size to the study we had visited the previous day. Wood panelling covered the left-hand wall from where we had entered. Two large, landscape portraits hung on either side of a large buffet cabinet which stood centred along the wall. A steaming pot and several cups were set upon a tray atop the buffet.

A large dining table running lengthwise through the room stood between the door and a stone fireplace in the opposite wall from where we stood. The last remnants of an afternoon fire still smouldered in the grate as the odours of burned wood and coffee mingled in the air.

Along the right-hand wall were two large, mullioned windows, similar to those in the study. They also looked out to the front of the house. Between these windows stood a small table, a leather-bound book placed on top, and two large chairs on either side of the table.

Upon our entering the room, the housekeeper announced, "Mr. Sherlock Holmes and Dr. Watson."

At the mention of our names, Colin Dunn, who was standing in front of the fireplace at the far end of the dining table, whirled quickly around. It was evident that he had not expected our presence. Basil Hart, who was standing behind one of the chairs by the farthest window, turned his gaze towards us and gave a startled expression as we entered.

Out of the corner of my eye I noticed a large, dark mass standing to our right against the wall. As I turned to get a better look, I recognised the huge shape of Mr. Cahn, standing impassively, looking at us both. As a precaution, I slipped my hand gently into my jacket pocket and grasped my revolver.

We all stood there, silently.

I watched as Colin Dunn, his expression ever-changing, began to put things together: the fact that Harvey Wise had not actually sent the telegram, the fact that Sherlock Holmes and I had instead presented ourselves for a meeting that was supposed to take place with Harvey Wise, and the fact that we most likely knew their secret.

After a few moments of silence, Dunn regained his composure, straightened, and said, "Thank you, Haddie.

That will be all." At this, the housekeeper gave a slight bow and withdrew from the room.

Holmes and I walked slowly into the room until we had progressed to the midpoint of the dining table, our eyes never leaving those of Colin Dunn. I saw that Dunn's eyes never left Holmes, and I'd wager that our other two adversaries were also locked onto our advance.

Finally, a bemused look fell upon Colin Dunn's face. Either he had decided that his plans had come to naught, or more likely he had been prepared for this eventuality.

"Well, gentlemen," Dunn said magnanimously, "forgive me if I say I'm disappointed that it's you. I was led to believe I would be seeing an old friend. I have been searching for my friend for some time and I was looking forward to seeing him."

"Yes," Holmes said softly. "I thought it best if we spoke first. I believe you were expecting Mr. Harvey Wise."

At the mention of Wise's name, Basil Hart's head turned quickly towards Colin Dunn in shock.

Colin Dunn nodded his head. "Yes. Yes. I don't suppose you know where I can find him?"

A slight smile crossed Holmes face.

"I have him."

"Oh, do you now?" Dunn asked, his eyebrows arching.

"Yes, and I have him somewhere safe. There's been so much murder about, lately. Don't you think?" As Holmes said this, he turned to look at Mr. Cahn, who stood impassively by the wall.

"Um, possibly," Dunn said. Then, "Well, perhaps we'll see him sooner than you think."

He then looked over at Mr. Cahn. "You can return to the warehouse and wait there. We may have need of you later tonight. But if not, you can resume your night watch duties for this evening. Basil and I will see you tomorrow."

We watched as, without a sound, Mr. Cahn began to move his bulk towards the dining room doors. There was no noise as he seemed to glide to the exit. How anyone, or anything, that large could move so quietly was beyond me. In moments he was gone. The entire room seemed to enlarge once he'd departed.

"We found him only four months ago," Dunn said, referring to Cahn, "but he has been invaluable at times. He stays in a small room at Holtz Manufacturing and serves as the night watchman, among other duties."

"*'Other duties,' indeed!*" thought I. My imagination ran rampant with what some of those other duties might be.

We turned back to face Dunn and Hart and as we did, we saw Hart step out from behind the chair he had been standing behind when we arrived. It was at that moment we saw he was using a cane to assist him in walking. He had a very distinct limp on his left side and when he had finally manoeuvred himself in front of the chair, he more fell into the chair than sat.

"Ah, Mr. Hart," Holmes said. "You appear to have injured yourself. Pray, tell us what happened?"

It was a sharp look that met Holmes' gaze. Hart's eyes narrowed for the briefest of moments and then he resumed a non-committal expression and waved his hand dismissively.

"Oh, I had an accident in the warehouse yesterday," he explained, not very convincingly. "We were moving some lumber and several boards fell upon my leg. It is not too bad."

"Well, you should be more careful," Holmes admonished. "You don't want to have another accident. The results could be worse."

"Yes," Dunn joined in. "I think he underestimated his task and will not make the same mistake again." His black eyes were focused on us both.

We all knew what we were talking about. Hart had been the other assailant the previous night, and it had been Holmes' cane that delivered the crippling blow. Whatever Hart had planned for the next encounter, he would no doubt take additional precautions.

As we all four stood in the dining room facing each other, we heard a knock on the dining room doors and the cheerful female voice of Frances Dunn call out.

"Colin," she said as she entered, carrying a tray with a pot and two cups. "Haddie told me we had visitors. Where are your manners?"

She continued into the room and placed the tray she carried onto the buffet next to the tray that sat there. After she had put everything down, she turned to Holmes and I.

"Good day, gentlemen," she said to us and nodded her head slightly.

"Mrs. Dunn," we both said with a small bow.

"I've brought some tea in for you both," she said, indicating the tray she had just put down. Then pointing to the tray that had been on the buffet when we'd arrived, she said, "This pot contains torrefacto coffee. If you are not familiar, it is a very bitter coffee that Colin and Basil have grown to prefer since their travels to Spain two years ago. I can hardly stand the mixture myself and I will not force it upon our guests. So, I have brought you milder tea if you care to partake." She said this last with a smile.

"Thank you, Mrs. Dunn. How thoughtful of you," Holmes said, also with a smile.

"Not at all," she said as she turned to leave. "Now I'll leave you gentlemen to your business. It's a pleasure to see you both."

And with that she left the room. I thought it was unfortunate that she had gone to so much trouble as neither Holmes nor I were inclined to have any tea, since our visit was not a cordial one.

After Mrs. Dunn left, Colin Dunn said, "Well, Mr. Holmes, exactly what is it that brings you and Dr. Watson to us today?"

"I would have thought that was obvious from the telegram that was sent to you both."

"The telegram led us to believe that we were to meet with someone else. We are meeting here, sir, under false pretences."

Holmes paused a few moments, then said, "And you really have no idea why we are here?"

Dunn looked over to Hart and both men shrugged their shoulders as though mystified by the entire affair.

"Well," Holmes stated, "I have an interesting and complex story that we have been uncovering for the past several days."

"A story?" Dunn said in mock surprise as he clapped and rubbed his hands. "This sounds like it could be fiction. A play, perhaps?" At this, Hart chuckled from his chair.

"It's a story that takes place over eighteen months and resulted in the murder of Simon Rhoads and another man, and then became the driving force behind the murders of five others and the suicide of a former Scotland Yard inspector."

Dunn glanced at Hart then focused back to Holmes, feigning surprise. "How was Simon Rhoads murdered? He was convicted of killing Paul Watts and executed for it by the English government."

"Simon Rhoads was framed for that murder. We know this because the real Paul Watts had emigrated to America and spent the past eighteen months there. It was upon Watts' return to London on Monday last that he was killed in the early morning hours on the London docks."

Dunn again gave a look of mock surprise and said, "Oh, that's sounds like quite a story. And *if* we were a part of it, that would be horrible. Please tell us this dreadful tale."

I could see that Holmes was becoming angry with the play-acting from Dunn and Hart. It was apparent that they believed they were untouchable for the atrocities Holmes was about to expose. But it was important to confront these men with their crimes and somehow make them pay for them.

#

"I believe," Holmes began, "it started almost two years ago. Paul Watts had already expressed some

255

frustrations to you, asking for some of his own clients, even saying he had considered emigrating to America. However, you stifled the idea.

"Later, in May, Watts and a friend of his, Jeremy Bales, travelled on a climbing expedition to the Pyrenees where they met Mr. Chris Ross. Watts confided to Ross his desire to make a significant change in his life and Ross encouraged him to make that change. Unfortunately, it was also on that trip that Watts' friend Bales died as the result of a climbing accident.

"When Watts returned from this adventure where he had lost a good friend, Watts decided it was time to make a change. The only real reason he had remained in London was because of his good friend and fellow climber Jeremy Bales."

Holmes eyes narrowed as he looked from Dunn to Hart and back again.

"I've contacted a friend of mine with the Spanish police, Inspector Estrada of the Security Corps. At my request he provided a summary of the death of young Jeremy Bales. He reported that the man's body was found in a valley below a popular climbing route. It appeared that one of his ropes failed as he rappelled down after securing to an abseil point. The police concluded at the time that as Mr. Bales attempted to descend, his rope failed, and he fell to his death.

"However, as I understand things, it appears that you both were on vacation in Spain about the same time as the young man's death. I wonder if one or both of you might have had a hand in his demise. I have asked Inspector Estrada to review the case."

Dunn had a serious look as he faced Holmes and said, "Careful Mr. Holmes. You would be facing a case of slander if you were to make such a statement publicly. Besides, just because we were in the same country does not mean we were involved in this young man's death. You yourself, as well as Dr. Watson, are in England, yet you are not considered to have participated in every death that takes place."

"No," Holmes confirmed, "I don't have direct evidence, but let me continue. With Bales' death, Mr. Watts was more determined than ever to make a change in his life. Perhaps it was because he saw his friend's death as a warning that death could come at any time. Whatever the motivation, after he wrote to his American friend, Chris Ross, concerning the death of Bales, they decided to start an export business together. Mr. Watts came to you and told you that he was going to emigrate to America. Perhaps this is where the idea of framing Simon Rhoads for murder had its beginning. I believe that this is where you both saw your opportunity."

"There you go with those slandering statements again. I'd be careful if I were you." I saw that Dunn was becoming concerned about how much Holmes had put together regarding their activities. Hart as well was sitting forward, listening intently to Holmes. Every once in a while, he would cast a furtive glance towards Dunn.

"Well, now that Watts' plan to emigrate had come together," Holmes continued, "you and Mr. Hart assisted him with disposing of his clothes and possessions. According to the records of the Randall House, you are both major supporters. And, according to their records, most of Watts' clothes went to that charity. It was a simple task to put some of his clothes aside for use in your scheme.

"Your 'volunteering' there also gave you unrestrained access to poor men willing to take on any task for which you paid handsomely. Once Watts had his travel plans established, I believe you solicited the unfortunate Kelwin Hooper and then separately, Harvey Wise, into your diabolical plan.

"On the night Watts was due to depart for America, you and Mr. Hart were in the Fox and Goose pub with Mr. Hooper, buying drinks for Watts and Rhoads, keeping their glasses full. We've spoken to the publican and he recalls two gentlemen sitting with a third man whose clothes were ill fitting. I suggest that was Mr. Hooper. It would be a simple matter to have the publican identify you both as the men who were buying drinks and who broke up the fight between Watts and Rhoads."

"Mr. Holmes," Dunn said as he raised his hand, "*if*, and I say *if*, I and Basil were to have concocted such an elaborate plan, how were we to know that Simon would go sleep under a tree in Battersea Park?"

"You both knew that Watts was leaving on his ship that evening. When Rhoads and Watts left the pub, Watts went on his way to his ship. He left Rhoads in front of the pub. I suggest that you both knowingly got Rhoads drunk that night. So drunk that he was easily guided to the tree in the park where you had him lie down and go to sleep."

Holmes paused a moment then continued.

"It was after you had Simon Rhoads asleep under the tree that you and Mr. Hart killed Kelwin Hooper with Rhoads' letter opener. After you killed Mr. Hooper, you ripped his clothes to disguise how poorly they fit. You also smeared blood all over Simon Rhoads' clothes. Then you left.

"But here came the critical part of your scheme. The next morning you had Harvey Wise merge into the crowd of onlookers as the police began their investigation. At the right

258

time – I imagine that you told him to wait until they took the sleeping man away or were searching the victim's pockets – he called out that the body was that of Paul Watts, an identification that the police accepted. But Harvey Wise recognised the heart tattoo on the arm of Kelwin Hooper; he knew you two had murdered him. That is why he never came to collect the money that was owed to him. It is also why he has been in hiding these many months.

"Even though you could not find Mr. Wise, the execution of Simon Rhoads was carried out as you had planned, so finding Mr. Wise became less of a priority as the months went by."

Holmes paused to look at first Dunn, then Hart. Then he continued.

"But then, four months ago, an event that threatened to unmask the whole enterprise occurred. Paul Watts wrote to tell you that he was returning to London. This would undo everything that you had established since the death of Simon Rhoads. You could not take the chance that any of Paul Watts' friends from the Alpine Club might see him walking around London. Or worse, that Mrs. Dunn might see him alive.

"You concluded that Paul Watts had to be killed the moment he stepped off the ship from America. Your hope was that the police would not recognise the name and associate it with the previous case. But you still had one other outstanding issue that needed to be dealt with. That was when you unleashed a second wave of death and destruction in a frantic attempt to find Harvey Wise.

"Over the next several weeks, you and Mr. Hart, along with the assistance of Mr. Cahn, hunted down friends of Harvey Wise in a desperate attempt to locate him. You even stayed out late to torture and kill those friends once you found them."

Holmes' voice began to rise in anger. "The murders of Messrs Estes, Norwell, and Hallis were for nothing! None of those men knew where Harvey Wise was hiding. In your desperate attempt to keep your plan from unravelling, you committed senseless murders!"

"You are again, making slanderous accusations, sir," Hart calmly warned from his chair. "Don't let your anger get the better of you."

Holmes paused for a few moments as he regained his composure. I, too, was seething at the arrogance on display.

"Finally," Holmes resumed, "the fateful night of Paul Watts' return arrived. He was killed in the same manner as Mr. Hooper in Battersea Park. But it was your bad luck to have Detective Sergeant Cummings investigate the murder, because he recognised the victim's name and the method of killing. It was he who uncovered that Mr. Watts had departed for America the very day Simon Rhoads was charged with his murder. Once this was discovered, Scotland Yard set us upon the case to uncover how such an atrocity could have taken place.

"I believe that you both observed us as we went to the London docks and then the Seaway Hotel. I suspect that it was one of you who fired the shot at us while we were outside in an attempt to eliminate Sergeant Cummings since you recognised him from the initial Rhoads investigation.

"And I believe it was you who were behind the murder of Sergeant Cummings and the attempted murder of Dr. Watson and myself Wednesday last."

"And how were we supposed to have done that?" Dunn asked incredulously.

"I know that Sergeant Cummings was beaten before being pushed in front of a startled team of horses drawing a wagon. And later that same day, a growler veered off the roadway and came at Dr. Watson and me as we were walking down Bond Street. I suspect you were behind both events."

Then Holmes turned to face Hart sitting in his chair.

"And I was attacked just last evening by two thugs. Fortunately, I was able to get the better of them."

Turning back to face Dunn, Holmes continued.

"And lastly, another casualty from this scheme was a retired Scotland Yard inspector. Upon learning that he had arrested and convicted an innocent man to hang, he took his own life. His grief was such that he felt he could not live with the guilt he carried."

We were all quiet for several moments.

Then Dunn sighed. "Well, in this fanciful tale of yours, Mr. Holmes, you seem to know everything."

"There is one point upon which I am unclear. I know the motivation for Mr. Hart to dispose of Simon Rhoads. He would, and did, gain full control of Holtz Manufacturing. But what was your motivation Mr. Dunn? Why would you devise and participate in such a long and torturous scheme?"

"Well, Mr. Holmes," Dunn said as he raised his hands in a noncommittal gesture, "*if* we had devised and participated in such a scheme, I would imagine you to be correct in Basil's motivation. He can now run Holtz Manufacturing unhindered. As to my motivation you have only to look at the obvious."

With a lecherous smile, Dunn said, "Simon did not know or appreciate what he had. And while he did not mistreat Frances, he did not treat her with the respect and kindness that she deserved."

Holmes, with a look of incredulity said, "You mean to say that you perpetrated all of this just so you could marry Simon Rhoads' widow?"

"Can you suggest a better reason? Look at her. Never have I seen anyone more beautiful. And let me tell you, she is every bit a woman as she looks." As he said this his leering smile became even wider.

I was so incensed that I was not going to have any of it.

"Why you blackguard!" I exclaimed as I took a step forward, fully intending to throttle the man.

All at once, Hart rose from his seat, his cane raised. Dunn took a step back and quickly withdrew a small derringer from his vest pocket, pointing it at both Holmes and myself. Holmes placed a restraining hand upon my arm and for several moments, everyone stood frozen, staring angrily at each other.

Chapter XXVII: Unfinished Business

The tension was finally broken when, from outside in the entryway, Mrs. Dunn called out as she approached, "Colin! Colin!"

Not wanting to burden Mrs. Dunn with the gravity of our conversation, I took a step back. Hart lowered his cane and resumed his seat while Dunn replaced the derringer into his vest pocket. As she walked into the room after a brief knock on the open doors, there was nothing to indicate that we had nearly come to blows just moments before.

Looking from us to Dunn, she said, "I'm sorry to interrupt you gentlemen, but Colin, I have given Haddie the night and the weekend off, so I will be preparing dinner tonight."

Turning to Holmes and myself she asked, "Gentlemen, will you stay and have dinner with us?"

"I'm sorry, Mrs. Dunn," Holmes replied, "but we have a previous engagement that we must attend to."

"Well," she smiled, "perhaps some other time." Then she turned to Hart and said, "Basil, you'll stay, of course."

"Of course," Hart said with a smile and a small nod of his head.

"Very well," Mrs. Dunn said. As she turned to go, she stopped for a moment and looked at Holmes. She finally said, "Good-bye, Mr. Holmes."

"Good-bye, Mrs. Dunn," Holmes replied.

We all watched her leave the room. Once she was gone, we turned towards one another again.

"Mr. Holmes," Dunn said, "you tell an interesting story, with many twists and turns, but you have not presented any evidence to go along with your, I must say, wild accusations. I dare say that if you had any evidence, you would be here with Scotland Yard in tow."

"Have no fear," Holmes replied, "Harvey Wise had already identified you both as the men who paid him to provide an incorrect identification of the body of Kelwin Hooper. He is willing to testify to that effect."

But Colin Dunn had a ready answer. "And who will the police believe? If we were to be identified, would they take the word of two prominent businessmen or the word of a day labourer?"

"Well," Holmes responded, "we have another witness who will also identify both of you as the men who broke up the fight and were buying drinks that night at the Fox and Goose pub."

"Ah. Who is that?"

"I'll keep the name to myself for the time being. I wouldn't want someone else to have an unfortunate accident."

Dunn paused a moment, then said, "I must also point out that if Scotland Yard were to bring a case forward, I suspect that word of an innocent man being hanged would be made public. Not a very good prospect for Scotland Yard or the justice system as a whole."

"Possibly," Holmes answered. "There might be some Scotland Yard resignations and changes to some judicial procedures, but the institutions will survive. I have no doubt that charges will be pursued."

"Are they willing to take that chance?" Dunn asked, but I noticed his confidence seemed to waver. Then he continued, "No, *if* we were involved in this scheme, I believe we would consider things at this point to be at a stand-off. We would not want to be publicly accused of carrying out such actions as you've described, and Scotland Yard would not want to be publicly accused of hanging an innocent man."

Dunn then thought another moment, then said, "It just might be best to let sleeping dogs lie and put the matter behind everyone. *If* I were involved in the scheme you have described, that is what I would propose."

"Um," Holmes said, "I'm not sure that Scotland Yard will want to 'let sleeping dogs lie.' One of their detective sergeants was murdered and a former inspector driven to suicide."

"Yes, I can see that they might want to take matters into their own hands. *If* I had perpetrated such a case, I would write a letter, detailing the acts as you've described, and send copies to several solicitors with instructions that if we were to disappear or somehow suffer an unnatural death, the letters should be sent to various newspapers. I think your story would make fascinating reading."

At this, a smile crossed Holmes' face.

"I suggest," Holmes said, "your position is not as solid as you believe, sir."

"How so?"

"Well, if you document your actions as I have described them in a letter, in an attempt to provide some level of protection for yourself and Mr. Hart, I believe you will simply provide more evidence against yourselves. Consider; first, you will be confessing to the murder of Kelwin Hooper and placing his body beside the sleeping Simon Rhoads. Second, you will be admitting to manufacturing and providing false evidence to Scotland Yard in an effort to convict and execute an innocent man for your crime. And third, you will be corroborating the testimony of Harvey Wise regarding your payment to him for providing a false identification."

Holmes chuckled, then concluded.

"No, sir, if you were to disappear and the public became aware of that letter, I'm fairly certain their response would be 'good riddance.'"

Dunn turned briefly to Hart and said, with false confidence, "I believe they're bluffing. Scotland Yard will do everything they can to keep this information from becoming public."

But I could detect the lack of assurance in his voice. Hart, too, seemed to have a worried expression on his face. I believed their arrogance was beginning to crumble.

We let it stay there. Our adversaries were now on notice that we had them in our sights and they were not as secure as they thought. Finally, Holmes decided we had discussed as much as we could.

"Gentlemen, I can assure you that this matter has not yet ended. I will communicate our discussions with the appropriate authorities, and we will determine our next steps."

Basil Hart rose from his seat as Colin Dunn said, "Remember, Mr. Holmes, *if* we had been involved in this case, I believe that our actions would soon be forgotten or discarded once it was learned that an innocent man had been hanged. In addition, there is no proof that anyone orchestrated anything such as you describe. I would tell your superiors to tread carefully."

"I believe our business here is concluded, for the moment," Holmes said, but then added, "Letting sleeping dogs lie would also mean that Harvey Wise no longer has to fear for his life. Something you should consider."

As we began to turn to take our leave, another thought occurred to Holmes. He stopped and faced Colin Dunn and Basil Hart again.

"One other thing; Have either of you had any medical training?"

"That's an interesting question, Mr. Holmes," Colin Dunn said as he smiled. "As it happens, when I started at university, I began with the study of medicine, even working as a hospital orderly between semesters. But I found that I preferred the certainties of mathematics to the vagaries of medicine, so I changed my studies to finance, and upon graduation, established my accounting firm."

"I see," Holmes said. Then in a tone absent of congeniality added "Very well. Good day."

And with that we left the dining room. As we collected our things from the table in the entryway, I noticed that the vase again contained fresh flowers. To my mind they presented an attractive image in a house where plans of murder and deception had been devised. Shaking off my thoughts, I followed Holmes out to our waiting cab.

On the way back to Baker Street we contemplated how our discussion with Dunn and Hart had gone. Neither man admitted nor denied any responsibility for the actions we had uncovered. They had simply stated that *if* they had been involved, they would have done everything the way we had described.

Our hope as we exited our cab and climbed the stairs to our Baker Street rooms was that Inspector Gregson agreed that with the help of Harvey Wise and the publican, we had enough evidence to bring those two, and possibly that Cahn fellow, to a court of law.

# # #

"Damn those scoundrels!" Inspector Gregson exploded as he pounded his fist upon the table. "Do they know no shame?"

It had been close to seven o'clock when Inspector Gregson arrived to our rooms after a full day of dealing with the death of former Scotland Yard Inspector Jack Hall. We gave him a summary of our meeting with Colin Dunn and Basil Hart, and I have to say his outburst summed up our own feelings regarding the matter. The nonchalant, sometimes flippant, responses from both men as we presented the facts of the case to them were as arrogant as they were sinister.

But their facade had begun to crack.

We were all silent for several minutes, each considering the various aspects of this case and how we had arrived at our conclusions. Occasionally, I would glance over at the photograph beside the boxes of evidence and wonder, with all of the evidence we had uncovered, whether we had enough to bring these rogues to justice.

After stoking the fire to stave off the night's chill, Holmes turned to Gregson.

"Inspector, perhaps in addition to charging these men for the deaths of Kelwin Hooper, Simon Rhoads and Paul Watts, we could find some other offences for which to bring charges."

"How do you mean?" the inspector queried.

"What about some sort of accounting fraud?" I offered. "Perhaps Holtz Manufacturing has not been operating legitimately."

Holmes thought a moment, then said, "That might be hard to prove with no outward evidence, but it is a possibility we should keep in mind."

After another moment, Holmes presented his idea.

"As I consider this case, I believe our adversaries, and we ourselves, have overlooked their biggest vulnerability: Cahn. He's a big brute, but not very smart. Inspector Lestrade could arrest Cahn for the murders of Estes, Norwell, and Hallis. Lestrade need only compare the sawdust he will find on Cahn with the sawdust he found on his murder victims.

"Once Cahn is in custody, let him know that if he doesn't reveal who else was involved with those three deaths, that he alone will pay the price for those murders. He most likely will break down and point the finger at Hart and Dunn, if it will save him from the hangman's noose. That will allow Scotland Yard to arrest them for those murders as well."

"What about Hart and Dunn's threat to go public about the execution of an innocent man?" asked I.

269

"Scotland Yard will correctly state that Hart and Dunn are desperate men trying a desperate ploy." Holmes replied. "In addition, if they *have* written that letter as they discussed and decide to publicize it, they will only be convicting themselves."

"That's a good possibility, Mr. Holmes," Inspector Gregson said encouragingly after a moment's thought.

"However," Holmes continued, "we must also accept the strong possibility that the assistant commissioner, the commissioner, and possibly the Prime Minister will lose their positions over this matter. I don't see any way to avoid it politically."

Inspector Gregson considered this for a moment, then replied. "Well, I can't speak for the Prime Minister, but with all of the deaths that have occurred because of this affair, I believe both the assistant commissioner and commissioner will graciously step aside if the need arises."

We were silent once again, each considering this potential path to justice as well as the consequences.

Finally, Holmes said, "Gentlemen, I think we should rest for the evening and reconvene in the morning. We are due to provide Mycroft and the others an update tomorrow evening. Perhaps we can further develop this idea and present it at our meeting."

"I can speak with Lestrade about his case tomorrow and get an idea of where his investigation is leading," Inspector Gregson offered.

"Let's meet here first tomorrow morning, if you don't mind, Inspector," Holmes said. "If nothing else, we will have to fabricate some reason why we may have evidence that could pertain to his case."

"All right, Mr. Holmes," Gregson agreed as he rose to gather his hat and coat. As he walked to the door, he turned and added, "I'll come by after ten tomorrow morning. Good evening, gentlemen."

We bade him good night and I watched the inspector descend the stairs and finally go out the door to the street. Then I closed our own door.

Staring into the fire, Holmes sat, no doubt replaying our recent conversation and evaluating our options.

"Holmes," I said, "I think you've hit upon a solution to this bedevilling case."

"Perhaps," he sighed. "The testimony of Harvey Wise and the publican will certainly cause Dunn and Hart significant discomfort in the courtroom. And if we can successfully exploit their vulnerability with Mr. Cahn, our adversaries may finally pay for their crimes."

As the night wore on, we spent some time discussing how the court case for the three murders might evolve. We both agreed that if the case went to trial, it would be a long one, with an uncertain outcome. After a couple of hours, I decided to go to bed, hoping that the coming new day would provide some new insight, perhaps a different aspect we had not yet considered.

Holmes said he could not sleep and would stay up for a while longer. So, I left him sitting in his chair, the curtains drawn against the night's darkness and the last of the fire burning low in the grate.

I spent a restless night tossing and turning as my subconscious mind wrestled with all aspects of the case. By dawn I was exhausted from a tortured night's sleep and decided to get up.

I went downstairs to the kitchen and made myself a cup of tea. As I sat and drank, I considered what we were going to tell Harvey Wise, who was still residing in Mrs. Hudson's basement. Could we truly say that he was out of danger? Could we tell him that he was now free of the fear that had enveloped him for these several months?

And would Scotland Yard agree to pursue the three murders as an additional means of delivering justice to Hart and Dunn? Would they risk having Hart and Dunn publicly claim an innocent man had been hanged? Even if Scotland Yard denied it, the accusation would be out in public. Assistant Commissioner Sanders had made it clear he preferred there be no trial of these men. Would he prevail?

As I went back up the stairs to our rooms, I had my doubts that this case was anywhere close to being finished.

Part VII
Day 6 - Saturday

Chapter XXVIII: Terrible News Received

Holmes and I finished our breakfast soon after ten o'clock. As we were assisting Mrs. Hudson in clearing away the dishes, Inspector Gregson arrived. From his tired eyes and dishevelled appearance, it was evident that he, too, had suffered a restless night.

After we poured our tea, Holmes turned to Gregson.

"Well, Inspector, have you had any additional thoughts regarding how we can bring these villains to justice? We can certainly arrest them and they will face Harvey Wise and the publican in the courtroom, exposing Scotland Yard and the justice system, not to mention the Prime Minister, to quite a bit of criticism. We can also arrest Mr. Cahn for the three murders and persuade him to implicate Dunn and Hart. I must tell you that I was up most of the night and have not been able to determine any other course of action that would suit our needs."

Inspector Gregson slowly shook his head.

"I'm afraid not, Mr. Holmes. I was also up most of the night but have very little to show for it." With a shake of his head he continued, "No, I think our best chance to catch these scoundrels is to arrest them and their public claims be damned. But we also need to pursue Lestrade's three murder cases, beginning with the arrest of this Cahn fellow. Perhaps these villains have left some additional clue or made some mistake that will be their undoing."

I had to agree it seemed our best approach. So, I followed on to what Inspector Gregson had suggested.

"Perhaps," I ventured, "Holmes, you could offer to assist Lestrade with his case. He did come to you Tuesday requesting your assistance. You could tell him that the case you were working on has been resolved, and then perhaps get a good look at his evidence to see what he has found."

Holmes considered the suggestion for several seconds, then sighed.

"Very well, gentlemen. We may be placing the Prime Minister, commissioner, and assistant commissioner at risk of having to resign their positions, but I don't see any other alternative at present. That may be our best avenue to have justice served."

We all agreed that we would have to present these possibilities to Mycroft and the others that evening when we provided our update.

"I believe," Holmes said, "that we should prepare a brief summary of the options we have discussed to present—"

He was interrupted by a knock on the door from Mrs. Hudson, who had brought the post up. Holmes took the letters, thanking her as he closed the door.

He began to quickly look through the letters as Inspector Gregson and I discussed what scant information we had regarding Lestrade's murder cases. As we were talking, we suddenly heard Holmes gasp and whisper "Oh no!" as he focused on one particular letter.

"What is it, Holmes?" asked I.

Without an answer, Holmes put up his hand indicating I should be patient as he read the letter he held. It was several minutes until he finished. I had never seen his face so shallow and drained of colour. A terrible shock had been borne. He slowly raised his eyes and looked at me as he handed me an envelope.

"This has just arrived," he said forlornly. "It is from Frances Dunn. However, notice the return address. It shows the Dunn residence, but the name is 'Mrs. Frances Rhoads.' She has used her name from her previous marriage."

I took the envelope and it was as Holmes said. In an elegant, feminine hand, 'Mrs. Frances Rhoads' had been written in the upper left-hand corner. As Holmes read the letter, I noticed that he had an additional sheet of paper in his hand.

Finally, he handed me the letter.

"Please read the letter aloud so Inspector Gregson may hear."

From Holmes' reaction, I was hesitant to discover the letter's contents. But I prepared myself as best I could and started to read, recognizing that same elegant, feminine hand. As I read, my stomach tightened and my heart sank.

The letter read as follows:

Dear Mr. Holmes,

By the time you read this letter I, as well as Colin and Basil, will be dead.

As I was in the entryway placing flowers in the vase, I passed by the dining room while you gentlemen were talking. I do not usually eavesdrop at open doorways, but when I overheard you say "the murder of Simon Rhoads," my attention was arrested and I paused to listen.

I heard the entire, horrible conversation.

How Colin and Basil helped Paul Watts donate his clothing; how they were in the pub buying drinks to get Simon drunk; how they killed that poor man and left him next to Simon in the park, paying someone to provide a false identification; and how they killed those other men when they learned Paul was returning to London, finally killing Paul upon his arrival.

Their efforts in the killing of Sergeant Cummings and then their attempt to kill you and Dr. Watson; all of it demonstrated they had no limits to what they would attempt in order to keep their secret safe.

As I listened, all of those actions made immediate sense to me from what I had observed over the past several months. The frantic look on Colin's face when he received that letter; the late nights; the evasive answers; all devised to keep their plan from being discovered and to keep me from suspecting what they had actually been doing.

As I listened to each of their transgressions, it was as if a body blow shook my soul.

And what made me sickest of all was hearing the motivations behind their scheme: Basil's greed and Colin's lust. His disgusting statements nauseated me. I have never felt so unclean.

The contempt I hold for them is only exceeded by the contempt I hold for myself. I know the fact that I married the man who instigated the execution of my husband would be a heavy burden for the rest of my life. It is a burden I do not wish to live with.

As I listened, I realized that they very well might get away with these murders. No one in the government would desire to have the fact publicised that an innocent man had been executed. I was unsure that justice would be served: for Simon, for Paul, for anyone.

It was an injustice too great. So, I resolved to take matters into my own hands and deliver the justice that was needed.

I knew what I had to do and how I would do it. I gave Haddie the night and the weekend off so that I might set my plan into motion.

Rest assured, Mr. Holmes, that had you and Dr. Watson accepted my invitation to dinner, I would have selected another night to dispense justice.

Our strychnine is kept in the green house for pests. I simply mixed the poison into their torrefacto coffee.

About an hour after you left, I had dinner ready. With a fresh pot of coffee, we all sat down to eat in the dining room. I sat at the head of the table nearest the fireplace. Colin sat to my right, Basil to my left.

You should have seen them, Mr. Holmes. I believe you had them worried. They sat across from each other silent, casting surreptitious glances, like petulant schoolboys. They would eat quietly and drink their coffee for a few moments, then one or both would sigh. Whenever I asked if something were wrong, they simply said it was nothing. But I knew they were concerned that their evil deeds were about to be exposed.

After about forty minutes, Basil began to feel some queasiness in his stomach. He said he felt like his food was unsettled. I offered him more coffee.

Shortly afterward, Colin too, began to feel out of sorts. His hands, arms, and legs stiffening, as if they had been exercised too much. I offered him more coffee. A few more minutes passed quietly as we continued to dine.

Then in a flourish, Basil flung himself onto the floor, gasping and knocking his dishes off the table. His eyes wide with fear, he began to retch and exclaim that his stomach was cramping. It was then that Colin looked strangely at me with narrowing eyes, before he too, fell to the floor and began to gasp and writhe in pain.

Did he notice my smile? I'm not sure, and it is no matter.

I folded my napkin, slowly rose from my seat as they writhed on the floor, and walked over to each of them. I had only pretended to drink my coffee. Their cries of pain became louder and louder. I began to speak to each of them. I had to raise my voice to be heard over their agonized cries. The more I spoke, the more hateful and spiteful I became.

I stood over them, raged over them, as they writhed and twitched. Then I fell to my knees beside each of them as they thrashed. I screamed that I was avenging Simon's murder. I laughed at them; I spat on them; I wallowed in their pain. At that moment, we were all screaming, their screams due to the poison in their bodies, my screams due to the poison in my soul.

It was a cacophony of madness, a rhapsody of death.

Finally, exhausted, I returned to my seat at the head of the table and silently watched. Their screams had become moans, their twitching had subsided to random jerks, yet their eyes remained wide. Basil had rolled over and attempted to crawl towards the

*windows, but he only progressed a few feet.
Only Colin, lying beside his overturned chair,
had managed to turn his gaze towards me.
Yet I could tell that his empty eyes no longer
beheld earthly visions.*

*You'll not think my actions those of a
Victorian lady, and you are correct. But the
designation no longer applied to me once
they put their plan into action and I married
Colin. In essence, I became a captured soul,
unaware of her bonds.*

I am free of my bonds now.

*For me, anger had turned to hate, hate had
turned to rage, and rage drove me to murder.
I fear I must say that I was unusually calm as
these deaths took place around me, knowing
that I had wrought such destruction. As I sat
and observed their death throes, a calmness I
had not felt in months settled over me,
engulfed me, comforted me. I'm afraid that I
may have taken too much comfort in
watching their deaths, and I will soon stand
before God to atone.*

It is no matter.

I have taken up my pen again after returning from clearing the evening dishes. I do not want Haddie to feel she is obligated to clean up after this horrid affair.

You can inform your superiors that their secret remains safe. I have left a note explaining that I have taken this action because for several months I was the victim of abuse at the hands of both these men. That may, perhaps, sully the reputations of Colin and Basil when the press is informed, but it will not compare to how they sullied Simon's reputation.

I have delayed too long, as the length of this letter can attest.

Please do not blame yourself, Mr. Holmes. You bear no responsibility for the way this affair has ended. Even though I begged you to warn me of this impending horror, I realize I had placed you in an untenable position. You were merely uncovering acts that had been carried out against Simon, the police, and others.

My fate was cast eighteen months ago, when Colin and Basil conceived and carried out their evil scheme and made me an unknowing participant. And I feel I bear some responsibility as well, for not seeking out answers to questions I should have asked. For this I am now willing to pay a heavy price.

I must make two requests of you, Mr. Holmes.

First, please ensure that someone 'discovers' our bodies before Monday morning. I do not wish for Haddie to carry the image of this room of death with her for the rest of her days.

Second, may I impose upon you to call upon my sister, Martha Hillsdale, and offer whatever assistance you can? You will find enclosed her address in Essex. In a separate letter, I will send her instructions that I wish to be buried next to Simon at our private cemetery. I also wish to have my headstone engraved as 'Mrs. Frances Rhoads.' When she asks you why I did such a thing, please tell her that I felt I had no other choice.

I am resolved.

I must finish this letter and do what I have to do before I lose my nerve. I know I cannot live the rest of my life with this revulsion and shame.

When I return from posting these letters, I will consume a cup of the poisoned coffee and pour out the remainder.

Good-bye, Mr. Holmes. Knowing what you know, I believe you can understand my reasoning.

Yours sincerely,

Frances Rhoads

In shock, I put the letter down on the table. We had all been struck silent, so overcome with the magnitude of her actions. She had single-handedly assessed the level of criminality that had been uncovered and, knowing that justice might not be meted out by any state authority, declared and administered a death sentence on her own, sacrificing her life in the process. No doubt, hatred and revenge were the motivating factors, but the end results were the same. The criminals had been brought to justice. But at what cost? I felt, as I'm sure we all felt, the cost was too great.

Holmes was looking down at his hands after having resumed his seat at the table.

"This case has taken a most egregious turn," he said forlornly. Then he suddenly struck his fist upon the table. "I should have seen it, Watson! I should have seen it in her eyes!"

Then he turned to me.

"When she invited us to dinner and we declined, as she said good-bye, she knew then what she was going to do. She knew it! And I didn't see it."

I'm not sure he ever really forgave himself for not seeing her intent, and I'm not sure that he could have prevented her actions had he noticed. I believe that by that time her anger and hatred was such that Colin Dunn's and Basil Hart's fates were sealed.

After several minutes of silent reflection by us all, Holmes finally said, "Inspector Gregson, I suggest that you take some men and travel to the Dunn residence to take charge of the police investigation. Perhaps take that Sergeant Collins we met the other day; he seems to be a capable one.

"Tell them that you are going to interview Colin Dunn regarding the accident that Sergeant Cummings suffered. Say that Dunn had come forward as someone else who had witnessed the tragedy and you wanted whatever information he could offer.

"When you arrive, walk up to the front porch and knock on the doors as if you are expecting entry. When there is no answer have someone, perhaps Sergeant Collins, look in the windows to the right of the front doors. Those windows give way to the dining room. He should be able to see the bodies on the floor, and once you're alerted you will have cause to enter the house."

"All right, Mr. Holmes."

Holmes then continued.

"Also, Inspector, take charge of the suicide note. It is most likely near Mrs. Rhoads. Review it just to make sure it doesn't, in fact, allude to the true reason for these deaths.

"You'll want to let the medical examiner determine the cause of death. Remember, all you know at this time is there are three dead bodies in the house and a suicide note."

Inspector Gregson rose to collect his coat and hat.

"Meanwhile," Holmes continued as he walked the inspector to the door, "I'll send a note to Inspector Lestrade telling him to take several armed men and arrest Mr. Cahn at Holtz Manufacturing for the murders he has been investigating. He need only compare the sawdust he will find on Cahn's coat to the sawdust he found on his murder victims. I'll also tell him to lead Mr. Cahn into believing that he has arrested Basil Hart and that Hart has confessed to the crimes. That should get Mr. Cahn to confess as well."

After another moment's thought Holmes said, "Perhaps that will fully bring this affair to a close."

Inspector Gregson left on his gruesome task and Holmes wrote out his note to Lestrade. In the meantime, I reread the letter from Frances Rhoads. *(I will refer to her by the name 'Rhoads' going forward)*. I could see the anger, the pain, and the wretchedness she felt in her last hours. I pitied the woman. Through no fault of her own she had become embroiled in such a heinous affair that it eventually cost her, as it had so many others, her life.

When Holmes had sent off his note to Inspector Lestrade, we gathered our hats, coats, and walking sticks and went for a leisurely stroll through Regent's Park in an effort to settle our nerves. Again, we were silent as we walked. There simply weren't adequate words to express the cauldron of conflicting thoughts and emotions that coursed through us. At once we were relieved, aghast, optimistic, aggrieved; however, the feeling of victory was not one of the emotions we experienced.

Upon our return to Baker Street, we rested for several hours. Holmes was still sore and somewhat impaired after his close call Thursday evening. A malaise again settled upon us which we fought to shake off.

I occupied myself by reading the newspaper accounts of the Olympic Games that had been taking place during the week. I found that on Tuesday, while Holmes and I were speaking with Mrs. Alicia Hunt in our fruitless search for Asa Bloom, England's Launceston Elliot became Great Britian's first Olympic champion taking the silver medal in weightlifting (after some unfortunate controversy involving Prince George). After reading further, I saw that England's George S. Robertson had won the bronze medal in men's doubles tennis two days later. Both were historical accomplishments and I must say that the descriptions were thrilling, but given the shadow of recent events, the excitement was lost upon me.

In a final effort to break our melancholy spirits, we decided to leave early for the Diogenes Club. Our stroll was slow as we made our way to what we expected to be our final meeting with Mycroft and the others regarding this affair.

Chapter XXIX: The Final Report

Holmes and I were looking out the bow window onto Pall Mall when Inspector Gregson joined us in the Stranger's Room. He presented a haggard look and I could tell that he was bothered by what he had found at the Dunn residence. With a heavy sigh he shrugged off his coat and placed it on one of the chairs, then joined us as we sat at the table.

"It was not a pretty sight, I can tell you," Gregson said as he ran his hands through his hair. "All three bodies were on the floor, curled up, teeth bared in a death grimace. Whatever beauty the lady once possessed, it was taken away in her last moments of life. The bodies are now with the coroner."

I didn't want to imagine the state of the corpses, preferring instead to remember these people, especially Frances Rhoads, as I had seen them in life. But being a physician and having witnessed victims of strychnine poisoning, I knew all too well what the inspector had observed and the horrible image intruded upon my consciousness, unimpeded.

"You found the note?" Holmes asked.

"Aye, I have it here," the inspector replied as he reached inside his shirt pocket, extracted a folded piece of paper, and handed it to him.

Holmes perused the paper and then handed it to me. As I read the note, I felt sickened, knowing full well the lie it contained.

It read thus:

To whomever discovers this scene,

Let it be known that it was I, Frances Dunn, who intentionally poisoned Colin Dunn and Basil Hart, and then consumed the poison myself.

For months I have lived an unbearable existence, suffering abuse, both mental and physical, at the hands of these two men.

I cannot and will not live like this any more.

May God forgive me for what I have done.

With sorrowful regrets,
Frances Dunn

I slowly shook my head. The press had already gotten wind of the story. On our walk to the Diogenes Club this evening we passed several newsboys hawking their papers with the headline "Double Murder-Suicide: Wife Claims Abuse." It would not be long before the papers realized Mrs. Frances Dunn had been the former Mrs. Frances Rhoads, and that connection would add another titillating sidelight to the narrative. But with the limited attention span of the press, I estimated that the story would disappear after three more days.

I handed the note back to Inspector Gregson, who put it into his shirt pocket. What a waste. This case had indeed taken a tremendous toll.

We sat silently until, not too many minutes later, Mycroft and the others came into the room. I couldn't help but notice the smiles that rested upon Assistant Commissioner Sanders' and Commissioner Haliford's countenances. For them, a crisis had been averted; a secret had remained concealed.

"Gentlemen," Mycroft began once everyone was settled, "I understand that this case has been resolved, although not in a way that we would have preferred." Turning to his brother, Mycroft said, "Can you give us a final update on the remaining aspects of this case?"

"I hope," my friend began, looking sternly at the two Scotland Yard officials, "that no one here believes this is a time to celebrate. We may have averted a disaster for Scotland Yard and the Prime Minister, but it was not by any clever planning or flash of insight. An innocent woman delivered the justice an impotent police force could not, and she paid a heavy price."

"I can assure you, Mr. Holmes," Assistant Commissioner Sanders stated flatly, taking great exception to Holmes' comment, "that we recognise the sacrifice this young woman made. However, I can also assure you that had she not taken such a drastic step, we at Scotland Yard would have found a method for justice at a time and place of our choosing." The assistant commissioner glanced at the commissioner, who nodded his head in agreement, then continued. "This young lady only accelerated the delivery of that justice and relieved Scotland Yard of the obligation. For that, we are, of course, saddened by her loss and grateful for her sacrifice."

Holmes and the assistant commissioner locked their gazes upon one another, neither willing to capitulate.

Finally, Mycroft, in an effort to calm the atmosphere, said, "Sherlock, if you please."

With a slow shake of his head, Holmes sighed, "As you wish."

He began to relate the events that had taken place since our meeting the previous Wednesday: That we had located and moved Harvey Wise to safer quarters; the attack upon Holmes that had occurred Thursday evening; Harvey Wise's and the publican's identification of Colin Dunn and Basil Hart from a photograph; the frustrating conversation we experienced with Dunn and Hart the previous day; the fact that we had resolved, with Inspector Gregson, to pursue murder charges against Mr. Cahn and to eventually bring a case against Dunn and Hart for the murders of Kelwin Hooper, Rhoads, Watts and the others; and finally, the murder-suicide that took place at the Dunn residence, including the letter we had received from Frances Rhoads.

Mycroft asked to read the letter, so his brother handed it to him. He spent a few moments reading the document, then folded it and placed it in his pocket.

"I'll continue to investigate the Dunn murder-suicide case," Inspector Gregson allowed. "I can stay on top of it and make sure it is closed quickly."

Gregson showed the suicide note he found at the Dunn residence to the group. Assistant Commissioner Sanders was particularly keen to review the contents of the note to ensure it made no references to the primary crime we had been investigating. Once satisfied, he handed the note back to Inspector Gregson, who would file it as evidence.

After a few moments, Holmes again spoke.

"Gentlemen, there remain only one or two points that still need to be addressed before we can bring this case fully to a close."

"And what are those?" Mycroft asked.

"I understand that Inspector Lestrade elicited a confession from that brute, Mr. Cahn. Is that correct, Inspector?"

"Yes, it is," Inspector Gregson said with a sad smile. "Cahn confessed to the murders of Estes, Norwell, Hallis, *and* Detective Sergeant Cummings. Lestrade will be the cock of the walk around Scotland Yard for the next several days. He is letting everyone know that not only did he solve his three murders, but he also solved the murder of a Scotland Yard detective sergeant. There'll be no tolerating the man."

Then turning to Commissioner Haliford, Holmes said, "Commissioner, I'd like to suggest that while you will want to keep Paul Watts' name as 'John Doe' for the official murder investigation, I think it would be appropriate to make sure his headstone, when he is finally buried, bears his real name. In addition, Kelwin Hooper was buried with a headstone bearing the name 'Paul Watts.' That should also be replaced with a headstone bearing his actual name. It would be a disservice to do anything less."

"Agreed," Commissioner Haliford said, making a note to himself as Mycroft nodded his head in concurrence.

"Then there is the case of Mr. Harvey Wise," Holmes continued. "He is the only other person associated with this affair who remains alive. He doesn't have any real idea of the larger crime and his role in it. He only knows that he was paid to provide a false identification eighteen months ago, and then lived in fear for his life. If he were to remain here in London, he might become aware of how his actions led to the execution of an innocent man; but then again, he might not. What should be done about Harvey Wise?"

This was an issue I had not considered, but what my friend had said was true. Wise had become a "loose end" for both Dunn and Hart; and now he was a "loose end" for Scotland Yard. How confident could Scotland Yard be that he would never become aware of his role in the initial murder case and try to turn it to his advantage?

It was Assistant Commissioner Sanders who proposed a possible solution.

"I have some contacts in Perth, Australia. If this man would consider relocating to Perth, I might be able to arrange for someone to offer steady employment. Mr. Wise must be a decent man and willing to provide an honest day's work. If he is agreeable to that, I can wire some friends."

"I think that is an excellent idea, sir," Holmes agreed. "I will present your offer to Mr. Wise and encourage him to seriously consider it."

This would indeed be at least one favourable result from this tragic case. If Harvey Wise could obtain steady work, his need for charity would end and he would be set on the path to a productive life. I was hopeful he would accept.

We all pledged to keep this case known only to ourselves and the Home Secretary. With the case now closed, the risk of a 'crisis of confidence' for the government had been avoided.

"Is there anything else?" Mycroft asked everyone in the room. No one had anything else.

"Very well," Mycroft said as he rose from his seat. "I'll provide an update to the Home Secretary this evening. He will be glad to hear the case is now closed."

There were handshakes all around, some grudgingly. As the assistant commissioner and commissioner were about to leave, Assistant Commissioner Sanders turned to Sherlock.

"Mr. Holmes, we may have had our disagreements over the past few days regarding this case, but I want to thank you and Dr. Watson for your assistance in this matter. The deaths of a detective sergeant and former inspector, as well as that of Mrs. Dunn are, of course, regrettable. But with the case now closed we can all move on from this affair. I thank you for your assistance in bringing this issue to a close."

Holmes smiled, and with a small bow of his head said, "Inspector Gregson and Sergeant Cummings were instrumental in uncovering the misdeeds that had been perpetrated. I am glad that we all were able to provide some clarity to a confusing case." It was as gracious an acknowledgement as Holmes could muster under the circumstances.

After both Scotland Yard officials had departed the Stranger's Room, Mycroft turned to his brother.

"Sherlock, I must echo the assistant commissioner's thanks to both you and Dr. Watson. The Home Secretary was quite concerned with whether this case could ever be closed and done with. He will be much relieved when I provide him tonight's update."

"Yes," my friend said, "I imagine he will be. But make sure to convey what the true cost was for closing this case."

"You can be sure of that."

We shook hands and said our good-byes to Mycroft, and then Inspector Gregson, Holmes, and I left the Stranger's Room, walking towards the street door of the Diogenes Club.

PART VIII

Chapter XXX: Aftermath

Once we were outside the Diogenes Club, Inspector Gregson hailed a cab. As a hansom pulled over to the curb he turned to us.

"I'll come by Baker Street Monday morning to collect the evidence boxes and return them to Scotland Yard." With a chuckle he added, "I will certainly make sure that the autopsy report for 'John Doe' is returned to Dr. Jackson."

"By the way, Mr. Holmes," he continued, "Jeffery Cummings' funeral will be held tomorrow in Norfolk. I and several others will be attending. If either of you would like to attend, I can let you know which church will hold the services."

"Thank you, Inspector. We will indeed make arrangements to attend as well. He was a fine young man."

We were silent for another few moments, remembering Sergeant Cummings' contributions and his unfortunate end. Then, with a sigh, Gregson climbed into his waiting hansom cab.

"Gentlemen, I will see you tomorrow."

"Very well, Inspector. *Au revoir*. Come along, Watson." And with that Inspector Gregson's cab departed for Scotland Yard and we began our stroll back to Baker Street. As we walked, I could not help but experience at once a feeling of relief that our investigations had finally come to a close, but also a feeling of remorse for how the case had ended and the ultimate cost it had exacted.

When we returned to our lodgings, we spoke to Harvey Wise, who was still residing in the basement. We informed him that the threat he had lived with for the past several months had been eliminated and he could resume his life in London if he wished. We also presented the offer of taking up residence in Perth, Australia, for his consideration.

It was the prospect of steady work that appealed to him and it was agreed that he would remain in Mrs. Hudson's basement until all the arrangements were made. He had been assisting Mrs. Hudson with repairs around the house and would continue to do so until it was time for his departure.

We then went upstairs to our rooms and replaced all of the evidence that was scattered about into the evidence boxes in preparation for Inspector Gregson's arrival Monday morning. As I handled the case notebooks from the Simon Rhoads investigation, I couldn't help but feel a pang of grief at the memory of Detective Sergeant Cummings and former Inspector Jack Hall. Both had become victims while simply doing their jobs. They each had much to live for when they died and had not deserved their fates.

The following day we took the train to Norfolk. The funeral for young Jeffery Cummings was, as all funerals are, a sad affair. Remembering a life cut too short. Holmes and I remained in the background until the service ended, then we made our way to offer our condolences to his mother and father.

Two days later, Mrs. Frances Rhoads was laid to rest next to her husband, Simon, as she had requested. Her sister and mother were in attendance, and after the service asked that Holmes and I join them at their home for tea. We thanked them for their offer but declined, saying that we had train connections to make.

To be honest, however, we both felt that they would want to know from us why Frances had done what she did, and we would have to tell a grieving family lies about their loved one. They wanted answers that we simply could not give them.

One week later, Holmes received a telegram from Inspector Estrada of the Spanish Security Corps. Through his investigations, he had confirmed that Jeremy Bales had in fact died as a result of some faulty equipment. He had verified that the rope Bales was found with had badly frayed and had *not* been cut. It appeared to have broken as he made his descent. Inspector Estrada concluded that there did not appear to be any evidence of foul play in the young man's death and the case would remain closed.

Holmes gave a "harrumph" as he read the telegram before handing it to me. I'm not sure that he ever fully accepted those findings as the true order of events in the demise of Jeremy Bales.

Three weeks later, we bid Harvey Wise farewell as he departed for his new life in Perth. Assistant Commissioner Sanders had arranged for Wise to be taken on at a small-scale, family-owned shrimp fishery helping with the maintenance and occasionally working on the fishing boats. It was an opportunity he was very much looking forward to.

As we said our good-byes and Harvey Wise left Baker Street to begin his new life, it truly felt, for the first time, that we had completely closed this case and that we could now get on with our lives. Holmes and I took time to assist Mrs. Hudson in restoring her basement area back to the state it had been prior to Mr. Wise's arrival.

A little over two months after we closed the case, we heard the sad news that Commissioner Haliford's wife, Donna, had died after a short illness. Holmes sent a handwritten note of condolences on our behalf.

Both Commissioner Haliford and Assistant Commissioner Sanders remained in their positions at Scotland Yard until their retirement several years after this affair. To my knowledge, no one ever informed Lord Oliver of the precarious position he and his government had been in during the days of this case. However, I will say that he never again publicly engaged in a debate regarding capital punishment.

Over the next several months, Holmes became engaged in several affairs. The two most prominent, of course, were the unusual affair of my old friend Bob Ferguson and the unfortunate case of Eugenia Ronder. As time, and circumstances, progressed, we set the sad memories of this case aside, but they were never far from our minds.

Chapter XXXI: Some Retrospection

Over the years that followed the events just related, Holmes and I attended any number of cases. Some involved the police; others were strictly private affairs better handled discreetly. By the time Holmes retired and moved to his bee farm on the South Downs, I had grown my medical practice considerably and my family had enlarged to include several grandchildren.

London, too, was becoming an even larger metropolis. So much so that I looked forward to visiting my old friend once or twice each year. The fresh air and warm sunshine always welcomed me as I took an open carriage to his house in anticipation of two to three days of remembrances and recollections of old cases.

It was on one such visit, about a year before his death, that we were sitting in his garden under the shade of a large oak tree, enjoying tea as we watched his bees buzzing around a planter of flowers that had recently bloomed. We were discussing the latest happenings with mutual acquaintances at Scotland Yard, before falling into that comfortable silence that friends often share.

After some moments, Holmes, holding his gaze on the flower planter, asked a question that at first startled me.

"Watson, do you ever think about the Simon Rhoads case?"

"Holmes," I replied turning to him as he watched his industrious bees, "there hasn't been a day that's gone by that I have not thought about some aspect of that case, all these many years since."

We sat in silence a few moments more, then Holmes expressed what was on his mind.

"I was thinking, you know, that the impetus of that entire affair was the death of Jeremy Bales during his mountaineering accident in the Pyrenees."

"Surely it was the greed and lust that Hart and Dunn felt that led them to conspire against Rhoads and commit those heinous acts."

"Oh, I think those two had contemplated any number of ways concerning how they might dispose of Simon Rhoads, and they most likely would have settled on some method eventually.

"But consider, it was young Jeremy Bales' death that finally convinced Paul Watts to break with his routine life in London and emigrate to America to start a new business with Chris Ross. That decision provided Dunn and Hart with the opportunity to dispose of Simon Rhoads by framing him for the murder of someone who had emigrated to America.

"They had very little to lose. If the false identification that Harvey Wise provided had been somehow questioned or discounted, Dunn and Hart would have simply had to come up with another plot to dispose of Simon Rhoads. But since the identification was accepted, they were able to hide their misdeeds for eighteen months."

"Until the real Paul Watts returned to London," added I.

"Yes, and that's what precipitated all the subsequent murders and eventually, Inspector Hall's and Frances Rhoads' suicides."

We sat in silence again for a few moments until Holmes concluded, "What a heavy cost that case extracted from everyone involved."

We decided to walk a bit and enjoy the pleasant spring air. We struck out along the road by Holmes' house, and we hadn't gone too far when a thought occurred to me.

"Well, one good thing that resulted from that terrible affair was the change in the fortunes of Harvey Wise," said I. "He married a widow with two children a year after he arrived in Perth. I heard from Gregson recently that he owns a fishing boat, and his sons are working with him."

"Yes, at least that turned out to the good."

Once we had strolled past his neighbour's house, we turned to retrace our steps. The country smells of peat, manure, grasses, and flowers were carried by the light spring breeze while the sun, high in the afternoon sky, cast our shadows in front of us as we walked. It was a pleasant change to the odours of London with its industrial coal fires and the city's overflowing waste bins.

Finally, Holmes asked me something he had never asked in all the time I had lived and worked so closely with him.

"Watson, do you think you'll ever chronicle the Simon Rhoads case? I believe it is a story that should be told. But it should be told at the right time."

"When would be the right time?"

"Well, you should probably write it while you still have all your faculties so you can accurately recall the events. But publication should probably be delayed until after all the remaining principals are deceased."

"And our pledge to keep knowledge of this case to ourselves; what of that?"

"As I said, it should not be published until after the principals of this case are deceased. We made that pledge to those principals. After they are no longer alive, the pledge expires as far as I can see."

We walked a bit more as I considered his words.

"You're not concerned that I might 'romanticize' the story too much?" I chided.

"Not at all," he replied in all seriousness. "I know you were as affected by the events that transpired as I. In fact, you yourself were made an unwitting participant, having to serve as the attending physician at Rhoads' execution."

Then he stopped and turned to me.

"And I don't think there is anyone else who could, by revealing their stories, provide justice to the dead. I believe this case deserves that justice, and I know you will deliver it."

It was this conversation that indeed prompted me, upon my return to London, to go back and collect my notes of this affair and to finally document the case as you have read. While I had my notes ready to confirm certain details, I wrote most of this narrative from memory, so instilled in my mind had these events become.

I have since placed a sealed box of several manuscripts, including this one, with my solicitors along with instructions that the box is not to be opened until fifty years after my death. At that time, I leave it to my heirs to determine if any greater purpose would be served by the publication of any of the box's contents.

My sincerest hope is that, if nothing else, this case can serve as a cautionary tale.

Acknowledgements

First and foremost, I must acknowledge Sir Arthur Conan Doyle, upon whose shoulders all modern-day mystery and detective authors stand. His unforgettable characters have inspired and entertained millions and we all owe him a debt of thanks. Also, my thanks to the Spout Springs Writing Group, who graciously endured my readings of various sections of this work as it was being developed, and who provided helpful feedback and suggestions. A big 'Thank you!' also goes to Christa and Bill for reading the initial drafts and providing valuable critiques. Thanks to my initial editor, Amaris Farr, who provided valuable insights throughout the text and helped to make this a better story. Her website is amarisfarr.com where she posts her own work and provides editing services. Thanks also to the editors at MX Publishing who helped pull this novel over the finish line, and to Steve Emecz, publisher, for his patience and guidance.

About the Author

Ken Courtenay is a musician, long-time IT systems consultant and author. When he's not writing music, he's writing science fiction, horror and mysteries which have appeared in a variety of on-line sites and anthologies. Ken is enjoying retirement and continues to write (stories and music) while enjoying life with his wife in their home east of Atlanta, Georgia. This is his first novel.

You can follow Ken on Facebook or on-line at Ken Courtenay